JC Wardon Books

Available in Print and/or ebook!

Mystic Thunder (*Book 1 - The Cavanaugh Sisters Trilogy*)

Touch of Lightning (*Book 2 – The Cavanaugh Sisters Trilogy*)

Tempest's Embrace (*Book 3 – The Cavanaugh Sisters Trilogy*)

Jewel of the Nile ~ *Cavanaugh Series - #4*

Sapphire Blues ~ *Cavanaugh Series - #5*

Diamond in the Rough ~ *Cavanaugh Series #6*

Luna's Landing ~ *Cavanaugh Series #7*

Celestial Liaison ~ *Cavanaugh Series #8*

Zeus: Unbound! ~ *Cavanaugh Series #9*

Apollo: Unleashed! ~ *Cavanaugh Series #10*

Blood Moon Rising ~ *Blood Moon Series #1*

What Reviewers are saying about…

JC Wardon's Mystic Waters Books

I would say that J.C. Wardon is a shining new star in the paranormal genre. MYSTIC THUNDER is the first book in a new trilogy that features three identical sisters who are blessed, or cursed at times, with mystical abilities. It centers around the three sisters, their tumultuous journey toward love, and the danger that seems to follow them. This was a totally engrossing story, unlike anything that I've ever read. It captivated me from the beginning and kept me hooked until the end." **Debra Taylor, The Romance Reviews**

"Wardon has crafted a page-turner with the first of the Cavanaugh Sisters Trilogy." **Karen Sweeny-Justice, Romantic Times Book Reviews**

"J C Wardon weaves a great story with memorable characters and a small town life found in the breath-taking atmosphere of the Great Smoky Mountains. I look forward to reading the next sister's story and finding out more about the murderer that is still living among the good people of Mystic Waters." **Susan, Night Owl Reviews**

"Wardon continues her Cavanaugh Sisters Trilogy with a second page-turner that ratchets up the action and the heat faster than the first book did. The romance between Rayne's sister and Garrison's best friend is a literal scorcher…." **Karen Sweeny-Justice, Romantic Times Book Reviews**

"Wardon concludes the Cavanaugh Sisters Trilogy with another page-turner that successfully mixes romance, paranormal elements, and the darker aspects of life." **Romantic Times Magazine, reviewed by Karen Sweeny-Justice**

"I very seldom buy books. Yet I bought all 3 in the series within 36 hours. The characters and story line are believable and there is the addition of the spiritual and paranormal. I look forward to more in the storyline." **A "Verified" Amazon Customer.**

Diamond in the Rough

Cavanaugh Family Series

J C Wardon

A Mystic Waters Novel

Mystic Waters Books
JC Wardon

Diamond in the Rough
Copyright © 2016, JC Wardon
Trade Paperback ISBN: 978-1-944454-98-2

Editing by Gilly Wright
Cover Design by Calliope-Designs.com
Stock art by www.thinkstockphotos.com

Digital release: August 2014
Original Trade Paperback Release, December 2014
Trade Paperback Release, April 2016

Media > Books > Fiction > Romance Novels
Keywords: Humorous, Witches, Romance, Contemporary, Deception

DIAMOND IN THE ROUGH

Will multiple magical misfires bring the danger of exposure to Dia's door?

Months before, moving into the secluded log cabin on the side of Mystic Mountain seemed the best solution for Dia to perfect a magic that often turned disastrous. But, for some strange reason, her elderly great-uncle rented out the next closest cabin to a single male, and he expects her to make sure the new tenant has everything he needs! The fact that Ryan Steward reminds her of Clark Kent, with the possibility of Superman hiding beneath the glasses, makes the chore so much more appealing. But she'll have to be very careful not to expose the family secret to an outsider, no matter how delicious she finds him. After all, what he doesn't know won't hurt either of them… Right?

With the Electronics Expo just a month away, and knowing his newest project will be all the rage, Ryan Steward doesn't mind being called a geek. However, when he learns he must travel to Mystic Waters to care for the mentally unstable father he never knew existed, he finds there is a world of difference between creating fantasy games and dealing with his father's inability to accept that witches do not exist in the real world.

Prologue

There was nothing better than having your hard work pay off, and for it to come to completion on his twenty-fifth birthday was just the cherry on the top.

Ryan Steward pushed his glasses up his nose as he knocked on his mother's apartment door. Barely suppressed anticipation filled him with what felt like superhuman energy, knowing she would be thrilled, in her subdued way, once she'd heard the news. He was a little early for the birthday dinner she'd planned on his behalf, but he hoped she wouldn't mind *too much*, even though her need for complete order and scheduling bordered on the manic side. His excitement kicked up a notch as he heard the multiple locks being released. He was smiling like a conquering hero, which he *felt* like, when she opened the door.

Shock, horror, and denial flittered through her eyes, coinciding with the dropping of her lower jaw. Never expecting such a reaction from her, his brows pulled together, and his glasses slid back down. "Mom?"

Instead of answering, she moved quickly to the couch

and snatched something up to shove into the pocket of her housecoat. Annoyed with his glasses, he took them off, tucking them into his shirt pocket, as he followed her into the room. He didn't know which was more bizarre, her behavior, or that she was already dressed for bed…or *still* dressed for bed. She gathered a pile of used tissues and headed to the wastebasket in her little kitchen.

Which was spotlessly clean, as there was *nothing* cooking.

Confusion turned to concern. He closed the door behind him and joined her at the bar that separated the kitchenette from the living room. "Hey Mom, what's wrong?"

Ellen Steward looked at him as if just realizing he was there. His concern turned to fear.

"Are you sick?"

When she nodded, frowned, and then shook her head, he became more concerned by the minute. "Whatever it is, we can beat it. I'll take you to a doctor right now. Give me the name of your physician. You put some clothes on while I make the call."

Ellen didn't move, just looked at him as her eyes welled with tears. She reached into the pocket of her gown reluctantly and pulled out an envelope, handing it to him. "That's yours."

Frowning, Ryan took the crumpled envelope, looked it over, and then put his glasses back on. It was addressed to him at his mother's address, which was weird, since he'd lived on his own since starting college years before. The return address said Mystic Waters Municipal Court, Mystic Waters, West Virginia. Baffled, he turned it over, surprised to see it was unsealed. Looking up, he frowned.

"What is this, Mom? I don't know anyone in Mystic Waters. I've never even heard of it." He said nothing about her opening his mail, since she was already acting so strange.

Ellen's features underwent several emotions before she shook her head. "I never wanted you to know it existed."

Since that made no sense, he pushed the irritating glasses up again, wishing he'd remembered his optometrist appointment. *But*, he'd been so close to finishing his project, and mega-excited the three-dimensional video gaming system was going to outshine the competition at the electronics expo next month, he'd completely forgotten to go.

Ryan put thoughts of his future away as he opened the envelope's flap before pulling out the folded sheet of paper. It was clearly a summons, but while reading one sentence after another, his confusion only increased.

"I don't understand. It says here I need to appear in court to take over my father's power of attorney and his care."

Ellen nodded. "Yeah, I know."

He stared at her, taking in her disheveled appearance, her hunched shoulders, and her watery eyes. "I *thought* my father was dead," he said evenly, while watching her every reaction.

"I know. I wanted you to. He's been dead to me for a long time."

Determined not to let rising anger take hold, Ryan tilted his head, indicating they needed to go to the couch. Ellen nodded and shuffled her way there. He waited until she was seated and sat himself. "I need an explanation as to why I've spent my entire life thinking I had no father."

Ellen nodded and bit her bottom lip. She released it on a sigh. "It's complicated. I don't know how to begin."

Ryan stared at her, exasperated. "*Try.*"

She nodded again and chewed on her lip for a minute more as her features played out her fear. Ryan almost told her to forget it, that he'd look into it himself, but the words wouldn't pass his lips. He'd spent a lifetime allowing her off the hook when she didn't want to discuss something with him, but this was too important.

"Mom!"

She sighed. "Okay, already. This isn't a story I ever wanted to tell you, but I guess I have no choice." She focused on her hands, which she rubbed together as if she'd just moisturized them.

"I met your father my first year of college, at a frat party. He was dark and mysterious, and I was free from my strict parents for the first time in my life. He had some...*pot* and we got stoned—a first for me." She glanced up at him, but when he didn't react, looked down again.

"He made me laugh with these stories of witches and magic that resulted in murder in this place called Mystic Waters. I thought it all so funny, that he was making it up to amuse me, or impress me... I don't know.

"Anyway, *at the time*, I thought it was so cool to be with him. Everything we were doing that night flew in the face of my very religious upbringing." Her gaze flittered Ryan's way briefly before her face filled with color.

"So we hooked up. You know, *had sex*. Another first for me."

Ryan placed his hand on the two of hers that were now tightly clenched together. He figured he knew where this was leading, but he wanted her to say the words "Okay, so you were a normal teenage kid. Go on."

She almost smiled, as if relieved.

"The next morning I went back to school only to find out he didn't even attend, just the friend of a friend of a friend, and no one really knew much about him." She paused and then swallowed hard. "You were conceived that night."

Ryan nodded. It was just as he had figured. "So, that's the last you ever heard of him."

Ellen shook her head. "I wish that were true. But…not exactly. Once I found out I was pregnant, my parents had a fit. My father forced me to tell them the whole story, and he had an investigator locate Clayton Davis. He was from Mystic Waters, West Virginia."

"So you *did* see him again."

Ellen shook her head. "No. He was in a facility for people with psychological problems. His stepfather was a policeman at the time, a really nice man. When my father took me there to see them, Mr. Grammar, his stepdad, told us Clayton's emotional problems started when he was a little kid, and since his mother had died years before, Mr. Grammar was raising him on his own." She cleared her throat. "He said Clayton was diagnosed as schizophrenic and would never be able to help out, but Mr. Grammar would set it up so I got a check each month to cover some of the expenses of having and raising the child…*you*. Of course my father got the money every month, and I never saw a penny." She shook her head. "But that's a story for another day."

Ryan nodded, understanding now why he'd never met his grandparents either. "Tell me more about my father."

"According to Mr. Grammar, Clayton believed there were witches performing magic in Mystic Waters. He also believed one died in his stepfather's house when he was little. The police chief said it caused *him* all kinds of problems, because his story had to be investigated, but of course, nothing came of it. Still, after all that, Clayton insisted he was telling the truth, and no one could convince him otherwise. Not even after years of medication and therapy. Because they couldn't help him see reality, he started cutting himself, and fighting with people who didn't believe him. He even broke a man's nose and nearly busted open another man's skull for calling him crazy. In other words, he became a danger to himself and others."

"Oh...."

Ellen nodded. "Yeah. Do you really want to hear more?"

Ryan nodded, though he felt a little ill that this man had sired him. "Yes. I need to know everything."

She cleared her throat. "Okay. At that point my father was done pursuing a solution to what he considered *my* problem. We went back home long enough to pack up all my belongings. I was sent to Memphis, Tennessee, to live with Aunt Grace until I had you. The only way I got to continue to live with her, once you were born, was to agree to never tell you or anyone about Clayton Davis. My family was afraid, if you knew, you'd try to contact him once you were old enough. And they wanted nothing to do with a nut case.

"With the exception of speaking with my father once, I never spoke to my family again after Aunt Grace died a year after I moved in with her. She was a mean woman, and she kept my father informed of my every move. Once she was gone, and *surprisingly* left me her house, I sold it and moved to the house you remember growing up in. But I saw the wisdom in keeping information about a mad man away from you. I was afraid you'd be concerned with the hereditary issues."

Ryan didn't know what to say, or how to react. Until she'd said it, he hadn't thought about the possibility of inheriting the condition. It was something he'd have to look into. But first, he needed to meet his father and see what was what, for himself. "I guess I'm leaving tomorrow for Mystic Waters, then. I only have four weeks to get my life in order before I show the world what video games are supposed to look and act like." He laughed, though he was not amused. "How weird is it that my games are all full of witches and dark magic?"

For the first time since he'd arrived, Ellen almost

smiled at him. "You finished it then?"

Ryan nodded, all his earlier joy gone. What if he'd inherited his father's craziness? What if what he'd thought brilliant fantasy for a nerd all these years was nothing more than hereditary memory? The though nauseated him. "Yeah, I finished it."

Whoop-de-do, and Happy Birthday to me!

Chapter One

"I'm sorry, Mr. Steward, but your father had to be sedated again this morning, so he'll be groggy, if he even wakes up. This isn't an uncommon thing with him, though I'd hoped the therapy and medication we've been giving him for the past six months eventually might make a difference. Unfortunately, with many of our patients, it never does for long."

"He's been in here for six months?"

The doctor nodded. "This time. We can only keep him until his insurance stops paying. Hospital policy." He grimaced. "Your father needs to be put somewhere permanently, for his own safety. But that isn't my call."

"So where does he go when he's released?"

The doctor flipped through a manila file and looked back up. "He used to go to his stepfather's house. But the retired police chief has gotten too old and feeble to handle Clayton. I believe the last time he was released he was homeless for about a week or so, then he was found lying in the street, smelling of liquor. When the police questioned him, he went right back to claiming witches had put him to sleep again, only this time, when he awoke, he could only remember he'd found them and had planned when he was going after them. He said he knew one was a cop, and he'd been watching her for months. It wasn't until he was brought here, and asked the date, that he claimed they'd wiped his memory as well.

"It wasn't the first time he'd told this story, or some variation of it. He's been telling the same since he was a kid."

"Did anyone check into his story?"

The doctor frowned at Ryan. "There is no reason to. Clayton has a lifelong history of mental illness. And no one in their right mind would believe the stories he tells."

A chill rolled down Ryan's spine. "Of course."

"Look, I know this is all new to you, but I've spent a career with these cases. The sad truth is your father should be able to live a normal life with medication and therapy. His condition hasn't improved over the years, and except for the way he acts out at times, it hasn't gotten any worse, either. That's actually pretty remarkable."

Ryan absorbed the information. "How does he act out, other than telling wild stories?"

"He cuts his skin. Since he's been here, he's found several opportunities to do so. No matter what we try to do to stop him. If we take away one thing, he finds something else. But there is usually a long lull between episodes, and since he's so close to being released, again, I'm trying to give him every opportunity to leave his room and socialize with the general population at meal times."

"You said he cuts numbers into his arm. What numbers? Are they significant?"

The doctor shook his head. "He keeps repeating elevens. At first we thought it was just straight line cuts, but a couple of months ago, when he came back out of his latest manic episode, he kept repeating the number eleven. When I asked him what eleven meant, he said he didn't remember, the witches took his memory, but he remembered eleven, and he had to keep saying it so he wouldn't completely forget what they'd done to him."

"So he still doesn't know what it means, even now?"

Again the doctor shook his head. "I'm sorry, but it probably doesn't mean anything. More likely, this number is a repetitive hallucination that torments him."

Ryan nodded, pushed up his glasses when they slid forward, and hoped his horror didn't show. He thanked the doctor before following an orderly down the long beige hallway of the hospital's psychiatric ward. They stopped at the thirteenth door on the right, which he thought appropriate somehow, as he waited until the door was unlocked. The orderly nodded and stepped back, but before he could make himself enter the room, he looked through the small wire enforced window to see his father lying on the bed.

He took a deep breath and moved forward. The door clicking closed behind him once he was inside sent another shiver down his spine. The entire facility gave him the creeps, but this room was even worse. It smelled like pine cleaner, rubbing alcohol, and bleach, a mixture that instantly made his head ache. He tried to ignore the smells and focused on the middle-aged man strapped to the bed. As if sensing his presence, Clayton opened his eyes, glared, and spit at Ryan, causing him to jump back to keep from being hit.

"Get the hell out of my room!"

Ryan stayed where he was, any hope of a good first meeting gone. "I can't do that. I need some answers."

"What the hell! I don't need other psychiatrist picking my brain!"

"I'm not a psychiatrist. I'm your—" Ryan nearly choked. "*Son.*"

That seemed to startle Clayton, which was good. At least it took the scowl off his face...temporarily. He squinted his eyes and looked Ryan up and down as much as he could.

"I don't have a son."

That question answered, Ryan moved closer. "You do. I'm Ellen Steward's son."

Clayton laughed, a rough gurgled sound that ended in

him coughing until spittle ran down his jaw. Ryan took a hesitant step and then another, before he reached for a tissue from the box on the nightstand and held it up. "Can I help?"

Eying Ryan warily, Clayton nodded and remained still while his son wiped his face. When Ryan resumed his distance, Clayton blew out a long breath. "How is she?"

Taken aback his father could recall her so quickly, he had to ask, "So you remember her?"

Clayton laughed, "I would think so. She's the only girl who every listened to me for more than ten minutes back then." He scowled. "And pretty much since." His smile returned but was distant. "So that night produced you. That beats all. Why didn't she ever tell me?"

Not wanting to go into that, Ryan shrugged. "It's a long story. We'll talk about it next time. I need to know something right now though."

Clayton studied him and then nodded. "You want to know if you'll end up in a place like this, with people constantly drugging you."

Surprised by his perception, given he probably *stayed* medicated, Ryan nodded.

"Let me tell you something, *son*, I am not crazy, at least I wasn't until they did all this to me. I told the truth from the beginning. I know it's hard to believe. But I did. I was a little kid, and I told people what really happened. Maybe if I'd been older, I would have known better than to argue with them when they didn't believe me. But I was accused of lying over and over, and I wasn't. And then this last time, I was still too drunk to think straight and hold my tongue, and damned if I didn't end up in here again!"

Ryan tried not to react to the foolishness his father spouted, since it was obvious Clayton believed what he was saying. "So you say witches are here, and they do things to you?"

Shaking his head, Clayton frowned. "No, not here. In the house I used to live in with my stepfather. And they didn't do *things* to me, only one thing that first time. I was knocked out cold for a couple of days right after I witnessed that woman doing things with my stepfather. And, last time? They did it again right before I was put back in this hellhole. Only this time they wiped my memory for weeks."

"Tell me about the first time. What *kinds* of things were done to a woman? And who was she?"

Clayton eyes grew wary. "Why? So you can laugh at me too?"

Ryan shook his head. "No. I don't find any of this funny. I'm just trying to understand."

"Well, I'm telling you!" He took a deep breath when Ryan jumped. "Sorry. Just give me a minute, okay? I'm not as eager to tell it as I once was." He looked around the room then back at Ryan. "For obvious reasons."

Clayton closed his eyes momentarily and then opened them, determination sharpening his gaze. "I witnessed them…uh, damn, doing unnatural things, with my own eyes, and then I fell asleep. When I woke up, it was two days later. But no one else knew that. Somehow the witch was gone, and my stepdad was going about his life as if nothing had happened and life was normal. Only it wasn't. He didn't even remember her, or…*well*, any of it."

Ryan took a deep breath. His father was completely delusional. But he was talking, and that was something. "Why did you think it was two days later?"

Clayton stared up at Ryan, his eyes filled with anger. "I don't *think*, I *know*. But in all the years I've told my story, no one ever asked me about that. They never got past me calling that woman a witch. They never believed she existed."

He took a moment to breathe in deeply and out slowly

and then sniffed. "Okay, I'll tell you how, but you have to keep an open mind."

Ryan nodded slowly. "I'll try."

Clayton nodded, his lips twisted. "That will be a first. But what the hell.

"I was in elementary school. A good student. A good kid, actually. I never lied to my stepfather or caused him any trouble. He was a good guy, and all I had, because my mom had died, and he kept me. He didn't have to, but he did. I was grateful. And he was kind. So when all this happened and he didn't believe me, it really hurt my feelings, and I was already scared shitless. That said, I'm going to tell you every detail I remember. Hell, you may as well know what has haunted me my entire life.

"The day I came home from school was a half-day, so I let myself in and went to my stepfather's room to tell him he forgot to be at the school bus stop to get me. But his door was locked, so I figured he was there but asleep or something. So I peeked through the skeleton keyhole." He grimaced. "That was my first mistake, but I was just a little kid and didn't know any better."

Ryan nodded and held his tongue. After all, what could he say?

"What I saw caused me to scream. I think." He frowned. "I *think* I screamed... It's so long ago now. I'm not sure about that anymore. But anyway, something alerted the witch that I was there, and all the doors in the house slammed shut. I jumped, startled, but other than blinking, I never stopped looking through the keyhole. My stepfather threw her away from him, and her head hit the nightstand before she landed on the floor. He screamed and hit the bed as hard.

"Then he was crying and screaming hysterically. Because he knew what had happened wasn't normal. And I think he realized the witch was dead, and he'd killed her.

I'm sure he never meant to, but he did."

Ryan scratched his head, trying to decipher all he was being told. "What caused you to scream? Or do whatever you did to get the woman's attention?"

Clayton stared at him for a full minute, his face expressionless. When he finally spoke, he did so slowly. "They were making love, although that didn't come to me until years later, but they were floating at least four feet above the bed while they were doing it. *That* made me scream."

Ryan backed up a step, his mind rejecting his father's words. "You know that isn't possible. Right?"

Clayton closed his eyes. "You may as well leave now. I knew you wouldn't believe me either. But I'm telling you, knowing I'm about to die in this shithole, it is not only possible. It happened.

"Just like the witches blanking out my memory right before I came here this time. That really happened too."

He opened his eyes. They were filled with defiance. "And when they are forced to release me this time, I'm going to prove it."

****

Calling himself all kinds of a fool, Ryan drove the continuously curving mountain road, wondering why he hadn't just gotten a hotel room in the valley below or, better yet, told the court he wasn't about to take on a mad man when his life was just getting where he'd worked so hard for it to be.

Still, since he wasn't one to drop any responsibility thrown into his lap, it would have made more sense to be closer to the hospital and the restaurants, but there hadn't been much to choose from. From the look of things, the town hadn't changed much in the past century. The only accommodations he'd found were on the extreme eastern side of the town. He'd made the effort to find more, but there was only the one motel, a single story building that looked as if constructed sometime before 1940. His only other option, according to those at the Main Street diner, was to go a couple of doors down the continuous line of stores and talk to a Frank Whitehawk, as he rented out cabins on Mystic Mountain to the tourists who frequented the area from spring to fall. Fortunately or, considering how far he'd have to drive to get back to town, *unfortunately*, there had been a cabin available close to the top of the mountain.

Sighing, he reached into the passenger seat and lifted the directions and address of the cabin he'd rented from the very elderly Native American, wishing he could just enjoy the view. But there was too much churning in his mind.

It wasn't that he believed his father was right or even sane, but there was something about his acceptance of never being believed that weighed heavily on Ryan's shoulders. Maybe it wouldn't bother him as much if it weren't the man who had sired him. Or maybe he could dismiss it all if the story were something Clayton made up as an adult. Regardless, Ryan knew he'd have to get some questions answered for his own peace of mind before he left Mystic Waters for good.

The clock was ticking.

Hoping it wouldn't take the full three-and-a-half weeks he had before having to prepare to showcase his new game, Ryan trudged on and then jerked his wheel when an explosion sounded and the road shook beneath the car. He grabbed the steering wheel tighter, praying he hadn't rented something close to a coalmine that would turn out to be a constant irritation. If that was the case, he'd go right back down the mountain, give that old man a piece of his mind and demand the rental fee back.

A few minutes later a reflective number stick, indicating he'd arrived, stood beside the gravel driveway he was to take. Ryan turned, surprised he couldn't see anything but thick trees. He proceeded slowly, glad the driveway was relatively smooth, but the more he drove the creepier it all felt, and he wondered if he'd been set up somehow.

Visions of horror movie plots he'd loved as a kid came back to haunt him now, and he kept glancing around him, waiting for something half-human with spiked teeth to jump out and attack the car. His shoulders bunched, his neck grew stiff, and he held onto the steering wheel tightly, ready to floor the gas pedal to run down anything that came his way. By the time the trees thinned and he arrived in the small clearing where a little cabin sat welcomingly, overwhelming desperation to escape and leave all his concerns behind had taken over.

He barked out a shaky laugh as he came to a stop before the little house, wondering if his father's stories had messed with his mind and questioning when he'd become such a dork. Pragmatic, staid, by-the-book Ryan Steward did not believe in things like monsters, witches, or any such nonsense, except where it came to creating interactive games. That his mind had even gone there embarrassed him, and he was thankful no one was around to see what a fool he was being. Especially his mom, who had fussed at him all those years ago when he'd gotten caught in front of the televised horror movies he'd regularly snuck into the house and watched while she was at work.

Still, he gave himself a moment to look around before unlocking the car's doors, and stepping from the vehicle.

He'd been told the cabin was in a remote area, he just hadn't expected *this*. He looked around, but with the exception of the small clearing, which might park six vehicles the size of his Volkswagen, there was nothing to see but trees. Ryan shook his head, wondering if he should just get back in the car now and head straight to the motel.

He sighed, discounting that option immediately. The

day had been endlessly long, and given the darkness that was falling ridiculously fast, there was no way he would consider it. At least not until morning.

Ryan reached into the back and lifted the two bags of groceries he'd purchased before leaving town. He grimaced, wondering what he'd do with the meat and dairy supplies if he headed back to more acceptable lodgings, but he hadn't expected any of this, so he'd figure that out in the morning as well.

He glanced at the single suitcase he'd brought, before shifting the bags into one arm to grab it as well. With his hands full, he looked longingly at his laptop in the passenger seat and decided he'd get settled first before coming back for it.

Until he'd spoken with his father, he hadn't planned on being in town more than a few days, a week tops. He was now afraid he'd underestimated the situation. Figuring out what to do with his father once he was released would likely take time.

The short walk and the three steps leading to the front porch took no effort, but digging for the cabin's key within the deep pockets of his jeans, while juggling his load, took a little more. He set the suitcase down, looking at the homey set-up. Hand-carved chairs sat facing the railing with a small table between them on one side, and a porch swing took up the other. He rolled his eyes, wondering who in their right mind would vacation somewhere where the only view while sitting on the porch was trees. Not him.

He located the key, unlocked and pushed open the door, retrieved his bag and stepped inside. Near darkness engulfed him immediately so he lowered the luggage again and felt around for a light switch.

There wasn't one.

"You have *got* to be kidding me."

Though not prone to curse, a string of foul words fled

his mouth as he set the bags down and returned to the car. He opened the glove compartment relieved to find the flashlight had batteries that still worked, grabbed his laptop, and returned to the cabin. He stepped over the groceries as he shined the light around the small room and his fear was confirmed when he saw the gas-chimney lamps and a large box of matches lying next to them on a nearby library table.

"You have got to be kidding me!"

Fury replaced disappointment as he lit one lamp after another. There was no way in hell he'd stay for more than one night. The groceries would no doubt go bad, and the drinks would be hot by morning anyway, so he didn't have to worry about what to do with them once he returned to town. If mice didn't dwell within the cabin he'd at least have chips and drinks tonight, then take the rest to munch on as snacks in the motel room once he got back to town. But the worst thing about what he now knew was a camping trip was he couldn't play his game, and check it, and recheck it, to make sure there were no bugs left in the new system or in the new game. Not if there was no damned electricity!

"Mr. Whitehawk, you had better plan to give me my money back!"

Ryan closed the front door and was relieved to see it actually had a lock. He stood in the glow of the little cabin and cursed again. When he ran out of words, he carried one lamp as well as the bags to the small island that separated the lounging area from the kitchen. To his surprise the light showed a small upright chest that had a sticky note attached to its front door, indicating it was the refrigerator.

Intrigued, he opened the small door and cold air hit him immediately. Curious now, he held the lamp up and moved it as far as he could around the box. There were no wires, but there was a hose attached to the back of it and he chased the hose. Ryan found it ran into the cabinet and then attached to the horizontal pipe leading to the vertical pipe of the sink's spigot. He could only surmise it ran cold water between the box's wooden exterior and the metal lining that would hold his supplies.

"Okay. Now that's pretty cool. But still not enough to keep me here."

The hard knock on the front door startled Ryan, and he yelped before pushing his glasses back up. Knowing he'd have to get a grip, and get it soon, he crossed to the door and moved a sheer curtain aside to look out the window. Fortunately, the person on the other side held a flashlight up so he could see it wasn't a polite monster, but a beautiful blonde instead. Pleasantly surprised, he unlocked the door and swung it open.

"Hi! I'm the Welcome Wagon."

She held up a basket filled with things, but Ryan couldn't take his eyes off her lovely face long enough to look down.

"Actually, I'm the niece of the guy who owns the cabin. My aunt Destiny texted me, because cellphone service sucks around here, and said I should check on you. She wasn't sure Great-Uncle Frank told you about the plumbing and things. So how are you? I know it can be crazy scary out here when people come for the first time." She stepped forward, and he stepped back. She went straight to the kitchen and then turned with a smile. "I see you've lit the lamps. That's good. Did you see how to use the icebox? Well, it isn't really an icebox anymore, since my dad made it into a water-cooled box. But same difference. You can't leave the door open like that, though, or it won't stay quite as cold. And you should probably close the front door. The temperature is dropping fast. It always does up here."

Ryan nodded and closed the front door once she took a breath and moved to shut the cooler. But before he could answer any of her questions, she started up again.

"This is a nice cabin. Not nearly as far back as mine. I wonder why they didn't send me here." She frowned, looked at an oil lamp and then nodded. "Of course. The lack of electricity. I don't mind being out in the boondocks, at all, but a girl has to use a hair straightener every once in a while." She grinned at him. "You don't talk much, do you?"

He slowly shook his head, a little overwhelmed.

She nodded, and continued. "Most men don't as far as I can tell. My dad is really quiet, and so is Uncle Tom. He's the owner of the cabin, by the way. My uncle Logan talks more than those two, but I think it's because he's a doctor and has to talk to people all day, so he's more social. My dad mostly talks to his wood and to my mom, but he can get going sometimes when it's just family around."

She pointed upwards to the loft. "That's your bedroom if you haven't already figured that out. I brought clean sheets and put them on earlier. My great-uncle would have done it, but I volunteered. He's nearly as old as these hills but would have a fit, if he *had* fits, which he doesn't, if I said so.

"You do have a bathroom over there," she said pointing again. "But only cold water. Unless you've kicked on the generator out back?"

Ryan shook his head.

"Figured not. You don't look like you rough it. Anyway, no city water, thank goodness. Only well water out here. Runs from the spring. Great for drinking, but cold as an Alaskan's snot to shower in, which is why it works so well to keep cold food cold." She grinned.

"Toilet's good though. Has a concrete box in the ground. Can't remember what it's called, but it does the trick. For you know, catching things. But anyway, I'll show you how to work the generator tomorrow, unless you want to shower tonight." She grimaced. "I'm just afraid it may have spiders since nobody has used the cabin for some time. I hate spiders. Don't you?"

Ryan nodded.

"Thank goodness. I was afraid you'd want to deal with that thing tonight. It isn't hard or anything. Just really dark out there. Oh! I nearly forgot!" She pointed to the fireplace. "I've laid you a fire. All you have to do is light it. The matchsticks you used to light the lanterns will do the trick nicely, just put flame to the paper stuffed below the wood. Do you have any questions?"

His mind whirling, Ryan simply stared at her. By the time he could think to ask her name, she was reaching toward his face.

"You have an eyelash on your cheek." She lifted it from his face and dusted her hands together. "Nice glasses by the way. Makes you look very scholarly. Are you a professor? Oh sorry, I'm being nosy."

Ryan was so jolted by her brief touch, he couldn't tell her the lash had floated onto her jacket, rather than the floor. Once he found his wits and was about to tell her, she was hurrying toward the door. She opened it and turned to smile at him.

"Sorry, I've got to go. In a bit of a hurry. But you have a good night. I'll see you in the morning. But not too early, unless you need me here early. A girl's got to get her beauty rest, you know?" She smiled again and pulled the door closed behind her.

Ryan just stood there staring at the door until he heard the sound of a motor starting. That propelled him forward, but by the time he could reopen the door, all he could see were two tiny red lights entering the tree line, and he realized the whirlwind was riding a four-wheeler through the woods to go back to wherever it was she'd come from.

Amazed he hadn't heard her arrive, he closed the door back and exhaled, wondering just how much stranger his life could possibly get.

****

Dia hurried back through the trail leading to her cabin, hoping she hadn't been rude. She didn't particularly like being out after dark, even though she'd grown up on this mountain and knew it like the back of her hand. But the darkness wasn't her reason for hurrying. She'd left a new potion brewing on her stove, and she was afraid after the small explosion earlier she still might not have lowered the ingredients quite enough to prevent it from happening again.

Her dad would have a fit if she destroyed a third stove. As would her uncle if she burned down his ancestral home. But it was finally spring, and the weather was already showing signs of warmth. Soon she'd be able to move her experiments back outside, into the cauldron her mother gave her as a housewarming gift when she'd moved in. Thank goodness, Great-Uncle Frank said the cutie had only rented the place next door for a month; otherwise she'd have to be more careful. The last thing she needed was someone around to hear her noisy failures—and get nosy.

She grinned as she sailed over a boulder that suddenly appeared in the path she was taking. They often made up the launching pads she loved to fly over. For those brief seconds she was airborne, and the feeling of freedom was as exhilarating as it was brief. One day, and she hoped it was soon, she'd find a spell that allowed her to fly for real.

She couldn't wait.

Dia pressed her lips together, trying to not let annoyance set in that Sapphire was the one who'd inherited the celestial gifts. Her sister, oldest by only a few minutes, didn't appreciate her own power, had denied it for years, and even now barely acknowledged it, as far as Dia knew. Not that she'd seen much of Sapphire since last October. *She* was too busy with her new husband and their pack of

28

Lycanthrope to devote time to Cavanaugh family matters, which was just fine. That meant Dia could work toward creating magic without her sister's constant judgment and condemnation.

Darkness aside, Dia loved the smoothness of the trails she always found while riding the four-wheeler. Since moving into Uncle Tom's one-room cabin all those months ago, she'd gotten to ride often while out looking for the wild growing plants she tested once mixed together, with the hope of finding just the right things to cast spells, or alter and create things. It always surprised her that such rough terrain allowed for such smooth travel given the thickness of the pines, and the rockiness of the acreage covering the mountainside.

She spotted the glow from the windows of her cabin and slowed as she passed it to reach the little hidden shed her father and Uncle Tom built for her experiments. She parked in the little carport they'd added at its side to keep her generator and transportation out of the elements. Thankfully, the generator was only necessary for the shed's cook-stove and the lighting within. Like she'd told her delicious new neighbor, a girl needed real electricity in her dwelling.

Dia hurried into the shed and breathed a sigh of relief. Her potion was still simmering, the aroma light and pure. She shivered, as the room had grown cool in her absence, and then gasped as an eyelash floated down, landing in the pot of potion she'd so painstakingly concocted. Dia lifted the sterling silver ladle and tried to capture the lash, but it disappeared into the gently bubbling brew, and no amount of stirring brought it back to the surface. Disappointment flooded her, but she'd have to hope no more of her lashes dislodged, and that the one that had didn't make any difference.

Biting her bottom lip, afraid she'd now ruined the day-long experiment, she nonetheless stirred the rosebud, honey, and wine brew she'd mixed with a peppering of the other lesser but still important herbs, then grasped a small vial with her tongs. She poured the brew into the test tube and swirled it gently. Smoke rose in a twirling rope-cloud, puffed, and eventually formed a shimmering valentine heart. Excitement caused her to shake so hard she nearly spilled the vial, so she poured what little remained back into the pot.

Have I done it? Did I really create a love potion?

Nerves skittered across her body, sending goose bumps over her skin. What if she had? What could she do with it? She couldn't tell anyone, if indeed she'd been successful. At least not until she tested it. But how?

Her mother would tell her to destroy the potion immediately and try something else. To mess with someone's will was taboo. Though not exactly dark magic, it bordered there as far as her family was concerned. Which meant she'd have to keep this a secret. Or destroy it. But how could she do that if she'd finally found success after so many failures? The one and only time she'd thought she'd succeeded had turned out to be a farce. Her attempt to make gold out of wood had ended up being a material that crumbled after only a few hours of looking like gold. Her family, mostly, had celebrated her finally doing *something* with magic, but that hadn't made her feel better at all.

Torn, but unwilling to throw out what might be her first real step into becoming the White Witch she wanted to be, Dia set the potion off the burner to allow it to cool. Once it had, *then* she'd decide what to do. Of course, there was nothing the mixture could do without a personal item from the one the spell was meant for, coupled with speaking aloud the centuries-old incantation her ancestor created and recorded in her short diary.

Unlike many of the diaries her family owned, which

had been passed down through generations of Cavanaugh women, Camellia Cavanaugh's thin diary was little more than a pamphlet of simple spells. Dia knew her mother must have either forgotten it was within the pages of the thick tome she had given to her youngest daughter, or she hadn't realized it was there. All either of them had expected from the gift was Dia would learn about the local plants and all their uses in her quest to create magic of her own.

Dia had spent days debating confessing she had it and then decided it wouldn't hurt to try one of the simple spells within before giving it back. Since there was no danger of this spell working until she had something personal from the person who the spell was meant for, she knew there was no danger in reading the words aloud either.

Besides, she just loved to recite the little spell...

Three hearts of the precious wild growing rose
Beneath the sun and starry sky, grows;
Three silver drops of honey so gold
Awaken the mysteries of bold, and old;
Three silver spoons of blood red wine
And thee shall be mine;
Thee shall be mine;
Until by will I set thee free
This is my will, so shall it be.

Though no longer on the heated coil, the brew went crazy, bubbling and boiling over the sides, sending smoke throughout the room. Startled, Dia ran to the doors and threw them both open, and stood outside coughing until her lungs cleared. Trepidation skittered down her spine as she watched the smoke spiral through the trees in the direction of the rented cabin, its form nearly that of a snake on the hunt.

"Damn, damn, and double damn!"

She wiped at her irritated eyes as she made her way back inside, hoping the guy had gone to bed and wasn't calling the fire department instead. Disappointment filled her, as it did every time she thought she'd made a breakthrough only to realize nothing had changed. She stared down at the pot. Her potion was now nothing more than glimmering crystalized rosebuds. As pretty as they were, she lifted the pot and threw it across the room, shattering the three little buds on the far wall. Dia watched them float down as red glitter to cover the pot that had hit the dirt packed floor.

Fury overtook her with a vengeance she'd never before experienced, and though her mind rejected the emotion, her mouth took on a life of its own.

"You win!" she screamed, as tears formed and fell from her eyes. "I'm done! I'm never going to be a witch, okay?" She ran outside and shook her first at the star-filled sky. "Did you hear me? I get it! I'm done! You win! I'll never again try to cast a spell! Ever!"

Once she caught her breath and could make herself reenter the shed, Dia walked over to pick up the pot. She extinguished the electricity feeding the stovetop, since she'd forgotten to in her earlier excitement, and placed the strangely clean pot on the same cold coil as before. She looked at the glitter left behind from the boil-over but didn't have the heart to deal with it yet. She surveyed the little room and wanted to cry, knowing all she'd done to make it her own special place had been a waste of too much time and effort.

Overwhelming sorrow weighed on her as she returned the small bottles of herbs her family had helped her gather and stock to their rightful place on the shelves her uncle had built. Everyone had pitched in from her mother, to her aunts, to her cousins, and even her uncle Tom.

Everyone, that was, except Sapphire.

Dia groaned, knowing her oldest sister would be the only one who wouldn't mourn with her over the loss of her dream. Of course, Sapphire wouldn't see it as a loss. She'd told Dia more than once, "You can't lose something that was never yours to begin with." And now, finally, Dia had to accept her words as truth. But that didn't mean she didn't want to sock her sister in the jaw just once. The only thing stopping her was Sapphire could now transform herself into a wolf, and she'd probably been waiting for a reason to bite Dia for years.

Having no idea what is was that had always caused such friction between them, Dia lifted the diary she'd spent the last few years filling with each exciting experiment and subsequent failure. This time there was no need to write down her concoction or its results. She was closing this chapter in her life, and she wouldn't look at the little book ever again.

Reluctantly, she locked up the shop for the last time and went to turn off the generator before heading to her cabin to get what she needed to prepare for bed. *Tomorrow*, she promised herself. Tomorrow she'd search for the gift that was her birthright, and she'd accept whatever fate had thrown her way.

After all, what other choice did she have?

Since she now reeked of smoke, Dia gathered clean towels and took the path that led to the shower house her uncle had built long before her birth. The freestanding facility was one she treasured, as the toilet had plumbing, but better still, it contained a large shower room that could hold a party of people if one were so inclined. The multiple showerheads allowed her to feel as if she were standing in a steady rain. It could be turned up to torrential, or down to a mist, depending on how much pressure she wanted. The tiles were beautifully designed and the knobs were realistically carved eagle heads, created by her uncle's talented hands. But tonight, the pleasure of the shower house was lost in the folds of her heavy heart.

The only good thing that had come of this failure was she was being forced to look forward, rather than back, and now she wouldn't have to worry about the delicious new neighbor discovering her secret. But what in the world would she do with her days? She'd done nothing since returning home after her post-college European trip but try to perfect a craft that was not hers to begin with.

Burdened by defeat, she made her way back to the one-room cabin she called home and locked herself in for the night. Not caring her hair and body were still damp, she fell upon the bed and prayed for sleep.

Chapter Two

Her lips were as soft as a rose petal, her scent as pure as the rain.

Ryan stared into sky blue eyes when she pulled back and smiled. He wondered how he had gotten so close to the woman who awoke him with kisses from her plump pink lips and ensnared his torso with her delicately muscular thighs.

"I want you."

Stunned by her words, it took him a moment, but only just that, to realize she was sliding her body downward. When she stopped and pinned him with devilment in her amazing blue eyes, her core teased his aching loin. He inhaled swiftly as his tip touched her moistness, and everything inside of him sprung to life, taking his ability to reason along with his breath. He pulled her to him roughly, desperate to take her mouth again, to taste her, to fill her, to drown in a need like none he'd experienced in all his life.

She gave him everything but that for which his body strove, tantalizing him into submission, then she pulled back and laughed with delight. Her amusement only fed his hunger, as it was that of a seductress satisfied with her power. She nipped his lower lip, then his chin, and when she rose slightly to stare at him hungrily, her irises spun and reshaped using all the colors of the rainbow, and some it had never known.

He knew he should have felt fear at the oddity, but he recognized only desire magnified beyond his control. As restraint snapped, he rolled, taking her with him, giving him the advantage as he pinned her to the soft wildflower-covered ground.

Her skin tasted of sunshine, of moonbeams, of pristine rain falling from a virgin cloud, as he suckled and nipped and kissed each spot within lips reach. Her hands sought him, fondling him, from shoulders, to chest, to hips, before she grasped his buttocks to pull him closer. Each touch enhanced already infernoed flames, but the tip of his penis nestling in the opening of her soft vaginal lips, stole his soul. He bit her shoulder, not meaning to harm, but her own actions begged for the harshness of his touch.

He meant nothing but to please.

He suckled the mark he'd left behind, making her moan, making him ache all the more. She called him by name; the word a caress, a question, and a demand he would willingly die to fulfill. He didn't know hers, but it didn't matter; she was the air in his lungs, the blood in his veins, and all things elemental to his very existence.

Exercising resistant, he slid back, wanting to pay homage. To taste, and tease, and tantalize each and every inch of precious flesh. His desire to pleasure her and make her understand and match his need was playfully thwarted, though, as she had plans of her own. She curled into him, locked her heels beneath his buttocks, pulling him forward sharply so his arrow found its mark, and his control disintegrated as if it had never been.

Breathless, Ryan awoke to silence and darkness for the most part. He inhaled and exhaled harsh shaky breaths, puffing steam clouds in the cold morning air. His heart pounded, knocking against his chest. His penis was filled to aching as he clutched the blanket covering him. He sat up swiftly and looked around, then remembered where he was, and why he was there. It took a moment more for him to realize the woman in his dream was the one who flew in and out of his life for that brief moment the night before, and he couldn't help but laugh at himself.

As if!

The natural light coming from the windows below the loft did little to aid his vision even after he pulled on his glasses. He figured it was expected, given the darkness of the wood ceiling and windowless walls of the tiny loft bedroom. As his head cleared and his bearings returned, he searched for the clean boxers he'd flung onto the bed the night before, following the cold shower that nearly froze the skin off his bones. Once he threw the covers off, the morning air was as wicked, and goose bumps dissolved the last physical remnants of his dream. But his head still reeled with memories and unsatisfied desire.

The remainder of his things were still downstairs, as his intention of dressing in fresh clothing and heading straight to the motel first thing had been his last thought before climbing into the amazingly comfortable feather bed, and snuggling under the softest blankets he'd ever felt, the night before.

The cozy bed, and the possibility of once again seeing the woman of his dream, was a lure to remain at the cabin Ryan briefly considered giving weight to. But he'd made up his mind, and leaving was the more practical thing to do. Rising, he pulled on the boxers before taking the ladder-like steps down to the main floor. As he'd suspected, the fire had gone out in the hearth sometime during the night. He debated trying to rebuild it and tinkering with the generator to allow for a hot shower before he dressed for the day, as he made his way to the kitchen area. As cold as it was, he knew those were the practical things to do since he couldn't possibly get a spot at the motel until check-in time, but both looked like monumental tasks at the moment, and he was ravenous for some reason. He looked into the basket the whirlwind brought the night before, hoping she didn't mind if he ate one of the large, individually wrapped banana nut muffins sitting on top, even though he wasn't going to continue renting the cabin.

Surely one night in hell warranted a muffin.

Ryan rubbed his growling tummy as he smiled to himself, willing to admit it hadn't actually been hell. He'd slept better than he had since conceiving the mystical game, building the program, and finally succeeding in making it something gamers would flock to own. His dissatisfaction at leaving it there had turned into a quest to build a system that would allow the game to do things his games couldn't do on the systems built by others.

Sure all those months of non-stop work were what had sent him into such a deep sleep, one that made his mind jump headlong into an erotic dream, he relaxed and took a moment to enjoy the here and now. He'd been on pins and needles for the past year, and were it not for learning about his father and meeting him....

Ryan shook his head as he glanced back at his open suitcase. No, he wouldn't be relaxing anytime soon. He'd be working to build the sequel to his new game, *Temptress Realm*, or obsessing over the system prototype he was about to show to the world, all the while trying to decide what to do with the mad man that had been tossed into his lap. He wasn't capable of relaxing anyway. He needed order, and he needed focus.

Time on his hands made him nervous. Made him feel lost. As OCD as he tended to be, it amazed him he wasn't having a hard time with the fact his clothing was no longer perfectly packed, nor was the luggage closed and stored. He couldn't believe he'd left it lying in the center of the room where he'd rummaged through it the night before. Of course, his thoughts had been on the blonde. Which was another reason his dream made sense.

Unwilling to let his thoughts to go back *there*, Ryan crossed to the ice box cooler and pulled out one of the six small orange juice bottles he'd stored the night before. The absence of a coffeemaker made him groan as he'd bought coffee as well at the little grocery store in town. But, given the lack of electricity, unless he wanted to start the generator and run an electrical cord off it to brew each pot, he understood the lack of one.

Another good reason to move into the motel.

He frowned. Perplexed. For some reason, which he couldn't quite put his finger on, the thought of leaving the cabin didn't hold quite as much appeal as it had. There was no good reason to stay, what with the seclusion, the lack of amenities, and the possibility spiders were running rampant outside, yet... *No*, he wouldn't stay, that would be ridiculous. The knock on the door startled him, causing the small bottle of juice to swish, and a few drops to splat on the floor. He looked down and frowned, grabbed a hand towel hanging on an apartment-sized stove, and quickly wiped it up as he yelled, "Just a minute."

It surprised Ryan anyone would come out to the cabin so early in the morning, but maybe it was the owner and he could lodge his list of complaints and get his money back without having to chase anyone down. Pleased with that possibility, he bent before his suitcase and extracted a pair of pajama pants and pulled them on as he made his way to the door.

After a quick peek out, another kind of pleasure swamped him. His dream woman was on the other side, her eyes shining with delight once she saw his face.

He opened the door, stepped back, and she breezed right in. A light and tantalizing scent trailed in her wake, and it suddenly occurred to him she'd smelled the same in his dream. She looked over the room quickly and then smiled at him.

"Good, I see you haven't put things away yet, and I'm so glad you're already awake. I normally wouldn't be, but I just couldn't sleep. So I thought I'd come on over and show you how to work everything, if you haven't already figured things out. And since you haven't even unpacked, that answers that.

"I'm glad to see you aren't a neat freak, too. My sisters are, but I'm a little more haphazard. Actually a lot more. But that's something you'll learn if we get a chance to get to know each other better. So back to the issue at hand. Do you need me to show you how things work?"

Ryan closed the door behind him because he couldn't make himself look away from the beauty chatting away in the living room. For some reason he had trouble making himself tell her of his decision, but finally his mouth started working. "Thanks, but it won't be necessary. I've decided I need to stay in town. I'll be leaving shortly." Even as the words were leaving his mouth, his mind rejected the thought of a lowbrow motel, eating every meal in restaurants, but mostly that his new neighbors couldn't possibly hold the appeal of this one. The disappointment on her face added to his sudden need to stay where he was, which confused the hell out of him. Being alone with a computer had always kept him content. Talking to people, women in particular, made him feel awkward, and often confused.

Thankfully, being a geek wasn't as uncool now as it used to be.

"Really? But you can't! Um, I mean, that's too bad. I was taking the day off, well, more than the day, and I don't want to deal with my family right now, which is my other alternative. I thought I could show you around. If you wanted, that is. The mountain is beautiful, and there are so many things to see, and," she hesitated, bit her lip, and then added, "I *really* just needed something new to do. Something different. With somebody different. Only, please don't think anyone would do, I mean, oh gosh, I guess I'm going through an identity crisis of sorts."

She shook her head, her eyes expressed distress and then self-depreciating amusement. Ryan was so busy trying to keep from walking up to her and kissing her pretty pink lips to calm her down, he nearly missed what she said next.

"But that isn't your problem, is it?" she finished, looking like she desperately wanted him to disagree with her.

She eyed him up and down with an interest he knew he had to be misinterpreting. Women had never looked at him like that, except in college when they'd wanted him to do their homework. And as far as he could tell, she wasn't a schoolgirl anymore. Though the thought of her dressed all prim and proper in a plaid uniform made him have to bite his lip, and wonder when, if ever, his mind had gone in such a direction.

"I'm sorry. I'm boring you. I tend to talk a lot when I'm nervous. I never unload on strangers. Or even family for that matter. I'm kind of the odd duck, you know? Different than the rest. They're so content with what life has handed them, and I wanted something different. Oh, Lord! You can tell me to shut up anytime now."

Ryan laughed at that and relaxed a little. He totally understood being the odd one in a group. And her chatter delighted him for reasons he couldn't fathom, coming from gorgeous lips aside. He barely knew how to respond, but it was obvious she was waiting for him to say something.

"Uh, no… I mean don't worry about it. I'm kind of going through an identity crisis of my own. And I don't *have* to leave. I guess I'm a city boy, feeling a little lost. But the truth is, other than visiting my father in the hospital, I had no idea what I would do with my time." *Liar.* "So that sounds great. I'll just get dressed and… Why do I make you nervous?" Ryan frowned. *Did I just say I was staying?* Given that it felt right to do so, his face muscles relaxed and then slid into a smile when hers did.

"Well, you're a man, of course. And we're all alone…okay, honesty time, because I'm up for an adventure if you are. You're, you know, very pleasing to look at and seem very nice, and oh my, my mouth is running again, and you don't even know my name. I don't think. Do you?"

Ryan shook his head, trying not to laugh again. Listening to her made him feel happier than he ever remembered feeling. Seeing he was not now, nor had ever been a people person, that just added to the list of strange things that had happened to him since arriving in Mystic Waters.

"It's Dia, short for Diamond. I hope you don't mind that I think you're kind of a hunk. I like that you're not obvious about it. Hunks don't come to Mystic Waters." She frowned. "Well, they do sometimes. Both of my sisters married gorgeous men, but they are theirs, and not my type. Amen-ra is Jewell's and looks like an ancient Egyptian statue, and Nicolae is Sapphire's and built, well...like crazy, and okay, drop dead hot, but like I said, not my type. Are you anybody's?"

Ryan took a few seconds to try to catch up, confused by the names, and even more so if she'd actually just called him a hunk. Given his studious ways, and the fact that he wore glasses he'd probably slid back up his nose half a dozen times since she'd entered the door, that wasn't a label he'd ever considered, much less been tagged with.

"Um...anybody's *what*?"

Dia laughed, a tinkling little laugh that stirred something in him. Not that he hadn't been stirred since he saw her face on the other side of the door.

"Anybody's, you know, *hunk*?"

Ryan shook his head, as much in disbelief that this gorgeous woman really did find him attractive, as to answer her question. Surely she was playing with him...but what if she wasn't?

Her smile flashed. "That's great. I mean, *if* it's great with you. I'm something of a mess, or so I'm always told, but I can be a lot of fun. Not that I want you to think that's why I'm here this morning. The number of times I've been alone with an attractive man who wasn't related to me could be counted by the number of fingers I hold up while making a fist." She laughed at her own joke. "I was thinking we could be friends and entertain each other, unless you had pressing business, which I now know you don't."

She took a breath. "Okay. I'm done talking. It's your turn."

****

Dia closed her mouth, wondering what in the world had gotten into her. No wonder her family thought her a flighty, flirty mess, though until now, she'd never thought of herself that way. Sure, Ryan Steward was a good-looking man, in that *Clark Kent has Superman hidden beneath the glasses* kind of way, but she'd actually asked him about his love life, and she didn't even know the guy. But that wasn't the worst of it. She'd had him on her mind since shortly after waking, couldn't wait to get to him, and now, she was making a complete fool of herself over him. He had to think her a complete loser.

"I like listening to you talk, and I'm…well, flattered. Why aren't you anyone's somebody?"

Dia studied him, making sure he wasn't toying with her. Satisfied his gorgeous turquoise eyes were sincere, she shrugged, realizing she didn't know the answer. It wasn't as if she wasn't interested in a relationship, but she'd been so caught up in becoming celestial, she'd not taken the time to put herself out there. Or even give it much thought. "I've been too busy, I guess. But now I'm not."

She grinned, relieved he was really interested if the pleasure in his eyes was any indication. "I'm declaring myself on vacation."

Ryan smiled and took a step closer. "That must make me the luckiest man on earth. I'm free until I need to go check on my father this evening. What would you like to do?"

Dia had to keep herself from doing a happy dance. But

she tried not to let her excitement show. "Hmmm, how about I show you how everything works here, then we'll take a ride on my four-wheeler, and I'll show you the lay of the land. If we're out long enough and get hungry, there's this little barbeque stand a couple of mile on up the mountain that makes amazing sandwiches.

She giggled. "By the way, aren't you a little cold?"

Ryan looked down. By the goofy grin he gave her, Dia was certain he'd only just realized he was shirtless and barefooted.

"Um…yeah, sorry. I forgot I hadn't gotten dressed. Give me a few minutes to clean up and put some clothes on, and I'll be ready for whatever you want to do."

Ryan reached into his open suitcase and pulled out jeans and a button down shirt. Dia watched his every move, more interested in the play of muscles along his back than the clothing he chose. She forced herself to look away, somewhat aghast she was actually lusting after a man, but she found herself watching him again as he headed to the bathroom next to the kitchen.

Smiling to herself, she shook her head. The man was simply visiting for a while, taking care of a sick father, and then he would disappear as quickly as he'd appeared on Mystic Mountain. But there was no harm in having a little fun while he was here. And she needed the diversion.

Desperately!

She'd awakened after only a couple of hours of sleep, completely depressed. That had never happened to her as far as she could remember. She'd always slept soundly and then greeted each new day with enthusiasm, barely able to wait to get started on whatever she had planned to try. But she'd felt an overwhelming sadness instead, which also never happened. The decision to quit trying to conjure seemed to take her drive to function as well, making her even more upset than she'd expected to be about giving up on *the craft*. Why she hadn't just looked at it as another in a long line of opportunities to try again, like she always had before, and then moved on to the next *experiment*? These thoughts played through her mind while she'd gotten out of bed, dressed, eaten a few carrots for breakfast, and then had nothing else to do but stare at the walls.

Never having felt so lost before, Dia had done the unthinkable. She'd straightened and cleaned her one-room lodge completely. Nary a stitch of clothing laid across the footboard of her bed and not one dirty glass sat in the small sink in the corner that made up her kitchen. Dust, which she normally considered irrelevant, had suddenly become the enemy and was fought and defeated. It wasn't until she'd gotten the text to check on her new neighbor that she'd not only felt a spark of interest, but was filled with exuberant excitement.

Great-Uncle Frank had made a point of making sure she, not he, *given his advanced age and all*, was checking in on their guest, to make sure he felt at home. When she'd responded that she'd checked on him the night before, she'd been asked to do so again this morning. What was particularly funny, other than the instant pleasure she'd felt, was the elderly American Indian was as spry as a teenager and rarely left anything to anyone else.

Knowing *his* mystical abilities, Dia wondered if Great-Uncle Frank hadn't foreseen her need of distraction, perhaps a touch of excitement for something other than the gift she would never have. If that was the case, she'd have to thank him. To think about something other than ignoring her locked shed was a must. However, now that she'd come over and had gotten another much clearer *in the daylight* look at her new neighbor, she was actually jittery with nerves.

"Do I need a jacket?"

Dia blinked, realizing she'd been staring into space,

then nodded. She could only hope the sudden thrill-chill giving her goose bumps didn't show on her face. "A light one, maybe. The mountain is cool this early in the morning, especially at this elevation. But we can shed them later if we have to, once the sun is higher. Though you'll definitely need one until we get out of the forest. With all the tall pines, it rarely gets all that warm here at ground level."

Ryan looked her up and down with a slight grin on his lips before he returned to his suitcase to close it. "Let me run this upstairs. I'll be right back down."

Dia bit her bottom lip as she appreciated the view of his jeans-clad gluteus while he made his way up the ladder-like steps. Though he had the face of a mathematician, his body was that of an amateur athlete, and she liked the combination. Very much in fact. Grinning to herself, she waited and, from the sounds coming from above, figured he was taking the time to make his bed and put away his clothes.

How cute.

From the look of things, other than the half-finished bottle of orange juice, and the wrapper he'd taken off one of the muffins her mom had made for the gift basket, he hadn't settled in at all. Which made sense, given his decision to leave. But now that he was staying, and since it was basically her fault he was, she knew she'd need to find a way to make him as comfortable as possible. And keep herself too busy to get depressed again in the meantime.

And yes, find out what this strange pull she felt for him was.

He returned with a smile, wearing a jacket that looked appropriate given their plans. He made his way to the little island and lifted the cellophane wrapper and carried it to the small garbage can sitting at the edge of the sink. And took another minute to wipe down the countertop while he downed the small bottle of juice, then disposed of it too, before shaking the towel out over the trash can.

Dia watched him, wondering if she'd been wrong. Maybe he was a neat freak after all. But that was okay, too. In fact, she couldn't think of a thing about him that didn't tug at her. Which was confusing to say the least. "You have dish cloths. They're in a drawer."

He looked from her to the sink and lifted the hand towel and looked at it with a frown. "What do I do with this?"

Dia smiled. He really was cute. "Just hang it back on the stove handle, and when we get back I'll take it with me to wash."

"Oh, okay." After doing as he was instructed, he grinned at her. "Do I rebuild the fire before we go?"

Dia looked at the hearth. She hadn't noticed the banked fire or how chilly the room was until now. "No, I'll show you where everything is, and we'll get it done as soon as we get back."

Ryan nodded. "Okay, I'm ready, but let's check out that generator before we go. That way I'll know what to do with it later. I definitely don't want to take another cold shower."

Dia would have kicked herself if she wouldn't look foolish doing it. She should have taken care of it all the night before. "I'm so sorry I should have helped get you settled in much better than I did last night. I promise I'll show you everything you need to know to keep the cabin warm at night, and the water hot for whenever you need it."

Chapter Three

Having his arms around a beautiful woman first thing in the morning was every man's dream, and Ryan couldn't believe he'd not only awakened from a dream filled with her touch, he was now actually with her. Her scent was as intoxicating as her features, and her zest for life was something he'd never before known. The world he lived in, *when he bothered to socialize*, was filled with serious people who did serious things all day to achieve a serious goal. She seemed to be a free spirit, one who could declare herself on vacation, and one who loved speed and flying over boulders in the wildest terrain he'd ever been in.

It was amazing to look ahead and see nothing but forest in their path, but she somehow knew exactly where to go for them to continue on their journey without hitting a tree he was certain was in front of them only seconds before. At first his heart had lodged in his throat, but as time went on, he realized she was as good as any of those racecar drivers he envied when secretly watching NASCAR in his youth.

When she finally pulled to a stop, they were beside a wide stream. She turned to him and smiled. "Let's take a break here and I'll show you the magic of this place."

The word magic took a little joy from the moment, but he knew he had two choices. He could let his father's irrational mind ruin this time for him, or he could pocket those thoughts until later, when he planned to once again enter the room of the delusional.

There was no choice to make. His father was a stranger

in every sense of the word. And though he felt the need to help Clayton in any way he could, there was no way he would ever believe the tales his father had told with such conviction. That would make him as crazy as his sire.

Ryan rose from the seat and took Dia's hand when she held it out. She swung her leg over and they stood side by side. He smiled at her, and she smiled back, and he was certain he'd never had a more perfect moment in his life.

"This is beautiful. Like a painting. I didn't expect green grass and shrubbery this early in the year."

Dia smiled. "This place is always green, though the ground cover is mostly moss here. The stream never runs dry or stops running, even when it gets cold enough for a layer of ice to form on top. That only happens in the dead of winter. What you see is the main water artery that runs from the top of the mountain down to the lake below. We call her *Neolia*, as she brings new life to any who drink her waters." Dia's brows pulled together before she looked up at him and smiled like she'd made a joke. "I don't know why I'm telling you all this. It's…you know, folk lore."

Though he didn't know what she was talking about, he nodded. "That's a pretty name."

Dia nodded. "Yeah, um, well, come see what she holds."

She took his hand and led him closer to the stream. He grinned as he glanced down to their clasped hands, wondering if she even realized how unusual it was for someone to be touched so casually, on such short acquaintance. Or maybe it was just him. Women didn't take his hand to lead him anywhere, ever. If his nose wasn't stuck in a technology book, he was calculating reactivity equators in his quest to build either the video games that had made him a rich man or the game system he knew would take the market by storm. Making him even wealthier. Not that he minded her ease with him, *at all*. As firsts went, this one was pretty exciting. He curled his fingers loosely and was rewarded with a slight squeeze.

As hard as it was to pull his attention from her touch, he forced himself to follow her lead when they stopped by pristine water, so clear he could see the multitude of fish following its path, as well as the mossy bottom that looked rather deep for a stream. They squatted down together and she released his hand, to cup hers together. She dipped them in, then brought the water to her lips and sipped. She made a sound of pleasure and closed her eyes as if the simple act of drinking was a sensual experience. For several seconds he just watched her, so taken with her beauty he could barely breathe. When she opened her eyes and looked at him, his heart tripped, as they matched the kaleidoscope eyes of her in his dream. As soon as his mind registered the oddity, her irises were back to sky blue, and he knew he was mistaken. She dipped her cupped hands in again before holding them out to him.

"Try it. It's the purest water on earth."

Ryan looked from her to the stream again, his confusion stumbling over his desire to please her. Though he would never consider drinking from a waterway, because of all the minute germs that could live within it, he debated briefly but then knew he couldn't disappoint her. Touching his lips to the side of her palm sent a jolt through him, but he tried not to react as he sipped. As if the initial shock weren't enough, a surge of energy built throughout his muscles as the water slid down his throat. When he was done, he almost felt dizzy and looked at her, torn between wonder and trepidation.

"That's...strange."

"What is?" she asked softly, her eyes studying him intently.

"The energy. Didn't you feel it?"

Dia gasped. "*You* felt it?"

Ryan nodded, as they rose to their feet. "How is that possible? What's in that water…besides fish?"

Dia swallowed and stared at him as if afraid to answer. She sighed and looked around behind them, into the forest, seeming concerned they might be overheard. She turned to him again, and though her gaze seemed cautious, she answered anyway.

"I don't know. I've never followed it to its origins. That is a secret, *sacred* place of my uncle Tom's people. No one is allowed to go there but him and his father. They are the tribal and spiritual leaders of their people. My mom says one day his sons, my triplet cousins, will be taken there to…" She shook her head. "But anyway, isn't it, um, *cool?*" she finished, rather lamely.

Ryan frowned, concerned by her sudden reserve. He wanted to ask what it was that she hadn't finished saying, but she looked as confused as he felt. So he sought a safer course. "The old man who rented me the cabin. He is the local tribal leader?"

Dia nodded. "Yes… He's very wise. Um…and quite a good story teller."

She giggled, but it sounded strained and didn't quite ring true. He cleared his throat, wanting information, but not wanting to scare her off. "Tell me his story about the water."

Dia's eyes were large as she stared at him. "It's just Indian folklore. And I barely remember, um…uh, I remember the story."

Ryan tried not to let his confusion show. It was almost as if she was telling him things against her will. He smiled, hoping she would relax, completely perplexed by her agitation.

"Tell me anyway, please. I love hearing about regional folklore. I rarely watch television, but when I do, it's to discover things like this. My mother brought me up watching the Public Broadcasting Station." He grinned at himself. "But I snuck in unacceptable viewing when she was at work."

After a slight hesitation, Dia nodded. "Well, let's see... When we were little, Great-Uncle Frank told us *Neolia* was born of Mother Mountain millennia ago, when the earth's plates fought for dominion over each other. When what is now called the Appalachians were formed by the plates buckling over each other in battle for supremacy, the Great Spirit became angry with their foolishness. He feared the mountain range would continue to grow in length and also eventually reach the heavens. And man, *being man*, would invade and desecrate the city of God.

"So he sent a giant bolt of lightning to the center of Mystic Mountain, as it was already taller than all the rest. It went all the way through each layer of rock until it reached the water far below the earth's crust. Because of the heat of the lightning, hot water spewed up as a geyser for hundreds of years, then it cooled and continuously ran down the mountain until it created a lake at the base.

"Many hundreds of years more passed, and the weight of the water broke through the rock separating the lake from the mountain's underwater cavern. And to this day, the water runs in a circle from the lake, up through the mountain, and then back down Neolia and her veins, to the lake again.

"Great-Uncle Frank says it's *The Circle of Life*. Each time the lake waters run back up the mountain for another trip they are purified and chilled again, so Neolia is considered to have given new life to the water as well as...."

"As well as what?"

Dia bit her bottom lip before speaking. "As well as those who drink it. Of course, that's just what Great-Uncle Frank and his people believe."

Ryan nodded, liking the story, but more fascinated that he actually felt stronger and more alert than he ever had before. He pushed his glasses back up his nose, just realizing they'd slipped, and then removed them when they seemed dirty. He unzipped his jacket and wiped them on the tail of his shirt, and then put them back on. But wiping them made no difference. He tried wiping them again, but the result was the same. Irritated, he glanced up to find Dia watching him, and he nearly jumped. Not because she was so close, but because he could see her clearly.

"What is it?" she asked, concern marring her features.

Ryan shook his head. "Uh, I don't know… I think my sight is clearer." He looked beyond her, but he still had trouble seeing distances clearly, although he'd swear that had improved as well. "Well, up close anyway." He looked back at her, bewildered.

Dia's eyes were large and her face was frozen as if she didn't know what to say. Slowly she looked from him to the glasses in his hand, her frown deepening.

"Well, isn't that interesting."

Ryan didn't know how to respond to that. Though it wasn't totally clear as far as distance, up close, at least as far as Dia was standing, his sight was as pristine as the water he'd drank. Which was actually very cool. He glanced back down at the stream and then at her. "Do you think it's possible that drinking the water did that?"

Dia shrugged, though she looked seriously concerned now. He hated seeing her beautiful face tight like that, so he changed the subject. "So tell me more about this place. Have you always lived here?"

Relief eased her features a little, and she nodded slowly. "Yes. My entire family does for the most part. There are quite a few of us."

"Since you are clearly not, it must be another branch that are Native American?"

Dia nodded again, but it seemed her discomfort extended to talking about her family. He couldn't blame her. He had no interest in talking about his. He was about to find another topic to discuss, but, surprisingly, she answered him.

"Yes. My mom's sister, Destiny, married Tom who is a Native Son, and they had triplet sons."

"Wow, triplets are rare."

Dia inhaled before biting her bottom lip. He got the impression their conversation was making her irritated, yet, instead of telling him to mind his own business, she laughed a little.

"Not in my family. They are actually quite common. But enough about me, are you ready to ride some more?"

Though he didn't know why, he felt relieved for her. She seemed to need an excuse to stop talking. Ryan opened his mouth to answer, but nothing came out when he spotted blurry movement behind her. He slowly slid his glasses back on and gasped as he stared past Dia's head. He let his glasses slide down, and then he glanced down at her. "Don't move. There's a huge wolf right behind you," he whispered.

Dia swung around, and he grabbed her to pull her against him while keeping his eyes on the wolf. He was certain Dia could feel his heart beating frantically at her back, but instead of sharing his fear she emitted a little laugh of pleasure, and then struggled from his arms to take a step forward. The wolf sat down, its tail wagging.

Ryan shoved his glasses up and held his breath as she approached it, disbelieving when she reached out to scratch behind its ears. She turned back to him with a smile. "This is Jaspon. He patrols the mountain with his pack." She turned back to the wolf. "Jaspon, this is Ryan. He's a friend."

The wolf barked once and Ryan would swear it was a

greeting if asked. He nodded, not ready to take the chance he would get a hand bitten by moving forward to join her next to the big male. He glanced between her and the animal, wondering if perhaps he was still dreaming. It was the only possible explanation to her being with him in the first place. Never mind the magic water that made him feel like a superhero, the improved sight, and a friendly wolf in the wild.

Ryan blew out a breath and relaxed, knowing he'd wake up before the animal or something else killed him. He was more than willing to ride out the dream, as long as it kept her at his side.

If nothing else, he could use the information to build his next game.

Going with the flow, he looked the wolf over. "Is he tame, then?"

Dia patted the animal's head and then returned to Ryan's side as Jaspon licked at the stream. Though it was hard to tear his gaze away from the danger, even if he was just dreaming, he forced himself to focus on her.

She grinned. "Not tame in the least, except with my family. He won't hurt you because I've introduced you, and he'll let the rest of the pack know you are welcome here."

Ryan didn't know what to say, but now that he knew he was experiencing a lucid dream, he would just play along until its conclusion. "How many are there?"

Dia shrugged. "Several, but don't worry about them. The only way they'd harm you is if they felt threatened by you, or you were a threat to my family. They take care of us, and we take care of them. It works out for us all."

This was really getting good and would make his previous mythical and mystical games look like child's play. He grinned, hoping like hell the entire dream played out before he awoke. Knowing that was a danger, since he was rationalizing everything, he delved into his role. "I've never known of wild creatures befriending people, but I haven't really looked into it either."

Dia laughed. "City boy?"

"To the bone. That's why I was about to head back to town to look for a place to stay. I'm out of my element here." Saying those words scared him, making him fear the truth would knock him out of this dream. He dug deeper and kept his eyes on her to hold onto the moment. It was a relief when she approached the four-wheeler and climbed on and everything still seemed real. He followed her, noticing the large wolf decided to nap at the edge of the stream.

He smiled, satisfied. "You are completely in your element though."

Dia nodded. "Yep. I've lived here my entire life with the exception of my college years. I know the animals and they know me." She paused, made a face, and added, "Although the wolves are fairly new to the area."

"And, still, they are so friendly?"

Dia shrugged and started the motor, causing Jaspon to look over at them before laying his large head back down. She turned as much as she could to look back at Ryan. "I know it seems strange, but they understand me and my family. I don't question it. And neither should you."

Ryan grasped her tiny waist when the vehicle jerked forward, curious her last statement sounded like a threat, even though it was lightly delivered. He pressed his lips together, fearful a bug might hit him in the face and end up in his mouth as he pondered the strangeness of the world he'd entered. Dream or not, bugs in the mouth weren't happening.

Mystic Mountain *felt* different than any place he'd ever been, even while dreaming. Though he couldn't explain the difference if his life depended on it, there was something about the very air he breathed. It was pure and though seemed filled with moisture, the air didn't make him feel hot and sticky, or even cold and clammy. The most surprising thing was it didn't seem altered by the exhaust coming from the four-wheeler they were riding on. He leaned forward and yelled over the loud motor. "How is it that this thing doesn't put out a smell?"

Dia slowed a little and tilted her head so she could respond while keeping an eye on her driving. "Uncle Tom's cousins produce the fuel from local plant oils. It isn't gasoline. Or even corn oil. Everything used for fuel on the mountain comes from the mountain. That way we are not polluting our home or desecrating the earth.

"Even before my family came to this land, it was treated with the greatest respect by those who called it their home. That has been lost in the rest of the country—and pretty much all over the world. Which is really sad.

"I had a hard time living away from home while I attended college."

Ryan digested everything she shared, as impressed with the reality of his imagination as everything else. He'd never given much thought to such things on a conscious level, but then he'd always only known places where concrete and brick were considered natural elements. He closed his eyes, not caring where she took him, but held on to the feelings so he didn't wake up.

He breathed in and out, just enjoying the vibration beneath him, the exhilaration of giving himself to the moment, and the scent of the woman whose life he'd currently placed in his mind. When they slowed and stopped again, he opened his eyes and followed to where she was pointing. Though not clearly, he saw a large buck standing proudly a short distance from them.

Ryan stayed where he was, but Dia rose and lifted her leg, causing her to fall back. Her bottom landed between his upper thighs, and his breath caught. He wondered how he could translate his purely male reaction on screen, but let the thought go when she giggled a little, before standing with her back to him. Without looking back, she moved forward slowly until she was only a few feet before the buck.

"Good morning, Wind Jumper."

The buck lowered his head briefly and then stamped his large hoof once. Ryan was captivated by the slightly blurry scene before him and finally remembered to breathe.

"He is our friend, Wind Jumper, and will bring no harm to your herd." She turned back to Ryan and waved him forward. "Ryan, come meet Wind Jumper. He's head deer on Mystic Mountain and very protective of his family."

Bemused, Ryan gained his feet and walked to stand by Dia's side, being careful not to make any sudden moves. The large buck stood feet taller than Ryan and had massive antlers that were sixteen strong, if Ryan counted right. Though he'd been to petting zoos as a child, he'd never been this close to a mature animal, and with the buck's weapons on full display, he had to admit, if just to himself, the creature was intimidating as hell.

"Talk to him."

Ryan turned to Dia, but could tell she wasn't kidding. He turned back, and nearly held out his hand. Clearing his throat, he spoke. "Hello."

The buck nodded his head and Ryan jumped back. He swallowed, embarrassed that he'd been the only one to react. "I'm Ryan. It's nice to meet you."

Even though he felt all kinds of silly, Ryan felt his acceptance by Dia's animals was a must for his acceptance by her. He stayed where he was as she moved forward and ran her palm against the buck's jaw, then remained transfixed with the thought of her touching him as gently. As if the buck sensed Ryan's thoughts, Wind Jumper's head came up sharply, his regal antlers standing so tall Ryan knew he'd never be able to touch those on top.

The animal looked him over, then turned to Dia and snorted. She laughed, but Ryan had a feeling he'd just been insulted. Dream or not, he wasn't going to look like a fool in front of such an amazing woman. He took a step forward and looked the buck in the eyes. "You don't even know me."

Dia's hand on his arm drew Ryan's attention from the buck to her. She smiled gently. "He means no disrespect. He has simply taken me under his wing and is protective." She turned back to the buck. "Ryan is my friend. As are you. Be kind."

If deer could glare, Ryan felt certain this one was doing it, but he held his ground, and after a moment the buck looked back to Dia and nodded his great head. Ryan wasn't certain, but he thought maybe he'd just passed some kind of test. Which was ridiculous, of course, but would play right into the game possibilities spinning in his head.

The buck pranced, turned, and leisurely walked away until he was out of Ryan's range of sight. Since Dia was still looking in that direction, her face pensive, he guessed she could still see the departing animal.

"How is it that you communicate so well with these animals?"

Dia turned to him, her eyes guarded. "I told you. I've lived here all my life. It isn't really that unusual."

Though Ryan had to disagree, he kept the thought to himself. He smiled at her, wanting to see her smile again as well. "I'm getting hungry. That muffin I had for breakfast is long gone. How about that barbeque place you told me about?"

As he'd hoped, her face lit up, and she smiled. "Definitely! I can't wait to see what you think about it. I keep telling the owners they should go international, but they, pretty much like everyone else from around here, like things to stay just the way they are."

****

Dia was glad the trip to the food stand would take them a good hour through the forest. She needed to think. Had she made a terrible mistake introducing Ryan to her wildlife friends? Maybe she shouldn't have, but other than her extended family and the Mystic Waters community, the animals were the only beings she happily associated with, and to bypass or ignore either would have hurt or insulted them.

But it was more than that. She'd felt compelled to share herself with him, and though she hadn't meant to, to be honest when he questioned her, as well. Still, she knew she'd have to be more careful. The last thing she wanted to do with her new found free time was place her family in danger. One of the things she liked most about Ryan was also the thing that could make him dangerous. He had no knowledge of mystics and magic. No idea her affinity with the animals was natural to them, where it was unnatural to others. She feared she may have breached one of her family's laws, to never reveal themselves to others because persecution had historically followed soon after. Not that she believed Ryan would hurt a fly.

Perhaps even stranger than her need to expose herself was his acceptance of all he saw and heard. She couldn't help but grin as she flew down the path, amused and more than a little proud he'd been willing to face down and protect her from both Jaspon and Wind Jumper, when it was so clear he'd feared both. She could just imagine how hard that had been for him. It was obvious he was completely out of his element. That he'd wanted to protect her filled her with pleasure. Of course just being in his company already did that.

She liked him—plain and simple—but she'd still have to be careful in the future and ask her family to tread lightly with him, if he ever got a chance to meet them.

It really wasn't fair Jewell found a man in the ancient past, for whom it was obvious from the start her family was full of mystics. And the same held true for Sapphire. Meeting and marrying a Lycanthrope pretty much took away any threat of exposure from him and his kind. Their need for secrecy was as great as her family's was. To reveal one would likely expose the other, once the need for help became clear. If Ryan had the slightest inkling he'd seen a werewolf—not just a wolf, as traumatic as *that* must have already been—more than likely the reality would have taken him over the edge.

Not that she had any illusions Ryan would end up being hers.

She had to remember that. Not let her deep attraction for him bind her heart in a way she'd be devastated once he returned to the world he knew. She had enough problems to deal with as it was.

The sight issue, however, was an immediate problem.

It killed her, but she'd have to contact her family and tell them she'd messed up again. Though none but Sapphire had ever said mean words, she knew her family thought of her as poor dumb Dia. Her clan was a mystical group of fixers, and she was nothing but a screw-up.

And now this.

Dia hadn't expected drinking from the stream to affect Ryan in any way. From her understanding, those waters only enhanced the ability of beings who were in tune with the elements, like the members of her family and the Lycanthrope pack. As the stream and the multitude of veins branching from it hydrated the rich soil, it also explained why all the plants and animals on Mystic Mountain were larger than life, filled with their own unique energy and power.

She'd always loved that the plants called to her, but

today, after already filling his head with the mystical, she had to ignore them. She didn't want to do anything else that might alert Ryan to just how different she was from other women he'd known.

After hitting a sharp rock, which threw them a little, Dia became concerned she wasn't able to find a smooth path for the four-wheeler to take. It wasn't something that had ever been a problem before. When she leaned back to apologize to Ryan for the rough ride, she noticed the flora she'd passed without acknowledgement seemed to wilt a bit in her wake. She slowed the vehicle and took a closer look. Sure enough, the plants that were lively before her were as they had always been, but those behind looked as if they were struggling to survive a drought.

Dia inhaled swiftly as excitement filled her. Was this her gift? Had she had it all along and was only now realizing it?

She braked again, this time so abruptly Ryan was thrown into her back. She turned to him again to apologize and froze. She couldn't find her voice and nearly choked while trying. Sitting against the four-wheeler's bumper was a large tree that hadn't been there before. Fearful Ryan would look back and see it as well, she mumbled an apology and sped off, knowing she had to bury her pride and seek out her family for help.

Chapter Four

Dia paced the floor of her aunt Destiny's cabin while she waited for the rest of the clan to gather. Her frantic text to her mother following lunch with Ryan had been necessary, though she'd hated leaving him behind earlier than their expected separation for the day, especially since his changing sight seemed to make him a little off-kilter. But she'd needed council, and since there was no one else she could turn to, she'd called a family meeting.

Knowing she'd have to keep the meeting relatively short, because she'd accepted Ryan's invitation to dinner following his visit to see his father, Dia was on the verge of biting her fingernails. She'd talked him into letting her take him so he didn't kill himself trying to drive the mountainous road with iffy sight, though she'd told him it was just because she knew the area so well. But time was getting away from her. So far only her mother, Aunt Haven, Aunt Destiny and Uncle Tom and her sister Jewell, who was days away from having her babies, had arrived. Apollo and Zeus were on their way from town, but fashion model Heracles wouldn't be attending since he'd gone to Destin for a swimsuit photo shoot, which would soon be turned into magazine ads. Her female cousins, Soleli, Celestia, and Luna, were also on their way, but were stopped on the other side of a wreck at the base of the mountainous road. The girls had to wait for law enforcement to clear the debris before they could proceed. She'd learned Sapphire was there as well, being one of the officers working the site.

As far as Dia was concerned, Sapphire could just stay. The last thing she needed now was her oldest sister's scorn.

Nearly an hour into her pacing, everyone who was coming had arrived and settled in the Whitehawks' large family room. Her mom and the aunts took the opportunity to make food while they'd waited, just as they did each time there was one of these gatherings. Though her mother kept sending her questioning looks, Dia wasn't ready to talk and would just shake her head. She didn't want to go into what she had to tell at all—and certainly not more than once.

Thankfully, the Hansen triplets finally arrived together to say they'd had barely missed being a part of the wreck. What had been a two-car accident had nearly been a three-car pile-up. Only Soleli's quick reaction kept them from hitting the two cars in front of them. Though they were unharmed, all three were filled with nervous energy, and Sapphire was still tied up dealing with the aftermath of the incident. Had it not been his day off on the fire and rescue crew, Apollo would have been there as well.

"Hi, all, since everyone has arrived, if you would, take your seats and we'll get started," Rayne said, wiping her hands on one of Destiny's many aprons. She motioned for Dia to come to the front of the large room to stand by her side. She looked her daughter over, her concern clear, as the chatter trailed off and the room became silent.

"The floor is yours, honey."

Dia nodded, unable to work up a smile. Now that the time had finally come, she didn't know where to begin. She looked around the room, and the concern and compassion that was sent back to her helped a little.

"I guess I need to start by letting you all know how much I love and appreciate you, and your support. I stand here knowing there will be no judgments, save my own, but I want to apologize in advance anyway for possibly revealing things about us to an outsider."

She waited a heartbeat to allow that to set in. As expected, curiosity and concern filled faces, but not condemnation. "The man who is renting Uncle Tom's cabin was with me today. I took him out into the forest on my four-wheeler, to entertain him, and because I needed a distraction."

Dia frowned, not ready to get into that. "I took us on a long ride to point out the beautiful plants and trees. I told him we were a big family, and I had lived here all my life, but of course I didn't say anything about our abilities. We eventually came to *Neolia*, and believing it would not faze him, but simply refresh us both, I offered him a drink."

Several eyebrows rose, and amusement was on as many faces, but no one said a word. Dia took a deep breath and continued. "What happened next is the problem. After he took the drink his eyesight changed."

This time those listening frowned. Her mother spoke up. "Changed how? And how do you know this?"

Dia nodded, glad for a specific thing to focus on because her head was spinning with what she'd yet to tell. "He wears glasses. Those dark-framed things that make him look like Clark Kent." She couldn't help but grin. "I know that sounds silly, but it's the only way I know to explain."

"So does he make you think of Superman when he removes them?"

All eyes turned to Luna in surprise. She rarely spoke unless directly spoken to and had little to say even then. Dia smiled at her timid cousin. "He does."

Luna smiled wistfully. "I love *Superman* movies. He's awkward like me until he removes his glasses. Then he's beautiful, and strong, and fearless. Sometimes I wish things were that easy to change."

Dia felt a flash of pity for her cousin, wishing Luna knew how truly beautiful she was, even if it *was* mostly on the inside by magazine standards. As far as Dia could fathom, Luna's introverted nature was what prevented people from noticing her. It also didn't help that, unlike the genetic blessings of all the other Cavanaugh children, Luna was the only one plain in feature and form. Not that it mattered to anyone. They loved her just the way she was.

Dia sighed, wishing she could do something to help her cousin, but the truth was she couldn't even help herself.

"I've found things aren't always easy either. Which brings me back to my situation." She looked around the room, and all eyes were once again on her.

"Like I said, Ryan wears glasses, and to be honest, I really find them attractive on him." The heat filling her face mortified her, and she had no idea why she'd revealed her crush on the man to her entire family, but there was no going back now. "Anyway, once he discovered his nearsightedness had cleared up, he realized his farsightedness changed too, but not nearly as much. He can use his glasses for distances, but it isn't completely clear either."

"Oh dear. The poor guy," Haven said. "Maybe I'll go see him and see if I can fix the other. I certainly don't want to undo the good that has been done."

"That would only make it more obvious we have power. Do you want to make this worse?" Destiny demanded.

"Well, don't go getting your panties in a wad, it was just a thought."

"Maybe you should keep your thoughts to yourself until you think them through!"

"Sisters!" Rayne injected, silencing them both.

Dia closed her eyes, knowing her actions were causing the sudden friction in the room. "I'm sorry. I didn't think letting him drink the water would matter."

Rayne shook her head. "It shouldn't have, honey. Of

all those who have vacationed here, no one has ever reported anything happening. You know each of the rentals gets water from the same source as we do, and your dad and Uncle Logan have never had any kind of a reaction other than liking it…a lot." She turned to Tom Whitehawk, who was looking at Dia speculatively.

"Tom?"

He shook his head. "You are correct, Dia. Drinking the water shouldn't have had any effect on him. So it must be something else. Have you been trying out any spells on him?"

Dia nearly choked but forced herself to speak. "No. I didn't do anything to him!"

Tom's smile was gentle. "I wasn't accusing you, honey. But you do have a tendency to try one thing, and something else results when you do your experiments."

Dia stared at him, debating whether to share the other predicament she'd placed herself in. First things first. "Well, I didn't do anything to him. All I did was give him a drink from my hands."

The adult's eyes lit up, and Dia looked from one to the other. "What?"

Rayne moved closer to her. "Have you noticed anything else strange lately?"

Dia grinned as excitement filled her. "Just today I noticed a couple of things. I think I know my gift."

Rayne smiled. "Go on."

"Well, I ride my four-wheeler all the time, and never thought anything about how smooth the path always was for me, or that a launch-shaped boulder would appear when I wanted to feel like flying. But today I noticed those things. Mostly because I was trying not to. If I don't acknowledge the plants I pass by, they seem sad and wilt a little."

Rayne laughed. "Thank God! You finally see what

we've all known for some time!"

Dia stared at her mother. "Are you serious? You knew and didn't tell me?"

Rayne's smile eased but didn't disappear. "It was yours to discover. If you hadn't been so focused on trying to claim Sapphire's gift, you would have noticed it sooner."

Dia nodded. "You're right. It wasn't until I decided I wasn't going to try to perform magic any more, last night, that I noticed all this today."

Surprise lit her mother's eyes. "Really? What made you decide to stop?"

Dia frowned, but kept her gaze on her mother. "I'm happy to learn I'm Elemental, like Aunt Haven, and I guess I just had one too many failures trying to be Celestial. But those aside, I'm still concerned about Ryan."

"Well, of course you are, honey. But never you mind. There is no way he can prove his sight change had anything to do with you or the water."

Dia looked from family member to family member, determined to come clean. "It's more than that. Jaspon came to the stream while we were there. I didn't want to insult the Lycan, so I introduced them. Of course Ryan just thought I was introducing him to a wolf."

Rayne stared at her before speaking. "Maybe he didn't think too much of it. Sometimes animals accept locals, even people besides us."

Dia knew her mother was throwing her a lifeline, but she couldn't take it. "There's more. I introduced him to Wind Jumper as well."

Jewell rose slowly, using the arms of her chair for leverage. Once she finally made it to her feet, it was clear the triplets inside of her were taking a toll. She frowned at Dia, and her emerald eyes sparked with anger. "Why would you do that? You can't really know this man! He's either going to think you're crazy or going to want to know why some pretty blond recluse speaks to animals. You are endangering all of us!"

Dia's heart nearly stopped as Jewell's eyes filled with tears and she fled the room as fast as her waddle would allow. She looked to the others, knowing she deserved her sister's scorn, but she still hadn't expected it.

Not from Jewell.

"I'm sorry, you all. But it was like I couldn't help myself. I couldn't lie to him. Or even evade his questions. I tried. I really did, but every time I started to lie, my mouth said just the opposite."

It was clear her mother wanted to go after Jewell, but she stayed. A concerned look passed between her mother and aunts, and Dia was afraid she was about to hear something ominous. Instead, they smiled a little at each other before her mother pulled her into a hug. "It will all work out, sweetheart. I'm sure you'll fix this. Just don't turn him into anything we can't undo. I need to go check on your sister. And don't mind Jewell right now, she's about to drop those babies and is frightened."

As her mother hurried to catch up with Jewell, Dia looked from her aunts, to her uncle, and finally at her cousins. Destiny announced food would be ready as soon as everyone had washed their hands.

A bit dumbfounded that everyone rose immediately and followed the matriarchs, Dia stayed where she was. She hadn't finished. She'd planned to tell them the *why* of all this. She'd wanted their support and, if she was honest, a little sympathy that her dream had been blown into glittering dust. But no one seemed interested. Let down, but just as relieved the meeting was over, she followed the rest, wondering what to do.

When she entered the kitchen, plates were being piled high, Jewell was being settled into a chair and handed tissues, and everyone was ignoring her to the point she knew she'd angered the entire family. Destiny's many chiming clocks sounded off, reminding Dia of the time, and she was glad for the excuse. "I have to go."

Several heads turned her way, and other than a nod here and there, no one questioned her, or even inquired as to her need to leave. Hurt, and more confused by the minute, she left the room, snatched up her purse, and headed to her car. She looked back once, but no one had followed her out, and for the first time in her life, she felt truly alone.

****

The trip back to Ryan's cabin was filled with self-doubt and as time went on, anger developed and grew. Since when did her family condemn one of their own? It wasn't as if she'd meant to expose them in any way. It wasn't like she'd purposely shown off to impress. In fact, she'd told the truth. For some reason she couldn't lie to Ryan. Taking several deep breaths, she tried to remember just what she'd done to get her in the position she was in, but nothing added up.

Sure, she was attracted to him. Very attracted. But that shouldn't have mattered to her family. It wasn't like she'd slept with him or anything, not that they had ever condemned for that either. She'd been a part of their female get-togethers, and sex was something to celebrate, not scorn. And none had ever belittled her, save Sapphire, because she'd wanted more than what was hers to have. So why now, of all times, had both her uncle and her mother mentioned her inability to perform magic in a way it was meant to be performed?

"Fine! You all be mad at me!"

Saying the words out loud did nothing to ease her anger or hurt. As Dia turned into the long driveway, she knew she'd have to try to help Ryan without spending any more time with him than necessary. Were it not for the mess she'd made of his sight, she'd ignore him altogether. But even as she had the thought, sadness swamped her, overriding the hurt and anger until she pulled up and saw him standing on the porch.

Like a balloon inflating she was suddenly filled with pleasure. She pulled to a stop and let thoughts of her family melt away when he squinted and smiled at her.

Dia stepped from the car and greeted him. "I'm sorry. Am I late?"

Ryan frowned as he looked down to navigate the steps and was still squinting when he looked back up. "Are we awake?"

Dia stayed where she was. "What?"

"Right now. Are we awake?"

Thinking he was making a joke, she smiled. "I am. I'm not so sure about you."

He nodded. "I took... I mean, were you here earlier?"

Completely perplexed since he seemed serious, she nodded. "Yes... Why are you asking me this?"

Ryan looked at her warily. "Did the water from that stream change my eyesight?"

Dia swallowed. What had happened since she dropped him off? He hadn't questioned anything earlier. "I don't...think so."

He frowned. "Did you talk to a wolf and a large buck?"

Shivering inside, Dia nodded. "You were there. Why are you asking me this now?"

Ryan shook his head. "So I was really awake. It wasn't a dream?"

As much as Dia wanted to laugh it off and lie, she just couldn't. But she could evade. "You thought you were asleep?"

Ryan nodded. "Are you a witch?"

Thankful she could answer that truthfully, she shook

her head. "Nope. I wish I was one, but life doesn't work that way."

The relief in his eyes turned to amusement. "I'm sorry. I'm just confused. After we got back earlier, I lay down and fell asleep, and when I awoke, I thought things would be back to normal. But my eyesight is still messed up."

Dia moved toward him. "That's...strange."

He grinned suddenly. "Well, I guess you're going to have to be my driver until I can get a new prescription for glasses. I hope you don't mind."

"I don't mind at all." She looked into his eyes, desperate to change the subject. "I was afraid I was running late."

He shook his head. "No. Perfect timing, actually. But I have to admit, I've been waiting for you ever since I realized I probably hadn't been dreaming." He laughed at himself. "I hope this doesn't sound creepy, but I missed you."

Relieved there was someone who was happy to see her, Dia sighed. "I'm glad. But I'm sure it's only because I'm the only person you know here. Besides your dad."

An odd flash of something crossed Ryan's face but was immediately gone. He shrugged. "I barely even know him. In fact, I only met him yesterday."

Dia couldn't imagine not having known her father her entire life. But she wasn't about to pry. The less they knew about each other, the better. "I'm sorry."

Coming close he pulled out his glasses and scanned the trees. "Right now I'm more concerned about my sight. I don't want to be a burden on you. Would it be possible to take me to an optometrist while we're in town?"

Dia nodded, relieved he'd thought of a solution on his own. "Sure. But it isn't a burden. I'm kind of free and frankly have no idea what to do with myself."

"Have you considered vacationing somewhere else?"

That's right. She'd declared herself on vacation. "No, I hadn't even thought of that."

She frowned as she considered leaving Mystic Water as an option to divert her troubled mind. Sure, the thought of going somewhere else to be entertained sounded really good. But the timing just wasn't right. Even though Jewell was mad at her right now, she loved her sister and wouldn't dream of leaving the area with her so close to going into labor. And she couldn't leave her cabin. What if someone broke into it or her shed and discovered her books of spells and potions? Then there were the animals and the plants. They needed her. Not so much for their day-to-day care, but because she was their friend.

Dia inhaled deeply, loving the smell of her homeland. But instead of the fertile earth and sweet foliage she knew so well, it was Ryan's scent that filled her, and she realized she was just making excuses, because what she really didn't want to do was leave him. He made her tingle inside. He made her excited that... well, he just made her excited in the same way flying across the boulders did; the same way dreaming of successfully casting spells would have, had she ever accomplished that goal. He made her want to reach out and touch him, just as she now knew the plants reached out to her. The truth was she wanted to be with him as much as she could. And she had no idea why that was.

If he had a clue she'd suddenly become so obsessed with him and was looking for any reason to spend time with him, he'd probably run the other way. How could she ever explain something to him she didn't understand herself? She couldn't. So she would just have to play it cool.

"I'm glad you aren't going anywhere else for your vacation."

Startled he'd broken into her thoughts, Dia looked at him, caught up in his pensive gaze. "Why?"

His smile was uncertain. "Because I really like you."

Relief swamped her. If the feelings she was experiencing weren't one-sided, then she could just relax and enjoy the time they spent together while she tried to figure out everything else in her life.

"I really like you, too," she admitted. "Don't you think that's strange?"

Ryan frowned. "Me liking you? Not really. Though I'm actually surprised you like me. I'm pretty much a geek. Now that I know I don't have electricity or Internet access, I'm not sure what to do with myself."

Dia laughed. "First of all, I didn't mean it was strange I liked you. I meant it was strange we both like each other and barely know the other. And who called you a geek? I think you are…" Dia was afraid she was going to make a fool of herself if she said any more, but he looked so pleased, she took the leap. "I think you are great. Do I sound silly?"

Ryan's smile nearly melted her as he shook his head. "I hope not, because I'm right there with you."

He frowned. "I've never had such a beautiful woman look at me the way you do. It's…I'm…oh…I'm afraid I'm about to make a complete fool of myself over you, and I don't want to scare you off."

Dia had to keep herself from leaping at him and planting a kiss on his lips. She understood how awkward it was to feel such a strong attraction but have no idea what to do about it. As crazy as her family thought she was, the reality was she was a complete innocent when it came to doing anything more than looking at the opposite sex—and wondering *what if?* Sure, she knew the biology of it all but nothing more. And she was certain, now jittery with nervous excitement and swamped with all kinds of crazy feelings, there was a lot more.

"I know what you mean. I guess the only thing we can do is be honest about how we feel with each other."

Ryan nodded and wiped his palms against his jeans. "That will work for me." He laughed, nervously. "I don't have a lot of experience with women. I feel like a complete idiot for having admitted this, but it hasn't been a priority."

Dia took a step forward before she realized she'd even moved. "Well, if it helps, we are in the same boat together. I haven't had any experience with men on a deep level. I mean I dated some in college, but I never felt anything for them and never let anything go anywhere."

"Well, okay, last confession before I completely crash and burn." Ryan cleared his throat and blew out a breath. "I've never even dated. I never had the nerve to ask out the women I was attracted to. I figured they'd laugh in my face."

Dia was stunned. Did he have no idea how attractive he was? Well, experienced or not, she would make sure he did. She grinned at him and dissolved the distance between them with a couple more steps. She looked into his eyes, forcing her hands to stay at her sides. "Well, Ryan, I find you completely attractive. So, just what are you going to do about it?"

Chapter Five

Ryan looked at the woman before him, wondering how his life had turned so drastically. She was serious. Of that he was sure. And damned if he was going to be a coward, just because she was more beautiful than any woman he'd ever met. He grinned at her and made himself relax. "I'm going to kiss you."

The resulting lift of her lips was all he needed. Ryan reached out and pulled her toward him but didn't immediately take her lips. Though he'd certainly kissed a few women, and had been kissed in return, he hesitated, because this time it mattered, more than an experiment for one of his game prototypes. He stared into her eyes, hoping she didn't find him inept.

Ryan lowered his head and gently brushed his lips across hers. When she just grinned a little, he did so again, only this time he lingered and slipped his arms around her. On his third pass he delved in, and tasted with his tongue, and knew he would come unglued when she slid hers across his. He finally broke the contact and waited for her eyes to open.

And his heart nearly stopped.

He hadn't been imagining it before. Her irises shifted and sparkled and slid, from differing shades of blue to a milky lavender, then light green, and touched on lemony ginger before returning to blue. He pulled back, only far enough to watch as they settled.

He wanted to ask what made it happen, and ask how, but he didn't want to destroy the moment with reality.

Whatever secrets she had were hers to keep, as long as she wanted to be with him. "I can do better."

Dia laughed, a light airy sound that hit him in his loins.

"I didn't complain. Besides I'm good at practicing things."

"I…" Ryan's brows drew together. "Don't take this the wrong way, but I've never felt this kind of connection with a woman before. This deep attraction." He shook his head. "I don't want to screw up with you, so please tell me when I do."

Dia tilted her head and studied him, her brows pulled together. "How is it that you are so unsure of yourself? I would think women would have been knocking down your door to be with you."

Ryan inhaled, so overwhelmed by her adoration, he didn't know what to say. He wasn't an emotional man. Probably because he'd been raised by an emotionless woman. He didn't know what to do about the feelings flooding his system. It wasn't just lust. *That* he recognized. It was something deeper, and for the life of him, he didn't know what to do with it.

He took a shaky breath. "You floor me." He laughed nervously. "I'm…."

Dia reached out and placed her palm against his cheek. He inhaled sharply, as the emotions inside of him skyrocketed. He pulled her closer and took her lips again; this time he didn't hold back and was rewarded with a hunger that matched his own. When they broke apart once more, she was breathing as harshly as he.

She looked at him, her face reflecting the same shock he felt.

"Do you believe in love at first sight?"

Ryan shook his head. "I didn't before. I always thought love was nothing more than a biological chemical reaction between two people whose chemistry collided and congealed. That sensory attraction, whether visual or aromatic, stimulated the mind and triggered endorphins in the brain. I believed it made that brain think there was something more happening than there really was. That's why, once the newness of the attraction waned, couples parted, looking for the same excitement to happen all over again."

Dia stared at him in shock, and he knew he'd said the wrong thing. Suddenly she laughed, and he felt like a fool. Before he could tell her he didn't think that anymore, she pulled him into a hug and then stepped back.

"I guess we need to test your theory."

Ryan shook his head, relieved. "You didn't let me finish. I don't know what love really is. I only know I'm more than willing to find out, if it's what I feel for you. If you're willing to do the same."

Dia nodded, her expression serious. "I'm willing, because I don't think I have any other choice." She stepped back then and bit her lip. "We need to get you to town. I'm afraid we may not be able to find an optometrist open if we wait much longer."

Ryan could care less about his sight at the moment, but he nodded anyway. He followed her to what looked like a brand new Jeep; he looked it over and grinned. "You seem to have a thing for all-terrain vehicles."

Dia laughed. "Yes I do. But I also have a hot little red convertible stored away in town, which I only use in the summertime and fall, before the danger of snow comes. It's too low to the ground to drive around out here, but I can't make myself sell it."

She grinned again, this time with devilment in her fascinating eyes.

"Just wait until I show you my dirt bike! Once you get your new glasses, we'll get it out of my storage shed, and I'll teach you to ride. It's…exhilarating!"

The thought of him on a dirt bike almost made Ryan laugh. He'd dreamed of riding on one, of knowing the freedom, of embracing the danger of speed, but had never expected to have the opportunity in the concrete jungle he called home. As he looked at the beautiful woman before him, he realized he'd allowed his upbringing to define him, but no more. He took the passenger seat as Dia jumped behind the wheel, wondering just what she did to allow her such nice toys. But he wouldn't ask. He would let her tell him in her own time if she so desired.

The thought of time made Ryan frown. He only had a few weeks to take care of this business with his father before returning to the world he knew. He let that settle on his chest and then threw it out the door-less vehicle when Dia put the Jeep into gear and flew down the long driveway. Tomorrow, or next week, would be soon enough to worry about how short his time on Mystic Mountain would be. Today, and for as many days as he could muster, he only wanted to *feel* what being in her presence did to him.

Once they reached the road, he embraced the speed, knowing he'd have a hard time settling for ordinary again. Because there was nothing ordinary about the woman who had somehow become the most important thing in his life.

****

Dia inhaled the land she loved as it flew past her. She loved the wind, the sound, the exhilaration of driving her newest toy. She glanced over at Ryan, tickled to see the joy on his face as well, and then returned her eyes to the ever-curving road. She loved that he wasn't as sure of himself in that way boys she'd dated in the past were. But mostly she loved that his lack of experience wasn't reflected in the way he kissed.

Dia knew she couldn't dwell on that while driving. It had been all she could do to stop kissing him, knowing he had business to attend to and glasses to replace. She chewed on her bottom lip, wondering if the water had indeed been responsible for his change in vision. She worried another sip could alter his sight again. She snuck a peek in his direction and then swerved when she caught him looking at her, his smile so huge it took her breath.

"Don't do that," she laughed.

His playful grin turned innocent. "Do what?"

Dia felt heat enter her cheeks, and she knew he had to see the effect he had on her. "Don't stare at me. You'll make me wreck."

Ryan turned his face forward, but she noticed when she looked again, he was still smiling. She wanted to pull over at the first opportunity and kiss the smile right off his lips. Even just thinking of doing so made her hot and hungry, and she had to force herself to concentrate on her driving.

She inhaled sharply when his lightly placed palm touched her just above the knee. She threw him a startled look, then shook her head and smiled as she was forced to pay attention to the road. "That isn't fair," she said, braking and downshifting on a particularly sharp decline that led into Dead Man's Curve.

Ryan removed his hand, and she actually mourned the loss as she navigated the dangerous turn, then she reached for his hand and placed it right back where he'd had it. Grinning, she refused to look at him, but she knew he was grinning as well. And if the surge of energy tingling throughout her body was any indication, she knew she was in serious trouble. They reached town forty-five minutes later and drove around the large lake. Dia smiled as Ryan put his glasses back on and was looking at it, rather than her.

"Do you fish?"

Ryan swung his head around to her and peered over

the glasses that had slid down his nose. He shook his head. "I never have. Do you?"

Dia shook her head. "I haven't either. Would you like to try it sometime?"

Grinning, he nodded. "Yeah. I will if you will."

Filled with a joy she didn't understand, Dia laughed into the wind flowing over the windshield. "You're on. My family loves fish, though we will have to get a tribal pass to be able to fish the lake. My great-uncle will take care of it, and then Uncle Tom will bless our journey." She grinned. "You're not in Kansas anymore, Dorothy."

Ryan laughed. "I've never been to Kansas, either."

Dia turned back to the road and slowed as they approached the town. Already the days were lengthening, but only by minutes, so she knew it would be dark by the time he finished with his visit with his father, and they had dinner. She took a deep breath, wondering if she dared to suggest they wait on his glasses.

"I've been thinking."

Ryan glanced over. "About what?"

Dia hoped she wasn't making a mistake. "What if there is a possibility the water had something to do with your improved sight?"

Ryan studied her a moment. "Then I'd say we better bottle it and patent it, and you'll make millions."

A thud hit her stomach. She'd never thought of the possibility of him thinking along those lines. But then she really didn't know him, even if it felt like she did. She struggled to find a reply. "What if it only affected *you* that way? Not others? I mean, others have drank from those waters with no…effect. But *your* sight changed immediately after doing so. Not that I'm saying one has anything to do with the other."

Ryan smiled while watching her, his brows drawn together. "Then I'd say I should try drinking it again, to see if that's a possibility."

He frowned, and Dia understood his confusion. She just wished she knew what to do about it. This was something she would normally turn to her family for help with, but she couldn't, not after the way they'd already reacted. If they knew she was even suggesting it, she'd likely get raked over the coals again.

The other alternative was to let him get new glasses, possibly drink from the water in his cabin, and then have to look at getting his prescription changed again. *If* that was what had affected him. She blew out a shaky breath. Either way, he'd know something was up.

"Dia?"

She pulled to a stop at the stop sign and glanced over. "Yes?"

"Is there something you want to tell me?"

Dia hoped the smile she was trying to form made it to her lips. "Like what?"

He shook his head and looked straight ahead. "Nothing. I just thought…" He sighed. "I don't know what to think."

And she didn't know what to say. He'd already asked if she was a witch, which she obviously wasn't, but the distinction would be lost on him. What could she say? "Ryan?"

"Yeah?"

Since he didn't even look her way this time, she pulled onto Main Street and slowly drove through the town she'd always known. Only this time she noticed things she'd never noticed before. Like the people strolling by the shops and cafés that lined the street, and the beauty of the flowers and trees that decorated the sidewalks. She couldn't imagine how a newcomer could drive into what she'd always taken for granted and not notice the perfection of it all. She glanced over at him, to find him staring at her over his glasses.

"I don't know what to say," she admitted.

He pulled his upper lip down and held it between his teeth before releasing it. "I thought we were going to be honest with each other."

Dia felt a pang. She was afraid to open her mouth, because honest words were what she felt compelled to share. But she had to ignore the urge or possibly endanger her family. "I was just making a suggestion. It was probably silly of me to even think it. So, if you want to go to the eye doctor before I take you to see your dad, that's fine."

Ryan frowned. "No. I want to go see my dad. He'll be waiting for me."

****

Ryan kept his eyes forward as Dia drove him to the hospital. He didn't know what to think. Nothing about them made sense. Dia was beautiful beyond imagination, and she was fun and funny, made him ache with want. But there were so many things that had happened since he'd met her that didn't add up. It wasn't just that her eyes did a beautifully strange thing, or that she spoke to wild animals as if they understood her. Or even that drinking water from a stream had possibly somehow affected his vision. But added together....

He wrestled with the possibilities, but nothing made sense. Unless his father had been right all along.

Ryan nearly doubled over at the thought. He couldn't look at her again and not let his doubt and, oh God, *fear*, show.

No! He wouldn't buy into his father's delusions. He couldn't. Witches were fictional. They had made him a rich man. His fellow geeks and nerds only got a chance to leave their world of numbers and certainties because of fantasies of the impossible he and those like him created. If there were even the slightest chance witches were a reality, it would rock the very foundation of the world.

Thankful the hospital was finally within sight. Ryan tried to stop the internal shaking that had taken hold and to focus on the large building. He knew its suddenly sinister outline was due to the riot going on in his brain and realizing the man he'd come to see might not be so delusional after all. When she stopped before the front entrance, he turned to her, and the sadness etched within her lovely face nearly made him stay. But he knew he couldn't. Not even if the pull to kiss her and make her smile tied him up in knots.

Had she bewitched him?

Ryan tried to grasp the possibility, and for the first time since meeting her, it took hold. He licked his lips and tried to smile. "If you can give me about an hour, I'll be waiting right out front."

Dia nodded, and he could tell she was struggling with his odd behavior. He wanted to reassure her nothing had changed, but everything had. He just had no idea where that put them. He nodded too and exited the Jeep and then made himself walk into the building without looking back.

The short consultation with the doctor revealed his father had been released from his restraints, and he could visit Clayton in the cafeteria. It was dinnertime and the best place for their visit. Staff would be present to make sure Ryan was safe. Though he'd hoped for a more private setting, he nodded and followed the same orderly he'd met before to the large room filled with round and square tables. To Ryan's relief, his father was sitting alone.

After nodding dismissively to the orderly, he took in the lay of the circular room. Seven staff members stood around the outside perimeter like guards as they continuously scanned the action at each table. Three of the large round tables held three or more people, and seven of the smaller square tables held individuals, like his father, who kept their heads down to either eat from the divided rectangular trays or simply stared off into space. He crossed to his father's table, his head filled with the impossible. When he stopped at Clayton's side, his father looked up. Surprise and pleasure lit his eyes.

"I didn't expect you to come back."

Ryan cleared his throat. "I told you I would."

Clayton nodded and indicated for Ryan to sit across from him. "They won't let you sit next to me. They're afraid I'll try to hurt anyone who comes close."

Ryan took the seat and placed his elbows on the table, clasping his hands. "Would you?"

Surprise preceded laughter. "No. I'm not manic, and I'm not crazy, contrary to popular belief."

"But you've hurt people in the past."

Ryan shrugged. "They had it coming." He grinned. "I was much younger then and not as inclined to allow others to call me crazy. Now I just accept that they are the delusional ones."

Since his father had brought it up, Ryan let the other go, and focused on the reason they were both here. "Will you tell me your story again?"

"Why?"

Ryan laughed quietly, though it was self-directed and held no amusement. "Because I might believe you."

The shock on Clayton's face turned wary, before excitement sharpened his gaze.

"Why?" he repeated.

Ryan slid a glance around the room, noticing his father's loud question caught the attention of several of the staff as well as some of those interned most likely, like his father, against their will. He turned back to find his father glaring at one particular orderly and saw the man glaring back.

"Dad?"

Clayton turned to him immediately, surprise again cloaking his face. "I never expected to be called that," he said, as tears filled his eyes.

Ryan hadn't given a thought to accomplishing any more than breaking the connection between his father and that staff member, but his own throat closed, as emotion filled him. "I guess I never thought I'd get to say it either."

They stared at each other before Clayton sniffed and wiped at his eyes. Though not a single tear had fallen, the action caused his dark lashes to shine with moisture.

"I'll tell you what happened again, and then you tell me why you might believe me." He glanced back to that orderly, then to Ryan. "But talk quietly. They try to listen to everything people say. And that one over there," he tilted his head back to the one who'd glared at him, "He likes to find reasons to take you down."

Ryan shivered and made himself keep his eyes on his father, not wanting to alert the orderly he was being discussed. But he'd make sure to speak to the doctor. Whether his father was mentally unstable or not, he didn't deserve to be abused. Since Ryan planned to tell his father what was happening to him as well, it worried him the staff might start looking upon him in the same way they looked at Clayton and the others in their charge.

Ryan listened as Clayton quietly retold his story, neither adding to nor leaving out anything he'd told before. When he was done, Ryan nodded and began to tell of his own experiences, but the orderly his father feared approached their table.

"I'm sorry, but visiting hours are over. You'll have to come back tomorrow."

Ryan and Clayton shared a look, before Ryan rose. "Could you give us just a moment?"

The orderly shrugged. "Sure. Just make it fast. I have to line everyone up."

Ryan nodded as the man turned and walked to the next table. He leaned forward over the table and kept his voice low. "I'll try to be back earlier tomorrow."

Clayton nodded. "I'll be waiting."

Ryan didn't know what else to do other than to nod as the orderly was once again at his side. He said his goodbye and headed to the door. There was already a line of men waiting to be taken back to their rooms.

Ryan nodded to them, and many smiled. With his heart heavy, he walked out and headed to the front entrance of the hospital, wishing he knew what to do once Dia picked him up. Did he hold his suspicions to himself or confront her? Did he take her out to dinner, as they had planned, or ask to be returned to the cabin? For the life of him, he had no idea which way to turn. All he knew was his head was telling him one thing, and his heart was hoping against hope it wasn't true.

Logic aside, something was off. He took a breath as he stepped out the door and saw her waiting in the parking lot. Since she was busily pecking at her phone, he slid his glasses up and took the time to study her. In profile she was perfection, just like she was head-on. Her finely sculpted forehead peeking from beneath almost white hair, her perfectly straight nose, and the pucker of her fill lips even in rest set a torch in his gut. Her slight form revealed a smooth shoulder and a lightly sculptured arm that begged for his touch. The rapid rise and fall of her breast indicated agitation, and he wondered whom she was texting with. He didn't know how he felt if the texts were about him.

Did she feel his suspicion? Or had her reactions to him earlier been because of the change in him? Ryan took a step forward knowing he'd have to decide quickly how he was going to proceed. If his suspicions were baseless, he'd mess up what could be the most important relationship of his life. But, if by some crazy chance he was right, and there was something mystical about her, then he'd have to reevaluate everything he'd ever believed.

Deciding he couldn't risk pushing her away, regardless of the circumstances, or maybe even because of them, he put a smile on his face and hoped like hell she bought it.

Dia looked up and over at him as he approached her side. She placed her phone in the console beneath the dashboard and eyed him warily. "Hi."

Ryan stopped next to the door-less Jeep, glad she'd removed them before he'd met her so there wasn't a barrier between them. "Hi."

She sighed. "How was your dad?"

Ryan shrugged, hating how awkward everything felt. "He was doing okay, I guess."

Dia frowned at him. "Is he terribly sick?"

Realizing she had no idea why Clayton was in the hospital and no knowledge he was actually in the psychiatric wing, Ryan took a moment to think how he should answer.

"I'm sorry. I didn't mean to pry." Dia looked away, biting her bottom lip.

Ryan couldn't do this. Not like this. Even if there was something off about everything happening, he couldn't hurt her or, for now, consider confronting her. "Dia, I'm confused about a lot of things, but I don't want us to be... *uncomfortable*, I guess is the word I'm searching for, with each other."

"I don't want that either."

He stared at her for a few seconds, and she held the contact. He relaxed and was able to give her a real smile. "Then let's not do that."

Relief softened the look in her beautiful eyes. He leaned forward and kissed her gently before pulling back to walk around the Jeep and hop in. Ryan reached over and took her hand when she placed it on the stick shift. "Before we go, I just have to ask you one question."

Though her eyes held caution, she nodded.

"Have you ever hurt anyone?"

Surprise pulled her brows together. "Of course not."

The outrage in her soft voice took any doubt he felt, and he squeezed her hand before letting it go. "I didn't think so."

"Then why would you ask me that?"

Ryan looked toward the hospital and shook his head. "I don't know. It's just…this sounds stupid, but I guess I just don't want to think what is between us isn't real."

She nodded as she looked him in the eyes, her own filled with concern. "Don't you think I'm afraid too? I've never felt what I feel for you for anyone. And I barely know you."

Ryan exhaled and laid his head back against the seat, knowing he'd let his imagination get the best of him. He'd spent years developing games filled with mystical possibilities and had a father who had almost convinced him they were reality. It was no wonder his mind was so clouded. He turned to her, hoping the truth of his words reassured them both. "Then let's get to really know each other, because I don't want to lose you."

Chapter Six

Dia was so relieved her eyes misted, but she blinked away the tears, ready to claim it was only the wind in her eyes if Ryan questioned it. She'd spent the entire time he'd been in with his father playing over every moment they'd spent together, afraid whatever was between them had ended before it really began. Jewell had texted her right before Ryan left the hospital to apologize for being so rough on her, and she'd already been close to tears as they'd both furiously texted how hurt they both were to be upset with the other.

Now that things felt more normal, and Ryan and she were headed for a meal, Dia knew she'd have to figure out a way to keep him from experiencing anything else that would jeopardize their time together. She knew he was only in Mystic Waters for a short time and had assured herself she accepted those limitations, but until the day he walked out of her life, she wanted to know and understand what it was about him that moved everything within her. If nothing else, maybe the experience would open her up to a lasting love, when and if that was hers to have.

Dia pushed away the instant denial she would ever feel for another what she felt for Ryan. If that was the case, she was afraid she'd have a long life of loneliness, and that wasn't what she wanted. She loved her large family and she wanted to add to it. But the thought of having children without Ryan's dark good looks wasn't something she could envision.

"Are you okay?"

Dia glanced over, her brows raised. "Yes. Why do you ask?"

"Because you're frowning."

Pulling into the parking lot of the pub that had only opened recently, Dia parked and turned to him. "I was just thinking about stuff."

"What stuff?"

"About you leaving in only a few weeks."

Ryan nodded. "Yeah, I think about it too."

They walked from the Jeep to the wooden door. Ryan stopped her by taking her arm and turning her toward him. "Does it make you think we shouldn't get involved?"

Dia's laugh was sad. "I think we are already involved."

"I agree. But you don't want it to go any further?"

Dia bit her bottom lip and shook her head as an amazing aroma drifted her way, reminding her she'd wanted to try out the bar and grill since hearing of its opening. "Let's go inside and order, then we'll talk, okay?"

Ryan nodded and opened the door, waiting as she entered. The dimly lit room was pretty typical of most bars, with illuminated colorful lights broadcasting the alcohols the establishment served. They were led to a booth with a high-gloss wooden table, and vinyl seats so new they still held the smell. Ryan waited until she sat then sat across from her and the woman who seated them smiled at them both. "I'm Clara, what can I get you to drink?"

Dia looked at Ryan, and he looked at her, grinning. "You're driving."

Relieved she could laugh naturally, she made a face at him and ordered a glass of wine.

"What kind do you want, sweetie?"

Waving her hands, Dia shrugged. "You pick. Whatever you think is good."

Once Ryan ordered a beer and an appetizer, the waitress left to put in their order.

"So, back to the discussion at hand. Do you want out?"

Dia shook her head quickly. "Absolutely not. You?"

"No way. So now that's settled, tell me about Dia White."

Grinning, Dia leaned back into the plush seat. She loved the richness of his dark brown hair, and the fact his chin stubble looked tailor-made, not lazy. The most amazing thing about his handsome face, though, was the unique turquoise of his eyes.

"You're stalling."

His teasing tone made her laugh. "No I wasn't. I was just enjoying the view."

Pleasure colored his cheeks, and Dia was mesmerized that she could affect him so easily. It was such a relief she wasn't the only one. "I'm twenty-four, just, and I have two sisters who share my birthday."

Surprise lit his eyes. "Triplets? Again?"

Dia laughed, and nodded, but kept the secrets of her existence to herself. Only the family knew, if tested, their DNA would be identical. It was something that was never revealed to anyone outside of the family. It had been hard enough for her mother to explain the different hair colors to the doctor who had delivered them all those years before. Thankfully they'd all had the infant blue eyes everyone else had at birth, so it wasn't until their eyes changed to the colors they now had that it became an issue as well. Her family just allowed anyone who knew they were triplets to assume they were fraternal instead of identical, and she knew Ryan could be no exception.

"I told you there were a lot of us in my family."

"That's amazing. I was, *am*, an only child."

"I can't imagine what that would be like. Do you have lots of cousins?"

Ryan frowned. "No. None. There was just my mother

and me."

Dia reached across the table and placed her hand on his just as the waitress arrived with the drinks and a large sample platter of buffalo chicken-wings, potato skins, nachos, and cheese-sticks. She looked at the mass of food and then him as he thanked the waitress. "That's a lot of food."

Ryan eyed it and then her. "I'm really hungry."

"Then dig in."

"Ladies first."

Dia lifted the small saucer the woman delivered with the food and filled the little plate with a small amount of everything. Though she rarely had the opportunity anymore to indulge in what most of her family considered junk food, because she rarely left her cabin and conjuring shed long enough to bother, the smells and visual effects of what was before her was too great a temptation to resist. Hoping she didn't look like a glutton, she dipped her potato skin into the small container of sour cream the woman had also delivered and took a bite. The moan that escaped her throat would have embarrassed her if it hadn't put a sparkle in Ryan's eyes.

"If it's that good, this is going to be fun."

Dia grinned around her chewing and watched as he took his first bite. With his lips sealed together, he grinned, too, and nodded his head. Once he'd swallowed and licked his lips, he took a sip from the tall frosted glass. Dia laughed and lifted her long stemmed glass to swirl the wine. She watched as the red liquid took on the life of a mini-hurricane and her smile faltered.

Three silver spoons of blood red wine… And thee shall be mine; Thee shall be mine….

Dia sat the glass back on the table and stared at it as her mind raced with the possibility she'd actually placed a love spell on the man before her.

"What's wrong?"

She pulled her gaze from the cursed drink to look into Ryan's eyes. Dia swallowed and shook her head slowly. "Nothing. I, uh... Maybe I should drink water. Or a soda. I do have to drive." She forced herself to smile even though she felt sick to her stomach. "My sister is a cop, and it would give her a big thrill to be able to pull me over and make me take a sobriety test."

"After just one drink?"

Dia was afraid she was going to cry. What if she'd cursed him? What if the attraction he felt for her was nothing more than a spell she'd accidentally succeeded in creating?

"Dia? What's wrong?"

She shook her head and fled to the bathroom where she splashed cool water on her face. With her chest heaving, she stared at her reflection in the mirror and allowed the water running down her face to land into the basin she was bent over.

"Hey, honey, are you okay? Your boyfriend sent me in here to check on you."

Dia glanced over to the woman who had waited on them and nodded. "I just got a little overheated. I'm sorry."

The woman smiled kindly and tore a couple of paper towels from the holder. "Here, honey. If you're sure you're okay, I'll let him know you'll be out soon."

Dia nodded and held out her hand. "Thanks. Would you take the wine away and bring me water, please?"

After she left Dia dried her face, glad she rarely bothered with makeup. She took several cleansing breaths and made herself leave the bathroom. Ryan was watching for her and stood when he saw her. "Are you okay?"

Taking her seat, embarrassed she was making a spectacle of herself, she nodded. "I'm so sorry. I suddenly felt sick and hot, but now I'm okay."

Ryan sat back down. "You scared me."

"I'm sorry."

"But you are really okay now?"

Dia nodded. "I am."

The waitress placed the water on the table and smiled as she lifted the glass of wine. "Let me know if you need anything else, honey."

Dia nodded her thanks and turned her attention back to Ryan. "What do you like about me?"

The question obviously surprised him. "Pretty much everything. Why do you ask?"

"It's just that this is all so sudden."

"I thought we'd already established that. Is that what made you feel sick? Doubts?"

Thankful she could be honest, at least for the most part she nodded. "Yeah. I don't want this to be a mistake."

Missing the double meaning, he shrugged. "I don't know what to do if it is. It's easy to see why I'm attracted to you, physically, I'm sure you have a mirror. But it's more than that. I like you. You're chatty and fun and have a sense of freedom of spirit I don't have. Never even knew how to have, if we're being honest. You know I'm worried about the same thing. What if we both just stop analyzing it every minute and enjoy our time together? If it ends badly, at least we won't have the regret of wondering. When the time comes that I have to leave, and things are going really well, which I expect, then we'll work that out."

Ryan grinned. "I can live anywhere. I work from home." He made a face. "Well, anywhere that has electricity and Wi-Fi."

Dia forced herself to relax, relieved he hadn't said things like he felt compelled to be with her, or he couldn't live without her. If he'd said those things, her fears would have been confirmed. She'd have no choice but to seek out her family to have his mind wiped clean, and his memory of this time filled with doing something else. She couldn't stand the thought of him never knowing they'd met, feeling like he had, believing he was less than desirable, when just the opposite was true. Worse, she'd have to live her whole life with the knowledge of how crazy she was about him.

"Tell me about your work."

Ryan shook his head. "I'd rather show you. You said your cabin has electricity, right?"

Dia nodded. "But not Wi-Fi. I haven't taken the time to have it installed."

"Good enough. I want to show you what I've been working to create the last few years. The reason I have to leave here in just under a month is, once I show it to the world, everything I've dreamed of since I can remember will come to fruition. You will be the only person to see it before I take it public."

Dia could feel his excitement, and she couldn't wait to see what it was that made his turquoise irises shine so brightly. "I'd love to see it. And of course you need electricity. We'll go get your things and take them to my cabin. But I have to warn you, it's a lot smaller than yours."

He bit his bottom lip and then released it into a slight smile. "Are you inviting me to stay there?"

Dia grinned and looked down at the smooth tabletop. She glanced back up and nodded slowly. "I am."

Though his eyes still held delight, they also carried questions. Dia pushed the pile of food to the side and held out her hand. When Ryan accepted it without hesitation, she took a shaky breath. "If we only have a few weeks to figure out what this thing is between us, I don't want to waste time being apart."

"You aren't going to get an argument from me. But I do have to come see my father and start taking care of his affairs." He frowned. "I'll tell you all about him sometime. I'm just not ready to talk about him yet."

Dia nodded, relieved they would table discussions about family for later. If Ryan was going to be more than a brief encounter in her life, he'd never have to know how very different they all were. "No talk of family. We just focus on us. Agreed?"

Ryan squeezed her hands. "Agreed."

"Then we'd better eat and go get groceries before we head back. Unless you like rabbit food, you're going to go hungry living with me."

Ryan laughed and released her hand to load a nacho chip with the messy chili and cheese topping. He placed it in his mouth and chewed, and the happy gleam in his eyes filled her with joy. No matter what had brought them together, she was going to live their time together to the fullest. If it turned out she had somehow put a spell on him, she'd take whatever retribution came her way and ask her family to fix his memories with kindness. Even if it meant she'd have to let him go with happy memories of these days doing something other than spending them with her.

He ate at a leisurely pace. Had it not been for the gleam in his eyes as he stared at her and spoke of inconsequential things, Dia would have wondered if Ryan was having second thoughts. Still uncertain, she finally worked up the nerve to ask him, only to make him laugh.

"Not hardly. You?"

Dia grinned. "Nope. Still working with first thoughts." They laughed together as he paid the bill, and Dia couldn't have been happier as they walked hand-in-hand to the Jeep.

Darkness had fallen completely, but it only took minutes to reach the grocery store. Once inside, however, shopping took quite a bit longer than normal since each possible purchase came with questions from Ryan.

"Do you have a grill?"

"Do you mind if I buy us one?"

"Gas or coals?

"Really?"

"How about gas instead?"

"I guess you don't have grill tools?"

"What do you mean, you don't eat hamburgers?"

"Who in their right mind would eat a turkey burger?

"Do you really eat that stuff?"

"Wine?"

"Beer?"

"Lemonade? Really?"

Dia knew the other patrons were as amused as she was. Ryan decided he had to have a gas grill and searched the aisles like a little boy on a treasure hunt for a cover and the large tools to cook with. When they went from the lawn and garden section of the store to the grocery section, he turned his nose up at anything she suggested that might be a healthy alternative to the pork and beef he was loading up on. She kept her thoughts to herself, since he was obviously having a ball, but she couldn't help but laugh when he looked confused once they reached their transportation. There was nearly too much to load into the small cargo space and back seats. Of course, the box containing the grill they'd have to put together took up a considerable amount of room. He'd somehow forgotten they weren't feeding a family of twelve and had chosen the largest one the store had.

She grinned at him as they sorted, packed, pulled things out, and then repacked them again.

"What?"

Dia glanced up to find him watching her. "I guess you love to grill out."

Ryan looked at the purchases and grinned sheepishly. "I've never grilled out in my life."

Stunned, she stood back. "Are you serious?"

Ryan nodded, frowning. "Yep. My mother hated the

outdoors, movies, socializing, and pretty much everything, so we never went anywhere when she wasn't at work and I was home from school or on summer break. I learned to entertain myself with books mostly. I eventually badgered her into getting me a computer by telling her it would help me in school." He grinned.

"She only agreed because she couldn't argue with the perfect grades I'd gotten from the start. I didn't get to watch much TV, but, as often as I could, I'd sneak out and get a horror movie from the grocery store a block from our home while she was at work. It never failed, though. My mom would eventually find them, then put me on restriction. Which was really a joke since I didn't get to do much of anything but study, and there was nothing to take away from me, except the movies she already wouldn't let me watch. Once I had the computer, I downloaded some she never knew about. But by then I was almost out the door anyway."

"She sounds…um…" Dia shook her head, unable to say what she was thinking.

"Mean? Yeah, I thought she was, too. Still do at times. I want to blame her sometimes for my social awkwardness. I ended up being this nerdy kid who got fantastic grades but had no idea what to do with people." He studied her, his brows pulled together. "*With girls* in particular.

"It was only after I left home that I had the opportunity to try to change. By that time I was pretty set in my ways and felt like such an outsider that I just stuck with what I knew. Other than finding other *older* nerdy college kids to hang out with, who also thought being in the sun was a health hazard, I didn't really embrace the experience most kids did. I entered computer and math competitions, built robots for the annual robot wars, and dreamed of being someone other than who I was. That's what got me interested in the project I want to show you. It will show you who I am beneath the glasses. I guess, at heart, I'm a dreamer."

Dia walked around the Jeep to stand before him. "I've had the world handed to me, but I don't think we're really all that different. In my own way, I guess I'm kind of a nerd too, except I'm not nearly as smart as you. I screw things up. All the time, according to my family."

Ryan shook his head. "I don't believe that. I think you're perfect."

Dia laughed. "Well, don't say I didn't warn you. When we go to put that monster grill together, you'll probably be ready to run me off with a stick before it's done."

Ryan pulled her into his arms and gently lifted her chin. "I would never run you off, with a stick or anything else."

He lowered his head and took her lips with none of his earlier hesitation. Dia melted into him, delighted with the gentle assault, but needing more. As if he'd read her need, Ryan lifted her so she had to lock her ankles around his narrow hips, and she felt his growing erection between them. She gasped, taking his breath within her, as she rode both shock and pleasure. She tightened her thighs and pulled him closer with her calves, making the gasp *his* this time.

Her tongue tasted and tussled, teased and was tormented as the kiss deepened, eased, changed to frantic pecks, then deepened again. She lost the strength in her legs, in her entire being actually, and had no choice but to let her legs slide down his, until she was dangling in his arms. He finally loosened his hold enough to allow her feet to touch the asphalt. Gasping for breath, she laid her head against the thunderous heartbeats coming from inside his hard chest. Her own heart was going as wild and she knew she was lost, as she desperately tried to catch her breath. When she found the strength to look up, he swooped her into his arms and placed her in the driver's seat. Dia laughed helplessly and watched as he rounded the Jeep. She waited, enthralled, while he took his seat, pulled her to him for one quick hard kiss, and then snapped his seatbelt buckle in place.

"Get us home, woman."

Thrilled with the possessiveness in his voice, thinking he definitely had no trouble knowing what to *do* with girls, at least this one, she threw the Jeep into gear and headed toward the mountain. Normally uncaring of her speed, as faster was always better, tonight she kept to the town's speed limits until she finally reached the usually empty lake road. Dia didn't want to take the chance of being stopped. Not because of the price of a ticket, but because she was desperately eager to have Ryan's lips, and hands, *and God help her*, his body, all over her again. Getting a ticket and being chatted up by some lonely officer, would simply take too much time.

It didn't help that Ryan couldn't keep his hands to himself, that each touch threatened to break what little concentration she had. As she headed up the mountain they continued to play, or he did, mostly, while she drove the increasingly curving road. She laughed with him and swatted at him when she wasn't shifting, but she had no desire for him to stop. Before she started up Dead Man's Curve she glanced at him threateningly, though it was all she could do not to laugh.

"You're going to get us killed!"

He laughed, as she was smiling when she'd said it, and settled back in his seat.

"Okay. I'd rather not do that. I have a completely different evening planned."

She glanced at him once more and caught his wink. Dia shook her head and slowed as the hairpin curve took all her concentration. She downshifted, eased up on the gas, and downshifted again until they'd passed the most dangerous section of roadway on Mystic Mountain. Once she was able to increase her speed, she still kept her eyes on the road. Though the threat of deer was small, there was always the off chance another nocturnal animal had found its way onto the asphalt, and she didn't want to chance hitting anything. Just the thought of killing one of her forest friends sent shivers down her spine.

She sighed in relief when they were once again on safer ground and slid him a glance. "Only about another ten minutes to your place."

Ryan smiled, and though the glint of pleasure was still in his eyes, they'd lost the playfulness. "I can't wait to get to yours."

It took just a little longer than she'd told him, and the remaining drive seemed endlessly long, but they finally made it to his cabin. She pulled out the flashlight she always carried in the Jeep and handed it to him. "Do you need help?"

Ryan shook his head as he leapt from his seat and rounded the vehicle to give her a quick kiss and take the flashlight. "No, just keep all your engines running. I'll be right back."

Dia laughed at his joke and bit her bottom lip. She couldn't believe what she was about to do, and she knew she'd still have to be careful not to reveal anything mystical to him, but there was no way she was backing away from the most exciting thing to happen in her life. The most exciting *man*, she corrected. She had no desire to coat it as anything other than what it was, at least not to herself.

Ryan thrilled her to the bone, whether kissing her or not. He was everything she hadn't known she'd been missing in her life. He was *nice*, in a world where people often weren't. He was extremely handsome, though he had no idea of it. And he treated her like she was *something*.

As much as she loved her family, none of them understood her. They loved her. They tolerated her mistakes, *mostly*. At least they always had before now. But they didn't identify with who she was. Her mother's amused indulgences, her father's unwavering adoration while he looked the other way, Jewell's acceptance that she was a screw-up, and even Sapphire's bare tolerance were what she'd always known. But not one of them questioned why she needed things they didn't, or why she couldn't settle for whatever life wanted to throw at her. She knew they thought her dumb at times. Although she'd never let it bother her—*much*—until now, having someone think her wonderful made their actions hurt all the more. She now realized none of them respected her.

But more than all those things, he was hers. As much as she wanted to deny she felt that way, there was no way to avoid it. She wanted him. And not just for a couple of weeks, even a month. She wanted the cute nerd, the awkward man, the genius who could dream for a lifetime. And there was no doubt in her mind he wanted her as desperately.

And thee shall be mine!

Dia shivered as goose bumps covered her body. She took a shaky breath as he returned to the car. She tried to smile at him as he loaded his things in the back and finally succeeded once she told herself to get a grip. Magic had always denied her, and now she was going to deny it!

There was no way she'd allow herself to believe she had put a love spell on him. Not after every other thing she tried had failed. There was just no way she would believe it… No way at all!

Chapter Seven

The drive to her own cabin was short and sweet, as Ryan kept taking her hand and kissing the back of it, or the palm, or even squeezing it in a way that conveyed his excitement to be with her each time she released the shifter. She pulled to a stop before the old cabin that had been built generations ago by the Whitehawk family, and smiled when Ryan exclaimed in wonder at the scene revealed by the Jeep's headlights. He turned to her, his eyes alight with excitement.

"This place looks like it's lost in time."

Dia grinned. "I know. Wait until you see inside. You may decide you prefer your place."

Shaking his head, Ryan looked into her eyes. "I don't care if the floor is dirt. As long as it has you and electricity, I'm here for as long as you'll have me."

Laughing, Dia placed her palm on his cheek. "You bowl me over with the romance of knowing electricity and I are equally important to you."

The seriousness of his gaze bespoke regret. "I didn't mean it that way."

After leaning in to give him a gentle kiss, and then another, Dia shook her head. "I was just kidding."

He grinned suddenly. "So was I. Electricity is much more important."

Dia laughed and smacked at him playfully. "You're going to eat those words."

"I'm counting on it."

He jumped out of the Jeep and was at her side

instantly as Dia struggled to unlock her seatbelt. But the more she struggled, the more stubborn it seemed to be. She turned to him in a panic. "It's stuck!"

Ryan looked from her to it. "I'll bite it off with my teeth."

Dia chuckled. "No you won't. This thing is fairly new."

"Then let me try. I'll not be defeated by a strap with a buckle."

Dia was released immediately and scooped into his arms. She glanced back and almost reminded him the lights were still on, but then changed her mind. It could wait until they were inside and she had turned on the floodlights. He sat her on her feet at the door and took her mouth in a kiss she felt all the way to her toes. When he released her, she figured the battery could die for all she cared, until she tried to open the door. Laughing at herself, she looked up to him. "The keys are in the ignition."

Ryan grinned. "Why does this always go more smoothly in movies?" He jogged to the Jeep, turned off the lights, throwing them in complete darkness.

"Maybe that wasn't such a good idea."

As her eyes adjusted, Dia could see a sliver of the moon's reflected light on the hood of the Jeep. "Stay there. I'm used to this."

She walked to the Jeep and slid her arms around his waist. "Just to let you know it's me."

Ryan kissed the top of her head. "Hi you. I'm starting to see, *a little*, now. Should we go on and carry everything in?"

"Maybe so. Everything except the grill?"

"Sounds like a plan." He lifted her hand and placed her keys in it. "Want me to turn the lights back on until you get in the door?"

"Not necessary. I'll turn on some once I get inside though. Give me just a second."

Dia hurried to her cabin and was inside in seconds. She flipped on the outside security lights her father insisted she needed, and she now fully appreciated, then hurried back out to help carry all their purchases in. Several trips later she laughed with him over the assortment of things he'd bought, some of which he didn't even remember putting in their cart. Ryan looked at her a little sheepishly when he realized she'd only picked out an assortment of fresh fruits, and then his eyes lit up when he saw she'd snuck in a can of whipped cream as well. They joked and jostled each other playfully while they tried to store so much, in so little room.

Once they'd accomplished their goal, Ryan took her into his arms as if he'd just been waiting for the opportunity, and covered her face with kisses. He pulled back to look deeply into her eyes. "Tell me you want this. That you have no second thoughts."

Dia leaned into him and hugged him tightly. "I've never wanted anything more in my life."

The truth of her words stunned even her. That she'd found something more important than magic felt like bondage, she'd never known she felt, disintegrating, and her spirit soared. She pulled his face down and took his lips pouring everything she was into the kiss. As if the earth shifted, the tone of his touch matched the seriousness of her heart, and he cherished her with his lips as well as his hands. They pulled apart, and she smiled up at him. "I want to show you something special." When Ryan nodded, she took his hand and led him out of the cabin, and down the path that led to the hidden bathhouse. He said nothing as he followed her inside, and then laughed in delight when she showed him the modern facilities: a toilet room and the small room added for the washer and dryer.

"Thank you! I was afraid to ask where the bathroom was!"

Dia grinned at him. "Wait 'til you see this!" She led

him to the much larger shower room and enjoyed seeing both the pleasure and speculation in his eyes when he glanced down at her.

"I'm liking your one-room cabin more and more all the time. Who would have thought something like this was hidden just beyond the trees?"

Dia bit her bottom lit then chewed on it. Now that they were together and alone for real, she was nervous. "Would you like to take a shower with me?"

"You already know the answer to that." He looked at her with love in his beautiful, honest, eyes. "I'm crazy about you fully clothed, but I'd be lying if I said I can't wait to get you out of them. You've completely bewitched me." Ryan ginned wryly, as if he thought his statement amusing.

She didn't as a thud hit her stomach, but she breathed through it and nodded. "Yeah. Okay, tell you what, let me run and get some towels and I'll be right back." She grinned at him, hoping her lips weren't quivering. "That way, if you need a little privacy…."

Ryan tilted his head. "I have a feeling privacy between us isn't going to be a concern of mine. But let me know when you need it." He grinned. "Whatever you want, that is mine to give, is yours."

Furiously holding back tears, Dia nodded as she turned quickly and headed back to the cabin. She knew that couples did all kinds of things in front of each other, but she was about to get naked in front of a man for the first time in her life. Anything else would have to wait until she was comfortable with that. But that wasn't what had her running for cover. She suddenly needed a moment to herself. To collect her thoughts, to give him time to use the bathroom if he'd needed to, but mostly to accept she was really going to make love with a man she feared she'd entranced with magic.

It didn't matter—she'd told herself time and again it

didn't matter—even if it was a possibility. She wasn't a deceptive person, and in her heart it really did matter. *So much.* The only saving grace was she really loved him, regardless of their short association. If in the end, she had to find a way to undo what she might have done, and he didn't really feel what she knew he was feeling right now, at least he would enjoy their time together. Of that she would make certain.

If I really have done this, please forgive me.

Determined to not be a coward, Dia hurriedly collected the new towels and matching washcloths she'd bought just days before. She'd convinced herself the impulse purchase was just because she'd loved the lavender color. Now she wondered if she'd hoped to one day have someone else to share them with, since she rarely bought anything she didn't need. Her focus had always been on magic, and since her cabin held little, and she wasn't a clotheshorse like Sapphire, the extravagant purchase had been completely out of character. She wondered what Ryan would think if he knew she had several clean towels in the cabinets above the washer and dryer and felt ashamed she was once again being deceptive.

Realizing she'd lingered too long, she hurried back to the shower house and sighed in relief when she opened the outer door and heard the shower already running.

"Dia?"

She carried the towels to the open shower door and stopped. Ryan was fully naked, his long body much more defined than she'd expected from a self-professed geek. He looked over at her and smiled as the water ran over his head and down the magnificent length of him. She stepped forward and placed the towels on one of the many built-in benches surrounding the room. Without hesitating, she pulled her dress over her head, and slipped out of her bra and panties. She knew he watched her every move and knew too, from the rise of his manhood, he very much liked what he saw.

"I was beginning to think you'd changed your mind."

Dia shook her head and walked into the spray, to stand before him. "No. I just needed a moment."

He nodded. "Are you done with it?"

She couldn't help grinning. "I am."

"Good."

Ryan reached out and grasped her skull, sliding his fingers through her hair. His gaze locked onto hers, he pulled her closer, before leaning down to place a gentle kiss across her lips. He licked his lips slowly, as if tasting her, causing Dia to take a shaky breath. He waited a heartbeat before taking her lips again, only this time he lingered and delved until she melted into him, and rock hard wet flesh met soft feminine wet flesh.

Once he pulled back he smiled at her with a gentleness that stole her breath. "I'm not making love to you in here. Our first time is going to be in your bed. But I have no problem working up to it for a while."

Dia nodded, unable to speak. She closed her eyes as he took a step back and then opened them to find him adoring her with his gaze.

"I'm going to touch and taste every inch of your beautiful body."

Dia was able to find a small smile, though she had no doubt he saw her lips trembling now. She held her breath as he reached out and ran a finger around the curve of her ear, before he leaned forward and placed a light kiss there. He allowed her hair to fall back down, as he inspected the curve of her jaw with as much gentleness, and then, again, kissed along the line where he'd touched. The length of her neck was next, followed by the line of her collarbone and rounds of her shoulders. He paid homage to each, before looking into her eyes again.

"You can touch me, too."

Dia inhaled sharply as his words were accompanied by his fingers sliding down the indention above her breasts. Her breaths rose and lowered quickly in her lungs' desperate attempt to keep up with the adrenaline rushing through her veins. She closed her eyes and panted as his fingers traveled downward then across to lightly brush a nipple. About to open her eyes, she moaned instead as wet lips grasped then suckled and licked, while he molded and then lightly pinched the other aching nub. Her knees buckled, but he caught her around the waist before she fell far. She looked up at the smile on his face and felt the heat that already flushed her body, fill her cheeks.

"I've never…. I mean I didn't know…." Dia struggled to find the words, but was saved the effort when he lifted her so he could kiss her, then nuzzled her neck through her mass of wet hair. By the time he lowered her to her feet she was completely undone.

"I love the smell of the shampoo. I've already bathed, if you'll let me, I'd love to take care of you."

Dia nodded, still unable to believe this man had just walked into her life and was somehow the most important thing that had ever been there. She allowed him to pour the fragrant shampoo onto her hair, and nearly melted again as he massaged the indigenes plant based liquid into a lather against her scalp. She hummed in pleasure as he lifted her and burst into giggles as the suds ran down her body and his, once she'd placed her hands on his shoulders and he raised her even higher into the spray. He kissed her softly as he lowered her, only to fill his palm with the conditioner also produced at her great uncle's factory to work it into her hair as if each blond lock was worthy of attention. After a second rinse Dia allowed him to wash her body with his large hands and knew by the slowness of his movements and the wonder in his eyes, he was enthralled with each and every inch of her flesh.

She was already blindsided by desire and barely able to stand by the time he lowered himself to his knees and nudged her wobbling legs apart enough to gently wash and rinse her there. He kissed her belly with adoring lips as he finished cleansing her body. His lips were again on her, capturing rinse water as well as flesh as he licked his way to her core. Were it not for the anchoring of his hands upon her butt cheeks, and hers upon his shoulders, she knew she'd melt onto the tiled floor.

She moaned his name and Ryan rose slowly, sliding up her body until she felt the full impact of his erection. He held her to him as he maneuvered them to turn off each of the many knobs and then took her to the bench where she'd left the towels. Dia knew she should help, but he'd stolen her strength, so she stood still and allowed him to wrap first her hair, then pat down and cover her from breasts to thighs, before lifting her into his arms.

"I'm going to need to get shower shoes," he said, laughing, as he struggled to slip into the expensive boat shoes he'd worn to town.

Dia smiled up at him, thinking that was the most romantic thing he could have said. "You don't have to carry me."

Ryan grinned. "Yes, I do."

He was careful as he took them back down the heavily wooded path that kept the shower house hidden from the view. Once inside the cabin, he set her on her feet. He gave her no time to think before unwinding the towels from her hair and body and tossing them into the small sink next to her refrigerator.

He lifted her face to stare into her eyes. "Not changed your mind?"

Dia shook her head slowly. "No. You?"

He laughed and let his masterful lips answer for him.

The kiss consumed her mind and flamed a fire already flaring throughout her body until she had to break away to gasp for breath. She dove right back in, her former lethargy replaced with empowerment that had her curling her fingers into the flesh of his back in her attempt to get closer. Her need transmitted to him, and he changed from being a gentle man to one willing to let his hunger reign. Before she knew how, the covers were thrown back, and they were upon her soft sheet. But by the time her mind registered the change, her body was being ravaged, and she craved and demanded more.

What Dia had expected was gentle love play. There was none of that. She reveled in her hunger for him as his mouth and hands were everywhere, tormenting and tasting, tearing and filling, all but where she ached most. She blindly let herself go, grasping and clinging, clawing and biting, loving that it only fed his own wild need. When he slid into her, she was more than ready, and the slight pain of invasion was something to celebrate to the depths of her soul. Ryan ravaged her lips as he rode her body and Dia fought to hold on to the rising tide of fire burning inside. But the pressure built too fast, and the explosion, when it came, tore her lips from his as her scream of joy ripped through the cabin's air. Ryan strained, stilled, and emptied into her, his hot seed bathing her own banking fire. He collapsed onto her but immediately rolled them so she was on top. As though he weren't spent, he continued the assault on her lips, until finally he gentled to wallow in one last kiss before he lifted her head back enough to look into her eyes.

He gasped, as his mouth fell open. "Your eyes!"

As if slapped from a dream Dia stilled, knowing what he saw. She lowered her lashes immediately, but he tilted her chin upward.

"Don't do that."

Dia struggled, wanting to get away, but he held her firmly against his body. "Please, let me up. I can't help it."

Ryan waited until she looked back up. "I mean, don't hide yourself from me like that. Your eyes are beautiful, but I've never seen anything like what they do."

Dia forced herself to relax. "I don't know why they do that. They just always have."

Ryan smiled teasingly. "So it wasn't just me."

Not knowing what to say, Dia bit her lip. She slid down slightly so she could lay her head on his chest. Swallowing was difficult because she searched for acceptable words, but there was no way to explain without revelations she couldn't offer. Not knowing how much of herself to reveal safely, yet knowing she had to find something to say, she opened her mouth and truth spilled out.

"They only do it when I'm very emotional."

Ryan stroked her hair. "Like angry?"

Dia smiled at his reaction. "Or happy."

"Or afraid?"

Dia nuzzled him and spoke through the kiss she placed on his chest. "Or excited."

"Or sexually satisfied?" he asked, amusement in his voice.

Dia laughed lightly. "Apparently."

She rode his deep sigh, wondering if her eyes really bothered him. It didn't feel like that was the case, but she understood why they would. He was silent for a time, and she was afraid to rise up and ask what he was thinking about.

"I meant to go slower."

Ah... She rose up then and placed her hands together on his chest so she could look him in the eyes. "That was the most perfect experience of my entire life."

He curled up to kiss her lips gently. "Mine too," he

said, relaxing back.

"So what do we do now?"

Ryan rolled them over and she giggled. "We have two choices. We can clean ourselves up and get out those strawberries and the whipped cream, or we can see if I can go slower on my second try."

Dia grinned and pretended to ponder her options. "Since I'm a little sore, maybe we could snack on something other than each other for just a little while?"

Ryan pretended to look disappointed but kissed her soundly anyway.

"*Or*, we could snack on the whipped cream *on* each other...."

A flash of light entered his eyes. "Now, you're talking!"

Ryan rose and pulled her up with him. They took a moment to play at washing each other at the sink, both fully aroused by the time they'd dried off, but had to take a moment to wipe down the water they'd splashed all over the side of the refrigerator and floor as well. The strawberries were washed, and Ryan insisted the stems and leaves be removed, before being placed into a bowl. He retrieved the can of whipped cream and turned to her with laughter in his eyes. Dia squealed as he approached her but stood her ground while he made pasties of the sugary cream. Her legs nearly buckled when he licked off the first, then tortured her nipple with lips and teeth.

By the time he'd addressed the other, she was ready to give as well as get. She snatched the can from his hands and ran a line down his center from breastbone to belly button, not yet brave enough to go lower. His eyes flared with surprise, and he held her hair back when she pitched the can to the bed and grasped his hips to lean forward. A tiny daring thrill allowed her to move one hand to the star of his show. She grasped his engorged penis and reveled in his swift gasping breaths. With a quick glance upward, she grinned, only to find him frozen in anticipation. Deciding to torment him, she stuck her tongue in his navel, causing him to flinch. Empowered, she licked like a kitten drinking from a saucer, her darting tongue taking only a little of the cream with each hit.

"You're killing me," he said breathlessly.

Dia grinned as she took another taste and then slid her tongue up several inches. As she held the cream on her tongue, she dropped her gaze to his straining member. Without hesitation she lowered her head and took him into her mouth, tightening her fingers around the base of his cock.

"Oh... my...God!" Ryan exclaimed as his knees buckled, and he grasped her shoulders, his fingers biting into her flesh.

Dia stroked him with lips and tongue as deeply as she could, knowing she'd yet to completely engulf him. Before she could adjust to take him deeper, he grasped her jaw and pulled her up slowly, but she tightened both hold and suction, until her lips caught on the swollen head.

"Dia, please," he said, breathlessly. "Not yet. Oh, God, not yet."

The chuckle from her throat was her only answer as she pushed his hands away.

"Please. I want to pleasure you first. I'm not going to last if you don't stop, now.

"*Dia!*"

With a slight shake of her head, he emitted a broken sound she was sure had never left his lips before. Delighted, she suckled her way down again, this time going a little further. His hands were once again on her shoulders, but now he was moving, sliding into her oral-strokes. As turned on as he, she continued, getting bolder and deeper each time. The subtle change in the stiffening of his legs alerted her he'd reached his limit. She stood with a last upward stroke and threw her arms around his neck while their lips collided. He lifted her, and she slid onto him and held on for the shattering ride she feared would take a lifetime to recover from. By the time she was on her feet again, neither of them had much strength to play at the sink, so the laborious cleansing took only minutes.

With the bowl of strawberries in one hand and her in the other, Ryan pulled Dia back to the blessedly welcoming bed.

Chapter Eight

Morning broke slowly for Ryan. He had no desire to awaken the amazing woman by his side. He lay facing her, looking from her beautifully disheveled head of nearly white hair to the long white-gold lashes that fanned out above her slightly flushed cheeks, and then on to the plumpness of her delectable soft lips. He inhaled sharply at the memory of what those lips could and had done to him the night before, which hadn't ended until long after they'd taken the strawberries to bed with them. He closed his eyes, not wanting to become so aroused he woke her. He knew she had to be exhausted and more than likely pretty sore.

That he'd been her first was beyond amazing. It could only be explained by her sense of self-value and the obvious stupidity of every other man on the planet. That she'd chosen him still bowled him over, but he was happy to take the fall.

"Good morning."

Ryan opened his eyes, so happy to see she awoke clear eyed and alert. "Good morning."

"I knew you were awake because you were smiling."

Ryan chuckled. "I could have been having a hot dream."

Dia studied his face. "Were you?"

He shook his head. "No. My hot dream is right in front of me."

She blushed, and his heart swelled, knowing she was still an innocent at heart, even after a night of ravenous lovemaking. "You are so beautiful, it takes my breath."

Dia leaned forward and kissed him lightly. "As are you. How is it girls didn't fall all over you, from the time you hit puberty?"

Ryan gave her question real consideration before he answered. "I guess I got some attention once I started college, but I was so young and awkward I didn't trust it. Like I told you before, I'm not good with people." He frowned. "My mother isn't either, and I guess I just took after her."

"You are good with me." She grinned, a self-satisfied gleam in her eyes.

Ryan nodded. "I am now. But I wasn't at first. I thought the looks you gave me were just you being naturally friendly." He frowned, realizing he'd always interpreted the looks women gave him that way.

"Are you feeling regret that you didn't, *I don't know*, take women's interest the way it was meant before?"

Amazed they were thinking along the same lines, he shook his head. "Not regret. I'm really glad you are the first woman I've ever been intimate with."

Dia smiled. "Me too."

He bathed in the sincerity of her eyes. "At first I was afraid I'd disappoint you, and then I realized if what was between us was real, I couldn't. Nothing has ever been more real for me. I'm completely in lo... *crazy* about you."

She bit her lip and then looked down so her lashes were once again shading her eyes. Ryan held his breath, knowing she'd caught that he'd almost said love. If she wasn't on the same page, which made complete sense given their short time together... He cringed, afraid he'd spoken too soon. She glanced back up, and her heart was in her eyes allowing him to test taking a breath.

"I feel the same way."

Relief swept through him and he pulled her to him. "You scared me there for a minute."

Dia snuggled into him. "I'm sorry. I'm just scared of us both feeling so much, so quickly. What if it doesn't last?"

Ryan couldn't imagine that happening and told her so, but there was something in her eyes... *Caution maybe?* The last thing he wanted was for her to hold back whatever it was she thought and felt. But he didn't want to push her and hoped time would take away whatever fears she had. Though he'd be more than happy to show her, again, just how much she meant to him, he knew he had to shift gears.

"I guess I need to go see my father. I told him I'd come back this morning."

Dia nodded. "That's okay. I hope he gets better."

It was on the tip of his tongue to explain about Clayton, but he held the words inside. With their relationship so new, and though he hated to admit it, tenuous, he didn't want to add crazy into the mix. "I hope he does, too."

Ryan kissed her soundly, relieved she didn't hesitate to kiss back. "Before I decide we can't leave this bed...."

Dia laughed as he wiggled his eyebrows. "I totally agree. Family before..." She looked away then back at him, the laugher gone. "Love," she added softly.

"To hell with that." Ryan's heart burst free and he ravaged her with his lips, hands, and male body. She was wild and opened to him in every way without hesitation. When they were both spent, they knew a shower was in order, but it too turned from an innocent facility of cleansing to an oasis for desperately erotic sex. By the time they were finally able to dress, the sun was high in the sky.

"I'm sorry. I hope your dad isn't mad."

Ryan shrugged. "It took twenty-five years to know he existed. I think he can give me a few hours." He frowned, hating that he resented having to deal with everything his father represented when his life had otherwise become perfect.

"Did he know about you?"

Shaking his head, the irritation waned. "No. That's the only reason I'm still determined to see this through. If he'd known and never made contact, I'd say to hell with him."

Dia approached him and wrapped him in her arms. "I'm sorry."

Ryan didn't want her sympathy. Everything else. But not that. "It is what it is." He lifted her chin and placed a chaste kiss on her lips. "But I guess we have to go."

The text tone sounded on his phone. Alarmed, since his mother rarely texted, and no one else but the hospital had his number, Ryan dug it from his computer case's pocket. Sure enough it was the doctor.

Tried to call. Your father overly agitated this morning. He escaped. Please contact me at earliest convenience.

His head reeling, Ryan looked up. "He's left the hospital."

Dia's brows pulled together. "Is he better then?"

Ryan shook his head, remembering his father's last words. "No."

"What's going on? You look like you're going to be sick."

Knowing he had no choice, he nodded. "I might be. My father was in the psychiatric ward. He's a dangerous man."

****

Dia's heart broke for him. To learn he had a father, and to find out he was mentally ill, had to be devastating. She crossed to face him, and gently took him into her arms. "What can I do?"

Ryan kissed the top of her head. "You're doing it."

"Where will he go? Does he have a home close by?" She stepped back to look up at him.

Shaking his head, Ryan led her to the bed and pulled her into his lap. "No. Not that I know of. According to the doctor, my father is homeless."

"Then they'll find him, right? He couldn't get too far, no matter which way he travels if he's on foot." Dia frowned. "Unless he's made it to woods. There are thousands of acres, and that would be harder. Do you want me to contact my sister? She's a police officer."

Ryan frowned. "A police officer?"

Dia nodded. "Yes. She and her husband are only a few miles down the mountain. I have no idea if she's home or not. She used to work nights but changed to days once she was married. I think her days off rotate though, so I never know when she'll be home."

She didn't add they weren't close enough for her to care much, either. If they were together long enough, Ryan would learn that on his own. The tone on her cell, indicating Sapphire was texting her, startled her. Dia wondered if her sister's ears had been burning. She frowned at Ryan and reached to the bedside table to retrieve her phone, then jumped up as excitement filled her once she'd read the message.

"I'm so sorry. I know this is a terrible time for you, but my sister, Jewell, has gone into labor, and I need to get to my mother's house."

Dia felt awful. He couldn't drive until he had new glasses, and he had no idea where his mentally unstable father had gone. And now she wanted to be with her family to celebrate the additions to their clan. "I'm really sorry, Ryan."

He smiled and pulled her into his arms. "Don't be. I would much rather go with you to a happy occasion than worry over a man I barely know. I can't see well, I'm completely lost in this area anyway, so there isn't anything I can do but wait for them to find him. If you don't mind me tagging along, I'd like to meet your family."

Dia nodded, though she had no idea what her family

would think of her bringing a stranger, one they believed could be a threat, to what was clearly a family event. But worse, she had no idea what he would think if everyone decided to descend at once, which her family was prone to do.

Relief washed through her. As far as she knew Jewell was still planning to have the babies at her parents' house, and there was limited parking spaces at their cabin. Of course, that wouldn't stop her aunts from popping in from thin air, which would be a disaster of major proportions.

But what could she say? "Of course, I don't. Come on. Let's go!"

Before they reached the Jeep, Ryan stopped her. "Your phone dinged again."

Dia looked down at the instrument in her hand. Sure enough Sapphire had texted her again putting an asterisk before adding Aunt Dee's cabin, not the parents'. Dia's heart sank immediately. Uncle Tom and Aunt Destiny had scads of room for the entire family to gather, so she knew what could have been a quiet birth would turn into a family party before the day was done.

She looked at Ryan, hoping he didn't regret inviting himself along. "Change of plans. We're going to my aunt and uncle's house."

Ryan nodded and joined her to strap in. "Not the hospital?"

"No. Nothing so simple. My sister wants to have a home birth." Scowling, she threw the Jeep into gear, backed up and turned, then headed down her long driveway, praying this wasn't all a big mistake.

It took only a short time to pull into the driveway that was as long as hers. This time there were acres of wide-open field once they reached the large cabin her uncle had built years before her birth and had added to after his triplet sons were born. Sure enough, there were lots of cars, trucks, and a motorcycle already parked to the far side of the driveway, and as many members of her family were sitting outside on the large wrap-around porch. She glanced their way as she parked and noticed she and Ryan were capturing the attention of her cousins.

She turned to him, catching his hand before he leapt from the Jeep. "I hope you're ready for this."

Ryan nodded as he glanced from those now standing on the porch to her. "The welcoming committee, or am I about to get the third degree?"

Dia shook her head as he laughed. "You might think it funny now. But they've never seen me with a guy, so the third degree is more likely."

He nodded and jumped down to walk to her side. He took her hand and looked deeply into her eyes. "Well, let's answer one question for them before we say hello." He leaned down and kissed her with gentleness, then straightened, making her smile.

"You are a *very* bad boy." Dia couldn't help but smile, but she was quaking on the inside.

Heracles jumped the porch railing at a dead run, only braking before he slammed into Ryan. Dia grinned at her favorite cousin, amused to see the challenge in his eyes when Ryan didn't flinch or react in any way. She cleared her throat pulling the internationally known model's attention her way. "Hi, Harry."

"Hey." He nodded toward Ryan. "What's this?"

Dia shook her head. "This is Ryan Steward. Ryan, this is Heracles Whitehawk. My cousin and self-appointed watchdog *apparently*."

Ryan grinned and held out his hand. "Hi, nice to meet you."

Heracles looked from his face to the hand and then reluctantly took it with a frown. He glanced at Dia and sighed, before eyeing Ryan up and down. "Yeah, you too."

He turned to Dia once their hands were back at their sides. "So why haven't I heard about him?"

Dia nearly laughed, but knew her cousin was serious. They'd been the closest of all the others, ever since all nine of the Cavanaugh children were born within minutes of each other. They not only shared the same birthday, she and Heracles shared the same sense of humor, the same love of the exotic, and had fought each other enough times while growing up that they even had the same moves.

"Because I wanted to keep him to myself for a while. Jewell's labor has sped that up."

Knowing Ryan wouldn't say anything about their short association if she didn't, she linked her arm through his and began pulling him toward the cabin. Heracles followed, and Dia could only imagine what was going through his head. She stopped on the porch, addressing Zeus, the oldest of the three Whitehawk boys. "How's Jewell?"

He nodded at Ryan, amusement in his eyes. "She's good. The moms are in there doing their..." He looked at her with a raised brow and Dia shook her head slightly. Nodding, he continued. "They're preparing the room and she's taking a bath, I think. At least she was when I came outside a few minutes ago."

Zeus turned to Ryan. "Zeus Whitehawk."

Ryan grinned and shook his hand. "Ryan Steward."

Dia took a deep breath as Apollo stepped up, and she repeated introductions. Apollo looked from her to him then back, and she prayed he wouldn't say anything he shouldn't.

"The girls are all inside. Why don't you go on in and check on your sister." He looked at her pointedly. "And tell your mother you're here. I'll introduce Ryan to Amen-ra and Nicolae."

"Where's the dads?"

Apollo smiled. "In the rec room. My dad and Logan

are plying your dad with some really fine whiskey, I imagine."

Dia glanced down the long porch to where Amen-ra sat in one of the many wooden chairs gracing the porch. He seemed to be throwing back and then refilling several glasses of his own. "Why isn't he with Jewell?"

Apollo chuckled. "She threw him out. Said he was smothering her. But the moms will call him back in when it's time.

"Have to say, that one has a mouth when she's in pain."

Dia couldn't imagine Jewell cursing, much less yelling at the man she worshipped. "I'll go in, but be nice to Ryan. He's mine."

"I'll be fine," Ryan said, delight filling his eyes.

Surprise lit Apollo's chocolate ones, but he merely nodded in understanding before turning to Ryan. "Welcome. Come on back and meet the father. I have a feeling he'll be wasted if they don't call him in soon. And then they'll have my ass for letting him drink in the first place. I can't believe he's let one little woman take him down like this."

Before Ryan turned away, Dia pulled his head down for a kiss and then glanced at Heracles with her brows raised. He glared at her for only seconds before amusement filled his chocolate orbs as well. "Got it."

Satisfied, Dia entered the house and headed toward the scents of jasmine, rosemary, and mint her mother and aunts would use to purify the house in preparation for the new babies and to ease the weight of the air for her sister. Though Dia knew her aunt did so regularly in her home, the three together would enhance the properties of each, to bring in love and protection and chase out any bad karma, though Aunt Destiny wasn't likely to let it in to begin with. Figuring her mother had prepared a hyssop bath for Jewell, she turned and headed to the rooms her cousins had once used before they'd moved out. Sure enough, the three matriarchs were slowly whipping the air with their burning herb ropes, and Sapphire was handing Jewell what was likely a magic-enhanced herbal tea. There were so many to choose from, Dia didn't attempt to guess which they meant to ease her suffering with.

"Hi!"

Jewell looked over and smiled before she burst into tears. Dia hurried over and squatted by the claw-foot tub. "Hey, it's going to be fine."

Nodding, Jewell wiped at her eyes. "I know. But I've chewed my husband's head off, and, ah, ah, ah, ah...."

Dia winced as her own abdomen clenched in sympathy. She glanced up at Sapphire, but she looked as lost as Dia felt. "Hi."

"Hi. Is Amen-ra still drinking?"

Dia nodded. A look of anger crossed Sapphire's face, and sparks shot from her sapphire eyes. "Hey, before you go out there, I need to tell you something."

"What!"

Dia wouldn't want to be Amen-ra if her life depended on it. "You can't show yourself. I've brought my...boyfriend, and he knows nothing about us."

"You did what!"

Rayne hurried over. "You brought a guy? You *have* a boyfriend?"

Dia smiled at her mother. "Yes. And yes. But he—"

"That's completely inappropriate!" Sapphire stated, her eyes flashing fire now.

"Sapphire, stop that now. She didn't throw a fit when you brought Nicolae home. We don't do that."

"You guys, these babies are coming, please stop, or get out. I can't take this right now."

All eyes turned to Jewell, and Sapphire immediately

calmed. "I'm sorry, Sis. I'm just going out to make sure your husband is sober enough to hold your hand without passing out on top of you." She turned back to Dia. "This isn't the time to ask anyone to hold back their power."

Having said that, she left the large bathroom to stomp her way down the hall. Dia glanced at her sister and then her mother. "I'm sorry. I couldn't leave him behind. It's the guy I told you about yesterday."

Rayne's brows rose, but thankfully she smiled instead of commenting on the shortness of Dia and Ryan's association.

"Is he special to you, then?"

Dia nodded. "He is."

"Then he's special to us too. We can do what must be done. He won't be in the room when the babies are delivered."

Relieved her mother was on her side, she turned back to Jewell. "Let me know what you need."

Jewell lay back and moaned deeply, her legs open wide. "I think the first one is coming. Please, get my husband in here!"

Dia looked up at her mother. "In the tub?"

Rayne nodded. "It will ease the delivery. Her children will be of water."

Not questioning how her mother would know such a thing, she hurried to help Sapphire get the ancient Egyptian in time to witness the birth of his children. She met Sapphire and Amen-ra in the foyer, and though his smile was big, his eyes were filled with panic. Dia glanced at her sister, who threw her an amused look.

"You might want to get out there. Heracles is flirting with your man.

"Really cute, by the way."

Both statements startled Dia, first because her sister was suddenly so friendly, and secondly because Heracles didn't *flirt* with guys. He was always in the tabloids with one starlet or another, and he was more than happy to tell of his sexual exploits whenever he came back from a photo shoot. She laughed, figuring Sapphire meant their crazy cousin was talking Ryan's ear off. "Okay, but tell Jewell I'll be right back. I'm not missing the births!"

Dia saw Ryan down the long side porch, talking as much with his hands as his mouth. Heracles was close, hanging on his every word. But so were Zeus, Apollo, and Nicolae. She stayed at the corner of the house, happy no one noticed her, just to have a moment to look at him as his animated face moved, smiled, laughed with her cousins, and then he went on with whatever he was talking about.

His concern that he was awkward with others wasn't apparent now. Though she couldn't distinguish their words over the soothing music her aunt must have turned on to bring additional tranquility to the birthing, it was clear Ryan was fully engaged in a discussion *or* demonstration. From the stances and looks on her cousins' and brother-in-law's faces, they found him equally engaging. He stopped talking, and she could tell he was listening with a nodding head as Zeus moved next to him and was now using *his* hands to form whatever it was which had them all so fascinated. Ryan reached up and pointed into the air between Zeus's hands, and Zeus nodded, then they laughed together. Heracles maneuvered between Zeus and Ryan, said something, only to have Zeus push him away. Again they all cracked up, and Dia could do nothing but smile at the abundance of testosterone held in check while they bonded and seemed to be welcoming Ryan into their fold.

He was so deliciously attractive he just took her breath away. For his beauty to shine in the presence of the company currently enthralled by his every word, said so much about him. She knew he didn't realize, geek or not, he was a man's man in every sense of the word. He could have been a ladies' man if he'd only allowed it to happen. She tore her gaze away to look at the others and marveled again that such works of art walked on two feet.

Zeus, Apollo, and Heracles were completely identical in looks, unlike her female cousins and sisters, though genetically each set of triplet children had, *if tested*, what science considered matching DNA with their siblings. The Whitehawk boys, deemed by their mother, *The Sons of Cavanaugh*—since they were the first males born to a Cavanaugh woman in over three thousand years—were darker of skin than the female cousins and were nearly an indistinguishable reflection of their father, minus the span of years separating them and him. The last full-blooded Native American male of his family line, her uncle Tom was still a visual force to be reckoned with at fifty-nine years of age, and his sons were blessed with his strong genes. As if that weren't unfair enough to the rest of the world, they'd also inherited the magic of both parents, as well.

Nicolae Lupei, Sapphire's husband, and Dia's newest brother-in-law, was off the charts when it came to looks. He was the kind of man who made women gasp when they first saw him, both because he was eye candy at its finest, but also because one instantly sensed the physical power that radiated from him at all times. As the Alpha Male of the local band of werewolves, who were now becoming as much a part of Mystic Waters as the Cavanaugh descendants, Nicolae had deemed his Lycanthrope pack as the protectors of Mystic Mountain. His males now took turns patrolling the mountain nightly in their natural form. Daily they worked as homebuilders for Nicolae's construction company in town in their human form.

Dia looked from one to the other and finally her gaze landed back on Ryan. As if he'd felt her presence, he glanced down the long porch, and his eyes lit up with pleasure. Her feet moved, taking her forward, even before her mind made the conscious decision to do so. She grinned at her cousins as they moved back, and then she walked straight into Ryan's open arms.

"Hi," he said and then kissed the top of her head.

Dia looked up, not caring that her family was looking on, and pulled his face down for a soft kiss. She inhaled his grin as if it was required for breath and then turned to the others. "Looks like you guys are having fun."

Zeus looked from Ryan to her, shaking his head. "You didn't tell us this was *the* Ryan Steward."

Dia made a face as she shrugged. "I told you his name. What do you mean *the* Ryan Steward?"

Surprise lit her cousin's eyes as Zeus frowned at Ryan. "She doesn't know?"

Dia turned to him. "What is it that I don't know about you, that my cousins do?"

"Just that he is the foremost popular game maker on the planet. His first game took the world by storm a few years back."

Dia glanced back at Apollo. "*What?* What games?"

"Video!" all three Whitehawk's said at once.

Dia didn't know what to say as she turned back to Ryan. "You didn't tell me that."

Ryan looked uncomfortable for the first time since they'd arrived. "That's the project I've been working on that I wanted to show you. We just never got around to it."

"You've got a new game?"

Ryan's discomfort with her instantly changed into a confident smile as he looked at Apollo. "Not just a new game. A whole new gaming system. I'm taking it to the biggest electronics expo in the country next month." He grinned. "It's going to blow gaming out of the water!"

Dia stood, stunned, as the men were once again talking excitedly. She hadn't ever played a video game but knew her cousins had been weaned on them. Her aunt Destiny had complained about how much they'd played when they were kids. She studied Ryan, realizing now why he was so confident with her cousins. He was in his element, talking about his passion, and he was in the company of men who obviously thought him a king. She smiled to herself, deciding it was time she learned more about her man and his talents, other than his ability to make her scream with sexual satisfaction.

"Dia? Are you coming or not? The baby is crowning!"

She whipped around but Sapphire was already gone, so Dia pulled Ryan's head down and kissed him quickly, but soundly. "You and I have a lot to talk about later. But I've got to go."

"Go! I'm fine out here."

"I can see that." She smiled at him and the rest before hurrying back into the house. She made her way to the bathroom just in time to see her mother lift the first baby into the air, its tiny body dripping. Sapphire waited until Aunt Haven clamped the umbilical cord, then handed Amen-ra a pair of surgical scissors to cut it. The baby girl was quickly placed into Destiny's hands, and she took it to the table that had been prepared with heat lamps, cloth diapers, and towels.

"Number two is coming!" Rayne said, her voice cracking with the emotion of becoming a grandmother. Dia's eyes filled as she was sure everyone's did. Jewell was blowing hyper-breaths as she moaned through the second delivery and then leaned back, resting her head against the tub while the second daughter was scooped up and the disconnection procedure was repeated.

Destiny had wrapped the first baby and, to Dia's surprise, thrust the child into her arms before running back to prepare for the next one. Dia's breath caught as she looked down at the tiny face and fisted hands exposed above the receiving blanket. The realization she was now an aunt tilted her world. She and her sisters were no longer the children of their family; there was now a new generation.

Seconds later Jewell groaned and pulled herself forward to push through the next contraction. After Aunt Haven handed the second tiny girl to Sapphire, she stepped back up to Rayne's side and was ready with another blanket once baby three was born.

Dia watched as Jewell settled back, her eyes searching the room to land on Dia and the child she held, then Sapphire and the baby she was cooing to softly. Finally she smiled up at her husband as he approached her with their youngest daughter his arms. Dia nearly stepped forward to show her the miracle she'd created, but the pleasure on Jewell's face transformed to shock as she curled forward and screamed.

Rayne, who was looking from granddaughter to granddaughter, turned back to face her child. Haven and Destiny were by her side instantly. Rayne glanced to oldest and youngest. "Take Amen-ra and the babies to the bedroom we've prepared."

Fear filled Dia as she hurried from the room, the sound of Jewell's hysterical cries following her out the door. Though she wanted to know what was happening to her sister, she didn't want the baby to become distressed or herself to be in the way. Sapphire was behind her, but Amen-ra wasn't. She looked back to see Destiny rushing up behind them with the youngest in her arms, pass them, then beat them to the bedroom.

"I'll leave this baby with you two. Amen-ra refuses to leave, and I need to get back in there."

She placed the baby in the center of the bed and hurried back out, leaving Sapphire and Dia to look at each other in fear. "What is going on?"

Sapphire's eyes filled with tears. "I don't know!"

Dia eyes filled as well as she tried to take even breaths. She sat on the side of the bed and placed her charge next to her sister. "Should we do something to identify which is which?"

Sapphire shook her head and placed the middle child on the other side of the youngest. "They have a marker in the other room. Aunt Destiny should have marked their birth order on each one's heel."

The sisters looked at each other and started unwrapping the babies. When each had a Roman numeral clearly marked, they sighed in relief. But it was short-lived as the sound of Jewell's scream reached them, making the babies cry.

"I have to go back in there!"

Dia shook her head, though she felt the same way. "We can't. Mom asked us to stay here."

Sapphire shook her head, nodded, and then put her face in her hands. Dia pulled on all the strength she had and started wrapping the babies back up. "Stop it, Sapphire! I'm scared too. But these babies are terrified and we need to take care of them."

Jewell's screams stopped abruptly and there was complete silence. Terrified, Dia shared another panicked look with her oldest sister. "I don't hear anything now," she whispered.

"Me either."

Suddenly the robust cry of a baby came through the door and she knew her face had to reflect the shock in Sapphire's. "Another one?"

Sapphire's tear-stained face transformed into one of joy. "Oh. My. Gosh! Can it be?"

They bundled the three little girls hurriedly, needing to get back to see if their sister was okay. Before they could get to the door Destiny arrived, carrying baby number four. She smiled at them.

"Welcome your nephew, girls."

Slowly they moved forward to look at the tiny little boy. Dia looked up in wonder. "Mom said there were only three. How did she not know?"

Destiny smiled. "This little troublemaker was hiding behind his sisters." She laughed. "I bet they'll make him pay for it many times in his life."

Sapphire, looked up, tears flowing down her cheeks. "Jewell is okay?"

Dia reached over and put her arm around Sapphire's shoulder with her free hand and then looked to their aunt for reassurance. "She is, or you wouldn't be so relaxed, right?"

Destiny nodded. "She's exhausted, but she's fine now. This little fellow wasn't expected. It terrified her when she felt him coming. She was afraid something horrible was happening to her body." She sighed. "Had us all pretty scared too."

Sapphire turned and placed the baby she held on the bed and cried harder. Confused, Dia looked to her aunt, but Destiny looked as perplexed. Sapphire didn't cry as far as Dia knew. Jewell was fine and now had four healthy babies.

"Sis? What is wrong with you?"

Sapphire glanced up and emitted a shaky sigh. "I think I'm pregnant."

Chapter Nine

By the time Jewell and the babies were settled, and the family had paraded through to congratulate her and Amenra, the men who'd waited out on the porch had the fire pit and the large barrel grills going strong. The smell of barbequing meat filled the air thanks to Apollo and Zeus, who stood over the grills sipping beers and flipping steaks, chicken breasts, beef ribs, and even burgers. Amazed that they'd gotten things going so quickly, Dia shook her head in amusement.

She'd always thought it funny her cousins were such meat eaters, when both of their parents only ate meat sparingly, after a great deal of apology and then thanksgiving to whatever animal had given up its life to nourish theirs.

Her mother and Aunt Haven had turned to the dark side some time back, according to Aunt Destiny, and not only ate meat frequently, they did so without apology, though giving thanks was still expected. Now the matriarchs, Sapphire, and the Cavanaugh-Hansen cousins, who had arrived just after the stressful event, headed to the kitchen to whip up side dishes to feed everyone. Dia was given a pass since her new man had been left alone too long according to her mother, who had gotten only a quick look at him, when Dia introduced him to each family member while they were *oohing* and *awing* over the babies. Rayne had said a quick *Hi and welcome*, gave him a hug, and then sent her youngest a wink before moving on to her next self-appointed chore.

Dia hadn't protested. Kitchen duty wasn't her forte, and Ryan most definitely was. But she'd sent him off and made sure everyone had something cold to drink before allowing herself to step out of the fray. Excited to get back to Ryan, she was grinning when she finally found him out in the field with Heracles pitching small corn-filled bags a good twelve feet into a point-marked board with holes. Deciding men were nothing more than large boys, she walked across the driveway and approached them to find her cousin was his usual happy, silly self. It was obvious Ryan, with his glasses back in place, was having a ball. He was new to the game of Cornhole and beating Heracles hands down.

"Hey cuz, your man's got killer instincts." Heracles's right brow lifted. "Probably from playing his games all the time."

Dia walked straight to Ryan, and he removed his glasses as she got closer. "This is fun. You want to challenge me next?"

She grinned and kissed his mouth. "Sure. Or we could take a walk and snuggle a little."

With a quick glance at Heracles, she raised both her brows, hoping her cousin took the hint. She wanted time alone with her man before the family sat down to eat. At that point, if they'd gotten her father sobered up some, Ryan was likely going to get as grilled as the cooked meat.

Ryan looked to Heracles, smiling. "Sorry, dude, duty calls."

Heracles laughed and nodded. "Whatever happened to *bros* before *hos*?"

Dia considered punching her cousin, but she had better things to do with her energy. She smiled up at Ryan as his grip around her waist tightened, but he was looking at her cousin, his gaze sharp.

"Since there aren't any hos here, it doesn't apply."

Startled by Ryan's tone, Dia glanced back to find Heracles's gaze filled with speculative amusement, before he shook his head as if he pitied her man.

"Looks like another one has bit the dust."

"He's kidding with you, Ryan."

Ryan glanced down at her then back at her cousin with a self-depreciating grin. "Sorry, dude."

Heracles brows pulled together. "No problem." He glanced at Dia. "You be nice to this one. He's a keeper." With that he turned and trotted toward the cabin.

Ryan kissed the top of her head. "I feel stupid. I don't know why him saying that went all over me."

Dia pulled his head down for another kiss, this time lingering until they were both breathing a little heavily. "Don't worry about it. Heracles speaks before he thinks, and he and I have called each other worse all our lives." She grinned at him. "You'd better get used to it. My family likes to tease and little is taboo."

Ryan's eyes were serious as he looked at her. "I've never had anyone to tease with, so I'll probably look like an idiot."

Dia pulled him back into a tight hug. "I know they're going to love you. My male cousins already think you are the coolest thing to ever walk through the door, from what I saw earlier. Which reminds me, are you famous?"

As Ryan's cheeks filled with color, he shrugged.

"Kind of. I played video games shortly after I started college, but they didn't challenge me, and I'd end up beating each new one pretty quickly. So I decided to try building my own. It wasn't as complex as what I do now, but it took off on campus. Out of the blue I was offered a ridiculous amount of money by one of the big game system manufacturers, and I took it. That allowed me to buy what I needed to start building bigger, and I've had great success with the games I've built since then. But they are nothing like what I've just created and am about to demo at the expo. I've made a gaming system that is like nothing out there. I won't just be selling games. The whole system is mine. I can't wait to show it to you to see what you think."

Dia stared at him, speechless.

Ryan grinned. "And if you're wondering, the answer is yes. I'm pretty loaded."

Dia frowned, shaking her head. "I wouldn't care if you didn't have a penny to your name."

He pulled her closer. "I know that. As special as you already are, knowing you want me, *just me*, socially awkward nerd that I am, makes being with you so much more amazing."

"Hey, you guys! Food's ready!"

"And here I thought we would have snuggle time."

Ryan stuck out his lower lip, pretending to pout, but the gleam in his eyes gave him away. Dia laughed. "Sure, pretend I look better to you than a steak right now."

"I'm finding I have dueling appetites." He wiggled his brows. "But being the realist that I am and knowing how much energy snuggling with you takes...."

"Come on, then. I sure wouldn't want you to pass out while I'm ravaging you."

She started to pull away but he pulled her right back. "Ravaging me? I'm not really feeling the steak right now...."

Dia giggled and swatted his hands away when they were suddenly all over her. She finally was able to grasp one to pull him toward the cabin. Several sets of eyes were on them. Her cousins, mother, and aunts were grinning. Her father, Uncle Logan, as well as Uncle Tom were not. She bit her lip as she stared at her father. "My dad is watching us."

"Everyone is. Which one is he?"

"The one targeting you with a glare."

Ryan chuckled. "Gotcha. I think I can take him."

Dia laughed and turned to him. "Behave. I'm his baby girl."

They made it to the front yard and Garrison took the steps a little unsteadily, meeting them front and center. "Hi, Daddy. Aren't the babies adorable?"

Garrison's gaze hadn't left Ryan until then. He glanced at her and nodded. "Yes. Very. Who's this?"

Dia had never seen her father even slightly inebriated, so she wasn't sure what to expect. "Daddy, this is Ryan Steward. Ryan, my father, Garrison White."

Ryan held out his hand. Garrison shook it but then took a step back, clearly off balance. He eyed their guest up and down. "So tell me, who are you and why are you all over my daughter?"

Dia nearly choked, horrified. She searched the porch for her mother, but it was clear she was enjoying the show too much to intervene. She flashed Rayne a look, but only got a laugh from the woman who had given her life. She turned back to her father. "Daddy, you're drunk!"

Garrison laughed and fell backward. Ryan caught him before he could lose his feet, but her father shook him off as soon as he was upright again, though still swaying. Thankfully, that was enough to get her uncles down from the porch. They positioned themselves on either side of her father, though both looked about to burst from holding in laughter.

Dia took a deep breath. She was mortified this was Ryan's first impression of the man she'd worshipped since her earliest memory. She turned to him, afraid to see his reaction, but he was smiling with kindness in his eyes.

"It's good to meet you, sir. Congratulations on becoming a grandfather."

Garrison nodded, importantly, and then smiled. "You too, son. No. No. Wait. Not you. You're not a grandfather." He glanced back quickly and lost his balance, but Tom caught him. Garrison sent him a dopey smile. "Where's Rayne?"

Tom took him by the shoulders and turned him toward the porch. Her mother was coming down the steps, not bothering to hold her amusement in check. She walked up to her husband, and Tom stepped back so she could loop his arm over her shoulders. She glanced first at Dia and then smiled at Ryan. "My dear brothers-in-law have plied my husband with whiskey, so I hope you'll excuse us while I find him a bed."

"No problem. Do you need help?"

Pleasure at his answer shone in her eyes as she nodded. "I do, but I'm going to let these two big oafs, who put him in this condition, take care of it. You stay here and enjoy yourself until I get back. Then I'll have to play the role of father and give you the third degree on my husband's behalf."

Ryan nodded, grinning. "I look forward to it."

Rayne handed her husband over to Tom and Logan, who were grinning for all they were worth. The retribution in her eyes did nothing but make them laugh. She turned back to Dia as they hauled him in the direction of the porch. "I'm sorry, honey. All I can say is...*men!*"

A resounding, *"Hey!"* came from her male cousins, making Dia laugh. "It's fine, Mom. I hope he comes out of it okay."

Rayne shrugged. "He's never had that much to drink in his life as far as I know. I just imagine he's going to pay the devil for it." She grinned. "Hopefully he won't be such a baby the next time one of you girls goes into labor."

She turned away laughing, missing the smile that froze on Dia's lips. She glanced up at Ryan, but she couldn't say anything in front of her family. From the furrowed browed look he gave her, she was certain his thoughts matched hers.

They hadn't even thought of protection.

His features smoothed out and he gave her a little shrug. "I know," he said quietly.

She studied his amazing eyes and spoke as quietly. "What if?"

A slow grin turned into a smile. "It would take some getting used to. But I think I'm okay with it, if you are."

A shuddering breath escaped, and she nodded. "Cross that bridge when?"

He nodded. "But talk about our future either way?"

Dia bit her bottom lip, released it. "Yes."

"Yes what?"

Dia knew everyone was watching them, wondering what their cryptic whispering was about. She swallowed and pulled his head down to place a gentle kiss on his lips. When she released him, she smiled. "Yes to whatever questions you might have."

He lifted her chin and placed a little kiss on the tip of her nose, then looked over at those watching. "So, where are those steaks?" he asked loudly.

Dia laughed as all but Nicolae and Sapphire hurried to act busy, like they hadn't been straining to listen in. Those two just stayed locked arm-in-arm looking at her and Ryan. Nicolae grinned, but Sapphire's eyes were filled with concern, and Dia knew their Lycanthrope hearing had allowed them to understand the entire conversation. She nodded to Sapphire when her sister tilted her head slightly, making it clear she wanted to talk in private.

Smiling up at Ryan as if she didn't have a care in the world, she pushed him toward the long food-laden buffet that had been set up as she searched for an excuse to leave him alone again. Relief swamped her. "Go make a plate. I want to check in on Jewell quickly, then I'll join you."

Ryan nodded. "Okay, but don't be too long."

"I won't."

She hurried up the porch and went into the house, knowing Sapphire was on her heels.

"Where are you going?"

"I need to check on Jewell."

"She's sleeping. Amen-ra, too."

"I still have to see."

"Why? You'll disturb them."

"No, I won't."

Sapphire grabbed her arm, stopping her from opening the door. "What is wrong with you? She just gave birth four times!"

"I know, but I told Ryan I was checking on her."

"So what?"

"So I have to."

Sapphire said nothing more but had her lips pressed firmly together in that way she did any time Dia annoyed her. Ignoring her sister, she opened the door a crack, just enough to look in and see Jewell was indeed asleep. She closed the door quietly and then continued down the hall until she was in Apollo's old room. She turned. "I don't like you listening in on my private conversations."

Sapphire's brows rose, probably, Dia decided, because she had never been the one to strike first. She shrugged. "I mean it. It's rude."

"You know I can't help it."

"Try. We're all entitled to our privacy."

Sapphire nodded. "That's true, and I'm sorry. But that man has no idea what you are, what *we* are. You can't go planning babies and whatever else it is you have planned, without letting him know who you really are. And you can't do that unless you're sure it's safe for everyone involved."

Her bubble of happiness completely busted, Dia nodded. "I know. I just don't know what to do. I can't let him go. I know you don't understand, but...."

"You're wrong. I do understand. When I met Nicolae, what I felt for him was instant, and it only got stronger as time went on, but he was never a threat to us. Do you even know this man? According to Zeus, you didn't even know what he did for a living until today."

Dia crossed the room to sit down on the edge of the bed. "I know. Nothing about what I feel for him makes sense, besides his being gorgeous and nice, and now I know successful. But I'm head over heels about him."

Sapphire smiled a little, settling at Dia's side. "Then you have to tell him. It's obvious he's just as crazy about you. He looks at you like you're oxygen for his lungs. Maybe he'll be shocked at first, then because he needs you as much as you need him, he'll accept it."

Dia knew Sapphire was purposely leaving out what would happen if he didn't. But that was only one of her concerns. If anyone had told her she'd be confiding in her oldest sister before anyone else, given their history, she'd have called them a liar. But she had to tell somebody.

"I think he looks at me that way because I placed a love spell on him."

The shock and outrage she expected didn't come. Instead, Sapphire burst out laughing and then covered her mouth to cut it off. Remembering why she shouldn't have chosen this sister to confide in, Dia let the insult settle before speaking. "Never mind, I should have known better."

She rose and headed to the door, but Sapphire was there as quickly, the merriment in her eyes belying her apology.

"I'm sorry, really, but come on, a love spell?"

Dia blew out a breath. "Yes. But you can't tell anyone. I was done with magic, but I know I've got to go back and figure out a way to undo the spell so I'll know for sure what he feels for me is real."

Sapphire's merriment evaporated. "You're *serious*? You finally succeeded and you've placed a man in love with you?"

Shrugging, Dia knew she was going to have to be honest. "I don't know for sure, but I think it's highly possible."

"Oh, my gosh, Dia. You have to tell Mom!"

Dia shook her head. "No, I don't. And neither will you. I'm an adult. I'll handle this." Tears filled her eyes. "I just don't know what I'm going to do if it turns out I've enchanted him, and he really doesn't love me."

Sympathy filled Sapphire's eyes. "I hope you're wrong and are still nothing more than a horrible witch-wannabe." She grinned suddenly when Dia's gaze sharpened. "There you go. That's much better than tears." Her gaze sobered. "But you have to be careful. If you did do this, then only you can undo it, and undoing a spell of the heart isn't as easy and is very dangerous. If you mess up, the heart might stop beating altogether. That's one reason we don't do them to begin with."

Feeling the heat of chastisement, Dia looked at the sister who'd inherited the gift she'd always coveted. "Do you practice now that the werewolves have been enchanted?"

Sapphire nodded, a slight grin on her lips. "I do. And you were right all along. It's great. But I would never attempt a love spell."

Dia pressed her lips together and nodded. "Yeah, I get that."

"Sorry. I don't mean to beat you over the head about it. I'm just worried for you. You could just leave it alone. Even if he loves you because of a spell, it's obvious he's happy. Think about it.

"I won't say anything to anyone, if you promise me you'll tell Mom before you try a reversal spell. Losing his love would be bad enough, taking his life…" Sapphire shuddered. "I can't even imagine how that would affect *you*."

Dia shivered, never wanting to find out. She couldn't imagine something so horrible. "I promise. But for now, I just want to enjoy our time together."

Several emotions played across Sapphire's face, all laced with worry. "I guess more time won't matter much at this point. Just be careful. His life isn't the only one in danger. Our family has a long history of star-crossed lovers and you wouldn't be the first Cavanaugh woman to die of a broken heart. As much as you aggravate me at times, it would break mine to lose you."

Dia was surprised, both by Sapphire's words and the hard hug that followed. When they broke apart, their mother was standing in the doorway looking from one daughter to the other.

Sapphire flashed her a big smile. "Guess what, Mom? I think I'm pregnant!"

At Rayne's squeal of delight, Dia blew out a relieved breath. She smiled at her sister as her mother caught Sapphire in a hug. Sapphire winked at her and pulled their mother from the room, talking babies and growing families.

Dia rolled her head to ease the tension in her neck and followed them all the way out the front door. She looked around and several fingers pointed to the side deck. Dia nodded her thanks and went in search of Ryan, for the first time in her life praying her sister was right about her being a horrible witch-wannabe. She needed to be wanted for herself, not because of a magical mistake.

The afternoon gathering bled into the evening, and Dia knew her time alone with her man would have to wait for quite a while. Her cousins had embraced Ryan into their fold as if he'd always been there. The males tried to outdo each other in competition, and the females simply enjoyed his ability to converse about any and every subject under the sun with an easy intelligence that impressed them all. Games of touch football were followed by horseshoes. A quiet round of putting commenced once flags were set out in the field, then replaced by a more boisterous round of shooting to see who could take the flags out first. That stopped immediately when Rayne came out threatening the boys' lives, since they'd awakened all four babies, right after they'd gotten them back to sleep following their first feeding.

Undeterred, and not the least bit repentant, the Whitehawk boys grinned at Ryan once Rayne's back was turned and declared another pig-skin war in order. This time, girls playing or not, tackle was the name of the game. Dia was delighted when all the dads and moms came out to join them for the second round, especially since her father had sobered up enough to give it a go, too. She was as proud of her all-female team as she was of her favorite nerd, since none of them buckled under the pressure of the very athletic Whitehawk boys. The girls might not have won, but they hadn't embarrassed themselves either.

Since everyone was too worn out to play again, the four-wheelers were taken from the large garage behind the massive house and raced around the parameter of the field before a mountain of pizzas was delivered all the way from the town below.

The pleasure in Ryan's eyes, as he embraced each activity, was nearly matched when he turned his gaze on her. So happy she could burst, Dia pushed away worries that popped up from time to time, determined not to let her concerns ruin what was the happiest time of her life. The evening ended with her father apologizing for being such a *doofus*, and Ryan assuring him he hadn't been. By the time they made it back to her cabin, they were both ready for showers and falling into the bed.

"I'm not sure I can lift my arms."

Dia laughed, and agreed. "I know. What were we thinking?"

Ryan rolled toward her, his joy-filled eyes shining. "I've never had so much fun in my life."

She raised a brow. "*Never?*"

He leaned forward and kissed her gently and then winced. "I think Heracles cracked a rib or two. He was supposed to be on our side."

Dia reached out to touch him, though she hadn't been kidding about being weak. Her arm felt like it weighed a ton. "Are you okay? Do we need to go to the emergency room?"

Ryan shook his head. "No. I'll be fine. Besides, I'm not sure I can get up." He laughed at himself and winced again.

"Seriously, do you need me to bind your ribs?"

"No. just let me look at you. That might be all I'm capable of tonight." Color blotched his cheeks. "I thought getting to the gym four times a week was enough to keep myself from becoming a complete chair potato, but I've never had a workout like the one today."

Dia smiled. "At least they didn't pull out their boxing gloves."

Ryan looked at her in horror. "I'm guessing you're not kidding."

She chuckled. "Nope. Those boys grew up pounding on each other, so my aunt finally made them start wearing gloves, with set rules. Not that they followed any when she wasn't looking."

"Okay. That's where I draw the line."

"Smart man."

He heaved a sigh and winced. "That doesn't make me look like a wimp to you?"

Dia couldn't believe he was serious, but the question in his eyes said he was. "Ryan, I wouldn't have cared if you had bowed out of everything today, for whatever reason. I think you a lot of things, but a wimp isn't one of them.

"I hope you didn't do all that to impress me."

He grinned. "Maybe a little. But I'm serious. I've never had more fun. Your family is amazing." He shook his head. "I've never been athletic or been around people who are. That wasn't exactly my crowd in school. But I wasn't blind either." He grinned. "Well, not completely. Your cousins are star athlete material. What do they do?"

Dia placed her palms together and tucked them between her cheek and pillow since it was obvious neither of them were capable of doing more than talking. "Well, Zeus owns a flower shop in the valley below, but he's rarely there so his staff really runs the place. We all thought it a strange business for him when he bought out the previous owner. He's so serious, and rarely smiles, so maybe it's best he isn't selling the flowers himself. No one questions that he flies out of town every week because he's Zeus, and none of us question Zeus about anything. He's so...*formidable*, I guess is the word I'm looking for, and always has been. In fact, today, with you, I can honestly say I have never seen him smile so much." She grinned at Ryan. "They all really like you."

His eyes shone with pleasure. "I really like them all back."

After another little kiss she settled back on her pillow. "Then there's Apollo. He works for the fire department in Mystic Waters and helps run the Boys and Girls Club on his days off. He hates seeing kids with nothing to do but get into trouble. He has a soft heart for people in need. My mom says Aunt Destiny worries over him the most. She's sure some girl will break his heart someday because he feels things too deeply.

"And finally, there's Heracles. He's a model. Underwear, jeans with no shirt, etcetera, etcetera, and is about as self-assured as they come. We all consider him the diva of the family, but he's a sweetheart in his own way. He jets around the world getting his picture taken for magazines and posters. He hooks up with an alarming number of beautiful women he doesn't seem to care for any longer than it takes to hook-up with the next one. But all three have always been athletic, probably because my aunt had to get them out from under her feet as often as possible to keep her sanity. They were in every sport imaginable.

"But, apparently, they also play video games."

Ryan laughed at that, and this time only blinked instead of his entire face contorting. "Thank goodness. We nerds have to make a living somehow."

"Apparently you nerds make a living just fine. But I'm serious, your money means nothing to me."

"I believe you. It isn't an issue."

Dia smiled. "Good."

"You know, I don't even know what you do."

Dia sighed, suddenly embarrassed. "I'm not sure myself. I used to try to invent things but have learned it isn't my calling. I'm good with plants and am still learning about holistic medicine, so maybe I can do something with that." She studied him. "Compared to you, I'm pretty much a loser.

"Still interested?"

Ryan grinned and groaned a little as he pulled her to him. "Definitely interested."

He proved his point by taking her lips and kissing her until she thought she'd pass out. She chuckled when he rolled back to his side of the bed with a look of consternation on his face. "Too much pain?"

Ryan looked over at her. "Too much everything, sun, exercise, food... I don't think I'll try so hard to impress you next time."

Dia reached over and took his hand. "Don't. Me either. How about we hold hands and go to sleep?"

Relief lifted his lips. "That sounds like a plan. Just don't hold it against me."

Dia yawned. "Not a chance. But you know, you asked about my male cousins, and not about my sisters and female cousins.

His eyes closed, he smiled with a contentment Dia found adorable.

"There were girls there? Hmmm. I didn't notice. I only had eyes for you."

Dia smiled as his sappy comment, loving it, and slid into sleep.

Chapter Ten

Dia awoke to the smell of bacon frying, and biscuits baking. She moaned as she sat up, wondering if every muscle in her body had declared war on her. She sent Ryan a tired smile, and plopped back down, deciding it was too early to move.

"Breakfast in five, sleepyhead."

She groaned into her pillow and then rolled around so she could watch him, loving her little one-room house more than ever. "So you cook."

Ryan grinned. "I've been on my own since I was sixteen, more or less. Somebody had to feed me, and at first I couldn't afford to eat out all the time. It was necessary I learn. Turned out I was pretty good at it."

Dia frowned. "*Sixteen?* Did your mother throw you out or something?"

Laughing, Ryan carried a perfectly cooked slice of bacon to her. "No. I graduated from high school at fourteen, got a full ride scholarship to MIT, and went straight into college. I've never lived with my mother since."

He held it out to her and she took a bite. Her attention was torn between the wonder of her happy taste buds and the intelligence of the gorgeous man who seemed to be good at everything he did. She smiled at how good he made her feel, whether touching her or just sharing the same air.

That he'd just told her he was truly a genius, so casually, would have made her breathless if she hadn't already figured that out for herself. She chewed slowly and decided she was going to have to get up for more, unless... She eyed him speculatively. "Breakfast in bed?"

Ryan nodded. "Only if you're a very good girl."

Dia grinned. "What qualifies?"

"When we're done, you wrap my ribs, and then ravage me."

Laughing so hard hurt all over, but she couldn't help it. "Deal. Are you in a lot of pain?"

Ryan returned to the tiny kitchen corner and pulled biscuits from the oven. He sat them beside the bacon and turned back to her. "Not as bad as I expected, but some. Let's just say I'm definitely not playing football with Heracles anymore."

"I don't know what got into him yesterday. I think you have a groupie." She grinned at the thought. "Which is cooler than you'd think. Heracles doesn't usually hang with the guys like that unless it's to pound on his brothers. He's such a pampered baby. I don't know if you noticed but he has no body hair. He says he gets his legs and *stuff* waxed for the cameras. My mom says she thinks he does it for the girls."

Laughing, Ryan turned back and cracked eggs into a bowl and then faced her while whisking them into a bubbly brew. "I noticed the plucked eyebrows but wasn't going to say anything. But I have to admit, I didn't look at his legs...or *stuff*."

They laughed together as he turned back. The sizzle of eggs hitting the hot skillet caused her stomach to make itself known. Hopefully the sounds of cooking covered its growl. "I'm glad you cook. I don't."

He glanced back. "That works out fine then. What do you say about breakfast, a trip to the shower house to take care of business, then an early morning ride? I'm thinking I'd like to go back to that stream and see if it has anything to do with my vision changing."

Dia didn't allow her reaction to show. She grinned at him instead, hoping he didn't realize he'd just thrown a wrench into her morning. "What about being ravaged?"

Ryan flashed her a smile. "I'm thinking ravaging in the open air sounds like something I'd like to try. Since meeting you, I'm finding there's a whole new world out there I knew nothing about."

You have no idea!

"Eggs are ready! Settle back, and I'll bring you a plate."

Dia did as she was told, fluffing up both their pillows before settling back on hers. She accepted her plate and held his while he went back and poured them both glasses of milk, before returning to sit them on the little table at his side and positioning himself on the bed. He winced only a couple of times, so she was hopeful none of his ribs were actually broken.

The food was delicious and they ate in silence, giving Dia time to worry over his request. She loved that he embraced so much so easily, but dealing with her big family was a lot different than accepting there were magical properties in the water that ran from the mountaintop into the lake below. She couldn't think of a reason she could share with Ryan to dissuade him from his intent, so she tried to think of things she might do to distract him once they were out and about.

"The cave!"

Dia threw a glance at Ryan when she realized she'd all but squealed the location she prayed was her answer. The instant flash of interest in his eyes tickled her.

He is so cute!

Her insides stirred, but she needed to calm down. Eat. Focus. And plan... She took a bite of steaming eggs, sure she'd fixed her immediate problem. He'd get so caught up in wonder of the crystal-filled cave she'd found as a child and had visited many times since, he would forget about everything else. *Hopefully.*

She turned to Ryan, to tell him more, only to find him watching her closely, making her wonder if she'd been just a little too exuberant. Dia smiled at his quizzical turquoise eyes, thinking she could get lost in them.

Focus!

"You'll love the cave. It's filled with beautiful crystals that poke out everywhere. I used to go there and pretend I was deep in the bowels of an ancient castle, and I was the little princess a hungry dragon had trapped there because he wanted to eat her. I'd always run through the tunnels from cavern to cavern hoping a handsome prince would find me and save me from certain doom." The memory made her smile. "It was so special to me I never told anyone else about it. But I'd love to share it with you. How about we go there first? It's on the way." *If I make a wide circle around the forest....*

Ryan nodded, his eyes filled with pleasure. "Sure. I'd love to see the place where you played as a child. It sounds amazing. We can go back to the stream later."

Concerned he was so focused on the mystical waters, she nodded, knowing once she had him in the cave she'd make sure they ended up exploring there a good part of the day. Especially if she took blankets and packed them a picnic lunch of fruits and cheeses, threw in a bottle of wine, and made good on her promise to ravage him…at least once. Delighted with her plan, she settled back and finished eating, thinking she could definitely get used to a sexy man serving her breakfast in bed.

It was obvious he hadn't figured out those waters also flowed through her faucets and that there were many branches of the stream that held the same properties. And she wasn't about to tell him. Dia slid a glance to her sink then lowered her eyes in shame. She hated she couldn't share the simple fix to his vision problems, if it really was what had cured his sight to this point.

Ryan took her plate as soon as she was finished and delivered it to the sink for a rinse before he returned and sat back down on the bed, this time facing her. "So, I guess we need to talk about birth control. I gathered from your reaction and our conversation yesterday you weren't on any, and I obviously didn't use any."

The switch of subject took a second to settle and Dia wondered just how long he'd been awake before she. Obviously long enough to cook a meal and think about several things. She shrugged, surprised at how uncomfortable she was talking about it. "I've never given any thought to needing any before, so I don't have anything here."

"I didn't expect you to. And I certainly didn't come here with the expectation of meeting you. So we need to talk about this and consider our priorities for the day. Do we want to hit a drugstore down in town or take more chances?" He grinned at her. "I am definitely not considering the other option."

Dia frowned. "What other option?"

Ryan looked her up and down and then leaned over and let his lips play over hers. When he was again upright, he pushed her hair behind her ear. "Not touching you."

Not willing to consider that option either, she gave his question serious consideration. "Maybe we should."

Looking slightly horrified, he pinned her with his gaze. "Should what?"

Realizing Ryan though she wanted him to keep his hands off her, she shook her head quickly. "Not that! I mean, maybe we should consider birth control, first."

The subtle blinking of his eyes and the way he suddenly stilled gave away he was surprised by her answer. Were it not for her concern he might walk out of her life once he knew the truth about her and her family, she knew she would have answered differently. Short association or not, she knew he was meant to be hers for a lifetime.

"So you aren't okay with the possibility you might already be pregnant?"

Dia didn't know how to answer and not sound stupid. Any *normal* girl would be horrified at the prospect of an unplanned pregnancy, given they were still only a few days into a relationship that neither had seen coming. Not that she was normal by anyone's standards. But worse, she had no idea if his desire to be with her was of his own will, or if she had forced it upon him.

"I think we need to wait and see, though I won't be horribly upset if I am."

She studied his gorgeous face and couldn't help but smile slightly at the turn of her thoughts. "A girl couldn't ask for a man with a better personality and genes than yours, when it comes to co-creating her child. And the fact you are eye candy doesn't hurt either. But I wouldn't mind us getting to know each other more before someone else enters the picture. That takes time, and once you get past the newness of it all, you might find I'm not really what you want for a life mate."

Ryan didn't respond immediately, instead, the confidence she'd seen growing in their short association seemed to have withered some. He searched her eyes, his own without the happy luster she usually saw. It broke her heart to know she had hurt him, even though it wasn't her intent. He finally nodded, his brows pulled together, his forehead creased with lines she'd never before seen. She wanted to reach out and tell him none of it mattered, but she still was unable to tell him a direct untruth. So she said nothing at all as he worked out whatever it was he was thinking.

"I guess that could be true for *you*. I've never made a personal decision *yet*—relying on my gut instincts—that turned out wrong *for me*. If there is one of us who wants out, it isn't going to be me."

Dia moved closer to him and put her arms around his neck. "I really hope that's true once you get to know me better. Because I can assure you, it isn't going to be me."

Ryan pulled her to him and kissed her with passion and purpose. "Then we are both worrying over nothing, but we can go to town and I'll take care of it. I know logically it's the responsible thing to do. There's just nothing logical about what we have together, and I think that's a gift most people never get to experience. I love that we found each other for all the wrong reasons, but it feels so right it has to be."

He frowned and shook his head slightly. "I *do* feel guilty the purpose I came here for has disappeared and is someone else's problem, but I don't want to think about him right now. You're the only thing I want to think about.

"You are the only thing I *do* think about.

"I want you in my life. Maybe more than I've ever wanted anything. The only thing that has come close to giving me this sense of fulfillment was building the worlds for my games and building this new system. Even as excited as I am about showing it to the world, it doesn't compare, though. At the end of the day, I turn them off, and there's nothing but a long list of things I have to work on the next day. But with *you* every minute is a wonder. If what I feel for you is love, and if that means kids, too, I think it's the greatest thing that's ever happened to me."

Overwhelmed, terrified, she shook her head. "Ryan…."

"No. Please let me finish. You are everything to me, Diamond White. Your beauty stimulates my body, I won't lie, but that is the least of your appeal. You are fun and lively, sweet and sensual, smell like heaven all the time, and no matter what you believe, you *are* smart. Your eyes shine with intelligence, and it's all I can do not to pick your brain every second we are together. You've opened my eyes. I don't look at anything the same way anymore. I haven't laughed and played so much in my life. I haven't looked forward to anything like I look forward to waking with you at my side. I've never thought about having a family, but after meeting yours I want a big one, but only because they would be yours too. I know I'm talking your head off, and it's probably all too much too soon for you, but I need you to know this is how I honestly feel."

Filled with so much love and as a result fear, it took all Dia had not to cry. She wanted everything he'd spoken of as well, but she knew she couldn't let go and accept what was happening easily. Not until she confessed. And she was too afraid to give him up to take the chance of doing so. Which only left her one option. She had to reverse the spell and pray he still felt the same way...if she didn't stop his heart while trying to make things right.

Sickened his heartfelt words only proved he was more than likely enchanted, she hugged him to her tightly, afraid to let go. Dia gave herself a moment, glad he was content to just hold her and not demand she respond. She still had a few weeks to live in the light of his love before he would leave Mystic Waters. If having his child or *children* was her destiny, and all she'd have left if he rejected her down the road, she had no desire for caution now.

Once she had herself under control, she eased back and smiled through watery eyes. "I don't want to go to town. I want to make us a picnic lunch, take blankets, and *my man*, and spend an afternoon in my cave. This princess has waited a long time for her prince to save her from that hungry dragon."

Ryan kissed her softly. "This princess may need the dragon to save her from this hungry man."

****

Though it had been years since she'd last visited her secret playhouse, nothing about it had changed. Dia figured it likely hadn't changed in all the years since its formation. The entrance was only easy to find because she knew the land so well, and had made the trip to it often when she was younger. Unlike many children who were brought up in areas where dangers lurked in the shadows and their activities had to be heavily monitored, she, her siblings, and their cousins, had all known complete freedom on Mystic Mountain. Not only because their mothers had placed a dome of protection above it, but also because Uncle Tom, who was in touch with Mother Mountain daily, had asked for her protection over all nine children be assured from below as well.

Ryan wore his glasses while they moved fast through the forest so he could take in the view on either side of them, but he took them off when she'd slowed or stopped to show him a particular plant and explain its medicinal or edible uses. He asked permission each time to gather a sample of those used to flavor food once she'd tell him what had to be done to make it palatable and in some cases non-poisonous. He chatted excitedly about the information she shared and then asked why she didn't cook with so much knowledge about all he was seeing. Dia's *because I'm lazy* got a smile and a headshake from him, but he was too busy searching to seem to care.

He sampled a leaf of sheepsoil and made a face before heading back to the four-wheeler to get his bottled water. Dia grinned while he took long drinks and laughed outright when he decided to reconsider taking that one. She grinned, remembering her own reaction to the bitterness when her mother once added its leaves to a tossed salad to give it a little *spunk*. Since she and her sisters, as well as their father had refused to eat more than a bite, it hadn't made it to their table again.

He spoke of his love of mushrooms and, after asking about the possibility of being poisoned, picked several of the haystack-shaped morels that suddenly popped up just a few feet away from where they happened to be looking. The same thing happened when she mentioned nettles and chickweed, both of which rivalled spinach, when he talked about his love for spinach.

Dia almost laughed when plantain popped up, finally realizing mother earth's desire to please her matched Dia's desire to please Ryan. Whatever he mentioned he wanted to try cooking appeared, even though it hadn't been on hand in that exact spot only seconds before. Thankfully, the very wise Mother Mountain was being discreet, and only Dia noticed the novelty of it all. Before they wrapped up his little gathering adventure he made her smile again when he declared he wanted to gather a few fiddleheads just because he liked the way they looked, and he wanted to make sketches to include all he'd found in the backdrop forest of the next mystical game he was now dying to create.

Once they were again flying across the landscape, whatever path she took once again smoothed out for her as it always had, only now she noticed and knew why. The pleasure of being in tune with her birthright made her realize how foolish she'd been to ignore it. With a silent *thank you* sent to the heavens, she made her way to the hidden opening of her childhood home-away-from-home.

Giant ferns hung from the jut of what looked to be a small cliff to the casual onlooker. What seemed like nothing more than plants growing downward completely hid the cave's entrance and was what had kept the secret place only *hers* all these years. Excitement stirred as she pulled to a stop and waited for Ryan to dismount. When she joined him beside their transportation, she took his hands and looked deeply into his eyes, her own filling with tears. "If you ever decide you don't really love me, at least remember this day."

The concern in his eyes bespoke his confusion. "I don't know why you think it's possible I'll stop loving you. I won't. I don't know how to convince you."

Dia nodded, wishing she could believe as strongly, knowing to say more would only ruin what could be nothing more than a happy memory for them both, once everything came to light. If all else failed and she had to confess, she had no idea how things would end for them. Though she hated to think it, Dia knew there was the possibility she'd be forced to have her mother wipe his memory. If that was the case, she could only pray *somehow* these moments, on this day, would linger, even if only in his dreams.

She made herself smile as she untied their picnic basket and blankets from the back and handed each to him, before taking the flashlight she always kept handy in the four-wheeler's cubby. Embracing the moment for all it was worth, she smiled at him. "Follow me, but stay close. I don't want to lose you in here."

Ryan looked up, his brows pulled together. "I thought we were going to a cave."

Dia laughed lightly and turned away. She began the process of parting the broad fronds, though she found she had to be careful to not let him see she no longer had to actually touch them. They parted as soon as her mind formed the thought, even if her fingers hadn't yet taken the action. Startled, she quickly made the motions as if she was pushing them away and blew out a breath of excitement that her gift, now she'd acknowledged it, was taking on a life of its own.

She glanced back to see if he noticed, but he was too busy looking around and jostling the load she'd placed in his hands. Relieved, she went through quickly and pretended to hold the leaves up when he stepped through to the small cavern she'd always thought of as the cave's foyer. Darkness engulfed them immediately when the fronds fell back over the opening, and she let it linger only long enough to inhale the scent of moist earth before turning on the flashlight.

"This is just the opening. Follow me, and I'll take you to my favorite place on earth."

Ryan nodded. "Lead the way." He paused and sent her a sheepish grin. "I've never thought myself claustrophobic, but I've never been inside a cave before either. It's a little creepy."

She hadn't thought of that. "Don't worry about it. Just let me know if you're bothered by being here. But I promise, once we get to what I want to show you, you'll forget about everything else."

Dia hooked her arm in his and slid the blankets from his arm to hers before draping them over her shoulder and handing him the flashlight. She knew she could walk with no light at all. Her memories mapped out each step she needed to take as if no time had transpired since her last visit.

"Thanks."

She looked up and grinned at him, seeing the relief in his eyes. "You're welcome."

Dia headed straight into the tunnel and he moved with her without hesitation. She was glad the rock formations seemed wider than when she was a kid and then bit her lip when she realized Mother Mountain was again accommodating his needs, this time for space. As they walked forward she reached out her free hand and allowed it to slide across the rock wall to express her appreciation and gratitude. Warmth in her palm was the mountain's response, making Dia smile in delight.

"This is really neat."

Glancing over at Ryan, she realized he wasn't

experiencing distress but was enjoying flashing the light beam over the sparkling rock wall. She'd always wondered if they were filled with diamond dust, but her selfish desire to keep this place to herself had prevented her from asking if anyone in the family knew.

They walked for some time before coming to the cavern she wanted to take. When they entered, Ryan gasped, and though she'd seen it all many times before, she felt as bowled over by the beautiful scene before them as he.

The ceiling and walls were only twenty or so feet in circumference, forming a large tunnel that ended at the opening at the mountain's side. Sunshine lit the room, throwing prisms of blue light all over the cave's ceiling and walls, and a shallow stream came from a tiny vein to their left, and flowed down the center to spill like a waterfall into the lake, miles below.

"This is amazing," Ryan whispered reverently, releasing her arm and stepping forward. He slowly walked the narrow edge millennia of passing time and rushing waters had left behind after forging the indention to narrow the water's flow so it no longer filled the entire cavern floor. He reached forward, then froze, before touching one of the long crystals that sat in clusters, spiking upward from the cave floor like ice blue prisms cut by a master jeweler's chisel. He glanced back at her, excitement reflected in his turquoise eyes.

"Is it okay to touch them?"

Dia nodded, as in love with his gentlemanly nature as with the man himself. She moved to his side and watched as he ran his finger down then back up the length of one before testing the sharpness of its tip. "Aren't they beautiful?"

Ryan straightened and smiled at her. "Yes. Are they amethysts?"

Dia shrugged. "I'm not sure. They're more blue than purple, although I know of blue amethysts. I always thought they were sapphires, except they aren't as dark as those my mom has in her personal collection." She grimaced, wondering why she'd shared that, and then was embarrassed to admit her lack of knowledge was due to selfishness. "I never told anyone about this place because it was my special secret as a kid, and I was afraid others would disturb something if they knew about it.

"I dreamed so many dreams in here."

She held her breath, only just realizing she'd connected with the earth even back then. The crystals hadn't filled the cave the first time she'd stumbled across it. It had been a dark dank cavern. If she hadn't been mad at Sapphire that day for whatever reason she'd had, she wouldn't have taken her mom's four-wheeler and set off into the forest. She wouldn't have found the hidden opening. And she wouldn't have braved searching the caves alone.

It nearly took her breath, knowing when she'd ended up in this cavern with the moon nearly filling the opening at the end, she'd been in a full-fledged panic because she'd gotten mixed up and couldn't remember the way out. And her flashlight batteries had been close to dying and the cave had grown dimmer by the minute. She'd cried out in terror and wished for light to scare away the darkness. To her delight the crystals had pushed from the rocky earth in clusters, and the light of the moon filled the cavern with prisms of magical light.

Dia stood frozen in amazement. How could she have forgotten all that? Why had she never questioned the mountain's ability to meet her desperate need? Sure, she'd only been eight at the time and knew their lives were filled with magic, but she hadn't recognized it was her own that connected her to all that was happening. Was it because it preceded her ascension? Or because her desire to be a

White Witch overrode the possibility her magic would come in another form? Was it because she always felt like the odd one and feared she didn't really deserve a *gift* of her own? The possibilities flooded her mind even as relief filled her soul. She *was* worthy of her family's heritage and now knew how blessed she was.

"Dia? Are you okay?"

It took a moment to pull herself together, to hold back tears that wanted to form in celebration of this moment of enlightenment. She swallowed, took a shaky breath, and wished with everything within her heart she could share this discovery with the wonderful man looking at her with such concern.

"I'm fantastic!" She reached for his hand, needing his touch more than her next breath. "Make love to me."

Chapter Eleven

Ryan smiled and pulled her into his arms. Her mouth tasted of mint, her scent that of a woman hungry for his touch. He was always ravenous where she was concerned. He had tried to temper his actions, knowing she still didn't trust the sustenance of his love for her to carry them through a lifetime. His intent to convince her of his devotion was quickly overridden by the desire to fulfill whatever had sent her into a wild, clawing, ball of need. She tugged at his jacket making sounds of frustration when her fingers couldn't find purchase. She clutched handfuls of his hair and pulled his lips to hers when he tried to move back enough to undo the garment that had angered her. She cried out in desire when he grasped her blond glory and forced her face upward, so he could devour the softness of her neck and try to catch his breath.

Knowing he had to settle them both down before he ruined everything by completing too soon, he lifted her, placing her on the other side of the stream. Her shock was plain, her hurt as much, and he shook his head with a grin. "Give me a minute," he said, breathless. "I need a minute or you aren't going to get as much pleasure from this as I am."

Dia's little laugh of delight was music to his ears, the colorful kaleidoscope irises topped by arched blond brows, though still surprising, filled him with delight. He loved the evidence of her heightened emotions, the wildness of her disheveled nearly white hair, and the urgency with which she shed her clothes. He loved everything about her and needed to find a way to prove it wasn't just lust for the amazing body she now displayed.

Ryan took his time undressing, keeping his eyes on hers, or her lips, or the perfectly formed globes topped by surprisingly dusky nipples. He slid off his shoes, his pants, and his socks last, empowered by her interest in all of him not just that which had every intention of filling her again and again, until she begged for merciful release.

He smiled at her and wet his dry lips, then glanced to the stream at their feet. In one motion he stooped down and scooped a handful, taking a drink of the ice cold water. An amazing infusion of energy filled him and he stood, wanting to tell her how much he loved the water on the mountain. But his excitement quelled as her smile faltered, her eyes were filled with fright, and she looked from him to the water like she couldn't believe what he'd just done. Ryan frowned, not knowing what had taken the gleam from her eyes and the joy from her expression.

"Dia?" He glanced down at the stream and then back up to her. "Is there something wrong with this water?"

She shook her head quickly and took a drink herself and then smiled at him a little unevenly. "It's just water."

Ryan nodded, trying to ignore the uneasy feelings her reaction evoked. Wondering... he looked to the far end of the cave and couldn't help but blink as his heart began to race. The distance between him and the opening should have had his sight deteriorating, but just like the last time he drank the local water, and his nearsightedness had improved, it appeared now his farsightedness was much better as well. He turned back to her, thrilled, but apprehensive that she wanted to deny the obvious. There were properties in the water that were special, and she *knew* it.

"That isn't just water."

Dia stared at him, but said nothing, and his heart sank.

"Do you want to tell me why you deny this water is more than it appears to be?"

"It comes from the mountain. I told you that before. Other people drank it. Many other people, but it hasn't affected any of them in any way. So I'm not lying to you. I'm just afraid you'll make something of it doing something special for you and draw others here. We are very protective of this mountain. It is sacred."

"Then why did you act like you knew it would do something special for me?"

Dia swallowed visibly. "Did I?"

Ryan nodded. "Yes."

"Did it?"

Again he said, "Yes. My sight is even better than before." He looked at her pensively. "Do you know why?"

She nodded slowly, but didn't speak.

"Will you tell me?"

She looked so frightened, so lost suddenly. He was certain she knew something, but whatever it was scared her into silence.

"Dia, I swear to you, I won't tell anyone, but I *have* to know."

Something deep within the earth rumbled and the floor of the cavern shook splashing the water onto their feet. Storm clouds suddenly appeared, throwing them into near darkness until lightning slashed across the opening at the end of the cave, illuminating the room with blinding light that burned his now healthy eyes. Ryan's heart jerked into action within his chest and he turned back from the mouth of the cave to tell her they needed to get out quickly. An earthquake could trap them, or possibly kill them if the cavernous ceiling gave way. But the words lodged in his throat when he turned from the light show outside to shout the warning, because the woman he'd entered the cave with was no longer there. In her place stood a woman aglow, with her white hair flying with static electricity and her kaleidoscope irises spinning with a multitude of violets, blues, greens, and yellow-golds that threw sparks from the corners of her eyes.

Though no wind touched him, her hair flapped, twisted, and turned as violently as the sky brewing with rage outside. He backed away as his mind tried to grasp what was happening and stumbled over something large enough to devour his balance. Arms flailing, he flew backward, and the last thought he had before pain sliced through his skull was his father wasn't crazy after all.

****

Dia fell to her knees, stunned by the power that had taken hold and transported her to places she never knew she could go. She'd been the moisture that made up the clouds in the sky, the rich soil that blanketed the earth, and she'd learned the secrets of the stars. Each experience seemed to take hours, yet she was certain only moments could have passed before she was once again herself. As sunlight filled the cavern, she struggled to her feet on legs so shaky she wasn't sure they still held bone. Weakly, she jumped over the now still stream, and nearly fell on the other side when her ankles gave way. She struggled through the few steps it took to drop at Ryan's side. Terror lodged in her throat, while tears of regret ran down her cheeks to splash against his arm.

The blood pooling as it seeped from the back of Ryan's head was her fault, although she'd had no control over the storm that had built from her fear of his discovery. Her own heart bled as she tested his pulse. Though there, it was as weak as his breaths were shallow, and her terror increased tenfold.

She swung her head quickly at the sharp gasps of alarm coming from the interior opening of the cavern. Though dizzy, relief washed through her, and the tears increased as her mother and aunts ran to her aide. Before she could relay the danger Ryan was in, blackness engulfed her mind.

****

"Good morning, sleepyhead."

Dia opened her eyes and stared into Ryan's happy ones, before she glanced around to find they were at the cabin she called home. Her breath caught as she struggled to remember how she'd gotten them back from the cave, but she couldn't grasp a thought long enough to finish it.

"Or, I guess I should say, good afternoon." He shook his head. "Your family must have really worn us out yesterday. I've never slept in this late in my life."

Dia turned back to him and frowned. "What?"

He laughed. "It's noon. And I'm starving. How about I make us a late breakfast?"

"What?"

Ryan sat up and stretched, but all she could do was look at the undamaged back of his head. There was no blood, no bandages, and other than being a little shaggy, his hair looked perfectly fine.

"Are you okay?"

Ryan turned back to pounce on her, and take her mouth in a hungry kiss before he pulled back enough to study her face. "I'm great. I'm not even sore. I thought for sure last night I'd be an invalid today!" He laughed again. "Your cousins are hard to compete with, but I think I held my own."

He doesn't remember? "What about the cave?"

For the first time since she awakened, he looked at her with questions in his eyes. "What cave?"

Certain now she'd been given a reprieve, she pulled him to her in a hug. Relief washed through her as she held on tightly. Her confusion nearly made her dizzy. Just like she'd been dizzy where her mother and aunts....

After a swift intake of breath, Dia exhaled heavily. *That*

170

was what had happened. She hadn't done anything to rescue them from the situation she'd created. It had been the three powerful mystics who had raised and loved her since her birth. She sent a silent *thank you* to her mother and aunts. She could relax and smile when he pulled back again.

"Good morning, or afternoon, or whatever it is." Dia grasped his face and pulled it to hers and poured all the thanksgiving she felt into the kiss. He wasn't hurt. He didn't remember her going all mystic on him. And his exuberant response sent fire to the tips of her toes. Once they were both gasping for breath, she released his lips, which only allowed them the freedom to forage to his heart's content. She wiggled and squirmed as he nibbled and lavished her body with erotic attention. She moaned and clawed when he bit a nipple then blew cool breath over it. She giggled when he found her most ticklish spot at the inside of her upper thigh, and rejoiced when he gave up the sweet torture to slide into her, filling her heart as well as her body. Finally, she screamed with delight when he took her over the edge of sanity and straight into ecstasy.

The hard banging at the door had them both freezing mid-pant as Ryan slid from her body.

"Dia! Are you in there?"

Heracles! She sent an apologetic look to Ryan before screaming, "Just a minute!"

Ryan's eye lit with laughter. "I think we were supposed to be back at your uncle's house sometime today." He frowned. "Weren't we?"

Dia couldn't believe she'd forgotten their promise to make it back to another family gathering and to check on Jewell and the babies. She allowed him to head to the sink first to quickly clean himself up and then joined him there for a quick wash down herself.

"I need panties!"

Ryan looked her over and grinned. "You need more

than that."

Dia shrugged. "He's my cousin. He doesn't even know I'm a girl."

Pulling her into his arms, he kissed her soundly. "I do. Cousin or not, you need more than panties."

Laughing, she headed to her little dresser and pulled out a camisole and panties before snagging a pair of shorts. Pulling them on as she went to the door, she glanced back quickly to make sure Ryan was decently covered before she unlocked and opened the door. Heracles stood on the other side, smiling for all he was worth.

"Good afternoon! The family sent me over to see if you two wanted to have lunch with us since they couldn't get you on the phone." He glanced past Dia and looked Ryan over with a smile. "You might want to put on some clothes. Garrison is already making noises about a shotgun wedding if you two can't keep your hands off of each other long enough for Dia to check on her sister. And Sapphire is in a snit because she says you're messing up her day." Heracles shrugged. "I don't know what that means, but she seems really irritated, and I'm not taking any chances with that one. One angry swipe and my career is over. This face is my ticket to stardom, and that girl can grow claws." He winked at Dia.

Knowing he was mocking her, Dia quickly but discreetly shook her head and glared at her cousin. She'd just survived the mistake of exposing their specialness to Ryan and she'd nearly killed him. Her cousin didn't need to be throwing it in her face, whether intentional or not.

Dia frowned, unable to believe her father would say such a thing, though she had little doubt he'd been informed of the family matriarchs' dash to save Ryan from her earlier folly. The gleam in Heracles eyes confirmed he knew, and Dia felt a stirring of irritation. "Just who sent you over here?"

"Your mom. She said to tell you to bring your man and come on. Seems you all have some girl things to talk about."

Dia groan inwardly and nodded, turning to Ryan. "You want to get some pants on? Seems I'm going to be taken to the woodshed."

Ryan grinned. "I want to see it too. I hadn't told you yet, with everything going on, but I have some of your dad's pieces. I saw his work online when I was furnishing my house and commissioned several pieces for my home office." His smile brightened even more. "I love the desk he designed. It stretches around two walls and allows me to go from one computer to all the rest." He grinned, as if he were embarrassed. "There are eight of them going all the time."

Glad he'd misunderstood, thinking she meant her dad's shop instead of the figurative *woodshed*, which her family jokingly referred to whenever any of them had gotten into trouble as children. Not that a Cavanaugh child had actually ever been spanked as far as she knew. Though, with the Whitehawk boys, she knew that could have gone either way.

"It's an old-fashioned term for a place where kids were taken to be spanked," Heracles stated, and Dia could have whipped him herself.

She glared at him again. "*Seriously?*"

Dia glanced back at Ryan. He was pulling on his jeans, and she couldn't help but admire how nicely the boxers hugged his butt when he'd leaned forward to step into the second leg. She turned back to find Heracles watching him as closely and punched her cousin in the gut.

Heracles brows rose and, amazingly, his naturally tanned cheeks filled with rich color. She frowned at him, confused, but he just winked back at her. Dia blew out a breath and pushed him back outside of the doorway he'd been filling. "Go tell them we'll be there shortly." And under her breath, "Stop now."

He just grinned and whispered back. "*Somebody's* in trouble."

Knowing he was enjoying her situation just a little too much, she sent him a mean grin. "Get lost!"

He turned away and swaggered his way toward the Jaguar his fame and fortune had bought him, glancing back once before he folded himself in the little car. "See you soon, cuz!"

"He's something."

Dia turned to find a delicious-looking Ryan standing in the doorway. Her heart threw a hard punch, and everything inside of her melted. Her feelings must have been reflected in her eyes because he was on her immediately, locking his lips with hers, returning her to a heightened level of sexual need she had no time to feel. Or no right.

She hugged him tightly when the kiss ended, knowing their earlier experience, *even though he didn't remember it*, was bound to happen again sooner or later. What scared her most was the lack of control she'd had while it was happening. As great as it felt, and much as she wanted to explore the power that had infused her, she knew waiting was her only choice. If they somehow managed to survive all the other obstacles that could tear them apart, Ryan was going to have to be told what she was, and in fairness, he needed to know she'd possibly enchanted him into loving her.

It was a good thing he already expected to spend time with her family. She needed to consult with her mother and her aunts, to see what they felt would be the best way to proceed. If it only affected her, she'd take her chances, but to reveal herself was to reveal all of them as well.

"I need to hit the head."

Dia looked up at him. "I do too. But you go first. I

want to straighten up quickly before we leave."

Ryan gave her a quick kiss and trotted toward the bathhouse. Dia returned to their bed and made quick work of straightening the sheets and blankets, then cleaning the kitchen area. When he returned, she passed him just inside the door and went to take care of her own needs. By the time she'd returned, Ryan was waiting with his laptop case strapped to his shoulder.

He patted the case. "I thought I'd take this and show you and the Whitehawk brothers. I know they'll get a kick out of it." He grinned. "And I know *they* have Wi-Fi!"

Dia smiled, relieved he'd found a way to occupy himself so she could converse with her mother and aunts. Of course, she'd have to look at it too. She'd been dying to see what made him so passionate about his work. "That's a great idea! I'm ready." *As I'm going to be.*

They made their way to the Jeep, and Ryan stopped all of a sudden and frowned as he looked out toward the tree line. He slid her a startled glance and then smiled so big it seemed to take up his entire face.

"I don't believe this!"

Dia turned to look at the trees but saw nothing. "What?" she asked, turning back to face him.

"I just now realized I can see *everything* clearly!"

Dia was certain her heart had stopped as she swayed, suddenly dizzy. He was at her side immediately and took her arms to steady her, his laughter filled with excitement. "I'm supposed to be the one falling over with shock." Ryan shook his head and looked all around them again, his joy palpable. "I guess it wasn't the water after all. This is amazing!"

Trying to embrace his joy as well, Dia hugged him hard. She had no words, couldn't think beyond the reality that though her mother and aunts had wiped his memory of their morning and repaired the injuries from his fall, they hadn't done anything to reverse the effects of the water. But then, they may not have known. Dia looked up at him, hoping he didn't notice how concerned she was. "We need to get going. My family will be waiting for us."

He smiled, too excited to notice anything, she imagined, as they boarded and strapped themselves in. With her heart in her throat she started the Jeep, hoping his day ended as well as he believed it had begun. And hoping her family would forgive her for falling in love with such a wonderful man.

****

The entire family had returned and was once again filling the porch or yard. The smell of barbequed pork permeated the air, and Dia knew the grills would be packed with ribs. Though she'd not eaten since their early morning breakfast, her stomach was in too many knots to appreciate that food was being cooked.

As expected, everyone on the porch stopped what they were doing and turned their way as she and Ryan exited the Jeep. As they approached the gathering, she searched the faces for her mother's and was alternately relieved and disappointed when she realized she must be in the house, probably taking care of Jewell and the babies. They arrived at the house hand in hand, Ryan joyously pulling her along, her trying not to let her unease show. They were greeted with exuberance by her cousins. It hurt, knowing her family's complete acceptance of Ryan would only make things more difficult for them both if things didn't end well.

Excitement increased when the Whitehawk boys realized the case Ryan carried not only held a new video game, but his new gaming system also. She shook her head, more tickled than she expected to be that their enthusiasm for her man's career made them look at her with more respect than ever before. She felt it should have irritated her, given the fact that she deserved it in her own right, but she understood in *their* eyes she was a screw-up and had only now, *finally*, done something right by capturing the heart of such a special man. Only she hadn't. Not legitimately. And it wouldn't be much longer before Sapphire wasn't the only one who knew the truth of it.

Dia allowed her male cousins to hurry Ryan into the house. They all headed straight to the back room to let him hook his system up to the 92-inch screen television Heracles had given his parents as an anniversary gift the year before. Of course, everyone knew the gift had been for him to watch sports when he and his brothers were over, since Tom and Destiny were always invested in each other, or their care of the earth and those around them, and rarely gave it a thought.

She could tell how excited Ryan was as he spoke with the speed of lightning, telling them what needed to be done to make the game work. She settled in one of the very long couches with everyone, except Heracles. He, of course, had to be first. Ryan held up a helmet that looked as if made for a cyclist except it had three bendable wires that came down from the front with what looked like suction cups attached.

"Okay," Ryan said, his voice quivering. "Sorry, I'm a little nervous." He grinned. "But this is good. I'd rather be nervous now than when I take it to the expo."

He blew out a breath, and everyone waited for him to get it together. Dia sent thoughts of peace his way as she was sure her family did. It was clear someone's had gotten through, because he grinned suddenly with confidence.

"This helmet has sensors attached that I will place against Heracles's temples and the center of his forehead. When he's ready for the game to begin, he simply thinks the word, *Start*, and the system will open whichever game is chosen. Of course, right now, there is only this one. If this goes over like I think it will, I'll be busy developing more."

"There are no hand held devices or cameras to watch the player's responses?" Zeus asked.

Ryan shook his head. "No. These sensors read your brainwaves, your blood pressure, and your pulse rate and send the information through a Bluetooth-like program to the motherboard. Your thoughts and brain-to-muscle reactions will be read by the system. The character in the game will be you short of it being able to breathe. If, say, you see an object in the game, and you want to pick it up, the system will read what you are seeing, what you want to do with it, how you emotionally react to it, and will have the player on the screen do the same thing as the player standing before it does even though there is nothing physically connecting you."

Dia knew little about the world of video games, but it was clear—in the body language and interest in her cousin's eyes—this was something special. She watched Zeus and Apollo slide back into the couch. She could tell they were dying to knock Heracles out of the way and get to be first themselves.

"I call this game Witch Warden. Gizzelle, my ancient, lovely, wicked witch has stockpiled the castle with items made of gold and beautiful jewels, the most precious of which is a diamond encrusted six-inch-high dragon. Millennia ago, in a fit of anger, she enchanted her lover when she learned he desired another whose youth and beauty surpassed her own. The enchantment not only captured him in a small statue, it enhances her charm for all time. He must look upon her daily and regret his decision to choose another over her. Her power over him only holds true as long as he stays within the castle walls. So, though she guards all her treasures with all her might, the loss of this dragon is her greatest fear."

Ryan took a breath and looked around the completely silent room, causing Dia to do the same. She didn't know

now if her family's intent gazes had more to do with the technology of the new system, or if everyone's look of wonder, like her own, was about his choice of game.

A frown furrowed Ryan's brow. "Is everyone with me so far?"

When all nodded but none spoke, he continued. "This is where the game starts. Because of her fear of losing all, Gizzelle believes anyone entering the castle is there to steal her treasures. The goal of the game is to find and take her dragon, which she moves constantly, then escape the castle. *But*, because of the many rooms between the high towers and the dungeon, the player faces many perils that can result in being captured.

"The length of time it takes to get from one quest to the next depends on the player's skill at outwitting the witch and developing savvy as the game goes on. If she does catch the player, though, she enchants them and then he or she becomes nothing more than another ornament in Gizzelle's collection and then *game over.*

"She considers every player a thief, and she uses all kinds of magic to keep them at bay. Because the game is inner-active with the player's brainwaves, she uses different magic on each player, never the same on someone who has played the game before. I've designed it so all a player's previous thoughts and moves are stored into the game, so memory of what happened the time before won't aid the player the next time. Every time the game is played, the goal remains the same. Unlike other games, the level of difficulty doesn't have to grow higher, because each time the experience will be different. If I've built it right, this game can't be beat."

A collective sigh went through the room, but the challenge of competition sparkled in her Whitehawk cousins' eyes. Dia smiled to herself, wondering just how long it would take one of them to prove Ryan wrong. When she looked back at him, she could see he was enjoying that they thought they could.

"Dia?"

She'd been so captivated with Ryan's explanation of his project, she hadn't realized her parents, Tom and Destiny, and Logan and Haven had entered the room to stand just inside the door. Her mother's look was one of amusement when she greeted Ryan, but her expression changed when she turned to her youngest daughter. "I need you to help me, if Ryan doesn't mind me *stealing* you away."

Ryan smiled at Rayne. "No. That's fine. Heracles will be replaced with another player in a matter of minutes. There's plenty of time for her to try it later."

The Whitehawk boys guffawed at Ryan's declaration, but he simply smiled back at them. Dia turned away and followed her mother, only to find her aunts following her. Her father and uncles stayed behind, and she didn't know if it was because they'd been told to, or if it was because they, too, wanted a crack at the game. They were the least of her concerns.

Surprisingly, Rayne led them into the room Jewell had taken over, so Dia left thoughts of a reprimand behind and greeted her sister. Jewell glowed with happiness as she held one baby to her breast, while the other three lay sleeping in their bassinets.

"Hey you!" Dia said softly, advancing. She stopped at the side of the bed. She reached out and ran her finger over the baby's soft hair. "Which one is this?"

Jewell smiled, her eyes filled with fatigued joy. "This is Rose, so named because it is the flower of love." She pointed to first one bassinet and then the next. "That's Lily because it was the flower of the Nile where I first met my husband, then Daisy whose name represents the fresh start our love brought to both of our lives. And finally, my little guy…" Jewell shook her head. "We have not yet named him." She grimaced. "Nothing we've come up with seems to fit."

Dia looked at the tiniest of the quads and nodded. "Naming him after a flower probably won't go over too well with him."

They shared a grin before Jewell lifted the now sleeping Rose and pulled her gown up to cover her breast. "Would you put Rose in her bed? I'd like to try to sleep until the next one awakens."

Dia nodded and took her niece, amazed the baby weighed next to nothing. She carefully placed Rose in the empty basinet and then smiled at her sister. "Rest," she whispered. "I'll see you later."

Jewell nodded and closed her eyes. Dia followed her mother and aunts from the room. No one said a word as they headed to the kitchen, though she was nearly knocked over when Zeus and Apollo flew past them as if the house were on fire. Dia cringed, knowing the front door would slam behind them, but it stopped and slowly shut without making a sound. Turning, she saw the glare of her aunt, before Destiny's features took on a speculative gleam.

"Those boys forgot they were cooking." She sighed. "I hope they haven't burned the meat."

Dia hoped not too. Though her stomach was once again in knots, she was pretty sure part of it had to do with hunger. She looked from her mother to her aunts and then back. "So, let me have it."

Surprise entered Rayne's eyes. "Let you have what?"

"The verbal spanking I deserve."

Laughing, Rayne pulled her into a hug. "What are you talking about? We wanted to ask you what happened. We were all here cuddling babies and the earth shook and the storm blew in. Haven knew immediately it had to be you, and at first we were all just excited. Then Destiny *felt* your great fear, and we were concerned you didn't understand what was happening. I zapped us all there to make sure you were okay, but you weren't. When we saw your distress over Ryan's injury we put you to sleep, cleaned up the mess, and did a small memory wipe in case Ryan had witnessed something he shouldn't have, before taking you home. If we timed it right, he shouldn't remember anything after falling asleep last night."

Dia stared at her mother, dumbfounded. They still knew nothing about what she'd done. As tempting as it was to rejoice with them over the development of her gift, and take the reprieve she'd been handed, she couldn't leave things as they were. "There are things I have to tell you."

Rayne nodded enthusiastically. "And I can't wait to hear them. Did you do it on purpose? Did you know you could?"

Dia shook her head in response to both questions.

"That's okay. I remember the first time Haven called in a storm. She was the only one to see it, but when she finally mastered her gifts and brought one on for the rest of us, it was breathtaking."

"Rayne, look at your daughter."

Rayne sent a glance to Destiny and then turned back to Dia, her brows raised quizzically. Her smile faltered and then disappeared. "Honey, what's wrong?"

Dia slid a glance at her aunts before addressing her mother. "I've really messed up."

"Well, I'm sure it isn't anything that can't be fixed. What happened?"

It was hard to know where to begin. Dia struggled in silence as they awaited her and then she blurted out, "I've enchanted Ryan."

Three pairs of emerald eyes looked at her without emotion at first, but each slowly changed to denial. Destiny moved closer to Rayne's side and held out her hand across the island. Dia looked from it to her aunt.

"That isn't necessary. I can tell you. I just hate that I have to."

"Then tell us, honey. Whatever you've done, we'll help you fix. But we have to know everything," her mother said, placing her hand on Destiny's arm. She smiled at her sister who gracefully moved away before Rayne leaned across the island to take Dia's hand herself. "In your own words."

"I have to sit down." Dia took one of the tall stools, which lined the counter that separated the kitchen from the large living room. She settled and placed her elbows on the counter before fisting her hands beneath her jaw.

"A few days before I met Ryan, I ran across a thin diary of spells written by Camellia Cavanaugh. It was inside the book you gave me containing the types and uses of the different herbs you'd chronicled over the years while studying Mystic Mountain's plant life."

"I'd wondered where I put that."

Dia looked down, ashamed. "I should have told you immediately, but I was intrigued by the simplicity of her spells. Everything I had tried to create on my own was so much more complicated, and it occurred to me I was trying too hard."

She glanced back up at the three women who waited expectantly, and she blew out a breath. "So…I thought I would try one."

Rayne shrugged. "So, did it work?"

This was the hard part. "I'm not totally sure, but I think so."

Rayne's smile returned. "Well, good for you!"

Dia shook her head quickly. "Not exactly."

"Why not?" Haven asked, studying her closely.

Dia looked from Haven to Destiny, before getting up the nerve to connect with the emerald eyes of her mother. "Because it was a love spell."

Silence filled the kitchen as the three matriarch's faces

froze.

"Oh no!"

"Oh, my gosh!"

"How could you?"

Dia shook her head. "I didn't mean to make it happen. I didn't think it had until later. I thought I'd blown it again, and I swore off magic at that moment. But everything that has happened between Ryan and I since points to it having worked.

"And that isn't all."

Rayne pushed away from the counter before walking around it to take a stool at Dia's side. "What more can there be?"

The weakness in her mother's voice killed her. "I'm so sorry, Momma. I was trying to distract Ryan from going back to the stream this morning, but all I did was put us in a position where he had another chance to drink the water within the cave, and now his sight is perfect. When you all wiped his mind, you didn't know that something significant had already happened."

The three sisters looked at each other and then past Dia, and all three mouths fell open.

"What are you saying?"

Dia jerked at the sound of Ryan's voice, and she froze before slowly turning his way. Behind him was the rest of the family, everyone looking at her like she'd just killed a baby rabbit. She rose from the stool, desperately wishing she had some idea what to say, wondering just how much he'd overheard.

"Ryan...."

He looked from her to the older women and then turned back to look at those who had followed him out of the family room. When he turned back again, the expression of shock and disbelief clouding his features broke her heart. The anger, once it formed in his eyes, took her breath.

"Everyone thought he was crazy! He's spent his life in and out of mental institutions." Ryan shook. "My father has nearly lost his mind because of you people. I didn't believe him. *No one* ever believed him!" He advanced on Dia, fury and confusion in his eyes. "Are you all for real? Are you witches?"

Tears filled her eyes, but she didn't allow them to fall. "Ryan…."

"Answer me, dammit!"

Dia jumped and nodded, knowing the distinction between witches and mystics would mean nothing to him.

His body shaking, Ryan looked her over with contempt before he tore from the house, slamming the door behind him. Babies started crying, her family started yelling, and all she could do was sit there as everything within her crumbled.

The sound of a vehicle starting penetrated the fog filling her mind, and she fled to the door and stepped onto the porch. Ryan was in her Jeep, pulling out of the spot where she'd parked. Without a backward glance he peeled out of her aunt and uncle's driveway as if the hounds of hell were on his heels, throwing up rock and dust behind him.

Chapter Twelve

Silence.

The motel room was filled with deafening silence, and after three days of wrestling with everything he'd overheard, it was driving him crazy.

Ryan couldn't concentrate, couldn't even stand to leave the television on because the noise was too much like being around Dia's boisterous family. He'd been staring at the dark screen for so long now, though, as he'd played every moment with Diamond White through his mind, he may as well have left it on. The few times he'd tried it only proved there was no use. As much as he wished it were so, his attempts to be distracted hadn't worked.

If only he hadn't left his gaming system behind. Or his car...but he'd been too distraught to go back to Dia's place when he'd fled he hadn't even thought about it at the time. And couldn't make himself later, once he'd caught his breath.

He couldn't look at her then, although he'd nearly give anything to have been able to leave Mystic Waters behind....

Ryan blew out a breath and wondered why he hadn't heard from any of them. They had to know where he was. It wasn't as if he had anywhere else to go until the situation with his father was dealt with, and the Jeep was parked right outside his door. They could have called the police and reported he'd committed *Grand Theft, Auto*. Or, apparently, they could have located him to wipe his mind. A chill went through him, remembering they'd said they had already done it once.

As they had his father's….

The knock at his door startled him, and Ryan almost laughed. So they'd finally decided to make a move, had they? Well, good. He wanted the confrontation over with. He wanted his mind wiped. If for no other reason than he didn't want to live with this overwhelming sense of loss. If he didn't remember being captivated by Dia's beauty, her personality, her adventure for life, then he could go on as he always had.

Ryan rose from the bed and pulled on the pants he'd been wearing off and on for days. The thought of work, work, and more work didn't taste as good as it always had before. *That* had been his life and until he'd found her. It had satisfied him once. And it would again, he promised himself, as he turned the knob and opened the door.

The police officer standing with his fist raised as if about to knock again shouldn't have caused such a sense of disappointment, but he did. So they'd sent the police to take care of him, instead of confronting him on their own. So be it. He just didn't care anymore. Still, he had to swallow whatever lodged in his throat. "Good morning, Officer. What can I do for you?"

"Good morning, sir. Are you Ryan Steward?"

Ryan nodded. "Yes."

The officer opened and glanced at the little black notepad he held in his hand. "You are the son of Clayton Davis?"

Surprised, as it hadn't occurred to him the visit had anything to do with his father, Ryan nodded again. "Yes."

"Sir, we've been trying to find you. Your father was found yesterday afternoon and returned to the hospital's psychiatric ward. He's terribly sick, sir, and the doctor asked us to locate you to have you return to the hospital as soon as possible."

Reeling, Ryan nodded. "Okay. Um...okay. I'll be along shortly."

The officer nodded and turned to leave, but Ryan needed to know more. "When you say sick?"

The officer shrugged. "When we found him, he'd been out in the woods for days. He's dehydrated, nearly starved, and has several lacerations. Mostly, from my understanding though, their concern is over his heart. He'd been off his medication during his absence."

"Okay...um, thank you."

The officer nodded again and looked him over with concern. "Are *you* okay, Mr. Steward?"

Knowing his confusion was showing, he nodded, and after one last doubtful look, the officer returned to his cruiser. Ryan closed the door and leaned his head against it before stripping off his clothes and heading for the shower. Even though he'd stop along the way and buy new clothes before going to the hospital, he had no choice but to put back on the ones he had. Thankfully the motel had soap and shampoo he only now realized he hadn't used while locked in the shock of the past few days. The stubble on his normally clean jaw would have to wait.

Once clean of body, he went about the room and gathered up the boxes and congealed food he'd had delivered but hadn't been able to eat. Since the shower had renewed him, *some*, he was aghast to realize he'd lived in such a stinky mess. His need for neat and orderly hadn't just flown out the door, it had disappeared with a poof!

Like magic.

The jerk to his stomach wasn't unexpected, but because it was so empty, it hurt. He'd have to grab a quick bite to eat on the way to the hospital...and a toothbrush, and some deodorant, and shaving cream and razors. All things he would have had with him if he'd had his belongings. Fury filled him, making him shake. Those evil witches had nearly destroyed his sense of self, just like they had his father's!

It took a few minutes, but as he calmed down, he had to plop onto the bed and look at the truth of his situation. *None had been evil.* They were fun-loving family members who had done nothing but give him a new perspective on life. If what he now believed was a reality, he was certain they could have taken everything from him. The clear sight he'd never believed was his to have. The outgoing personality he'd have given his life for while growing up. And the chance to love a gorgeous woman, who at any time in his past would have been so far out of his reach, he never would have considered letting himself fall in love with her to begin with. Even if she somehow cast a spell on him to make him love her, he knew he would have anyway. Just because she was her. *Dia White.* The most thrilling thing to have happened in his life.

As he pondered all he knew about them, the reality was that none of them were old enough to have harmed his father in any way. And…if his mind had been wiped of the events preceding the last morning he and Dia made love, the only logical explanation was that for him to have remembered, could have threatened them in some way.

"For a man who makes his living creating fantasy games, you sure have acted like a jerk."

Ryan jumped up and grabbed the keys to Dia's Jeep. Just as soon as he dealt with whatever his father needed, he was heading up the mountain and taking back all that was his.

Including the woman he loved.

****

It was hard to look at the man lying on the bed and believe it was the same one he met the day he arrived in Mystic Waters. Clayton had lost considerable weight, his skin was ashy, and he looked like his last breath could come

189

at any moment.

Unlike before, his father wasn't restrained. There was no need. He'd fallen into a coma.

"What would you like us to do, Mr. Steward?"

Ryan turned to the doctor, his brows raised. "What do you mean? I'd like for you to fix him, of course."

The doctor smiled a little at that. "We're doing all we can for him physically. But I'm talking about once he recovers, if he does."

"Oh, yeah. I'll be taking him off your hands. I need to make some calls, but I'd like to have him put in a home where he can get help, and I can keep an eye on him."

The doctor's expression made it clear he didn't think help was an option, but now that he knew what he was dealing with, Ryan hoped he could find a way to bring peace into his father's life. "I'll be back in the morning to check on him. I would appreciate it if you'd text me with any changes."

The doctor nodded and wrote on the chart in his hands. "Will do."

Left alone with his father, Ryan took his hand and squeezed gently. "I promise. I'll do everything I can to help you. You aren't crazy. You never were. I know that now. And from here on out, things will be different. Just get better."

Surprisingly Clayton's eyes fluttered, but they didn't open. Ryan sighed, and left the room, wondering just what kind of power the local witches had....

Chapter Thirteen

Spider webs.

Dia cringed as she pushed those closest out of the way and moved further into the shed. She hadn't thought enough time had passed since she'd been here last to allow for so many, but then dark and undisturbed were their favorite places to hide. The arachnids had taken full advantage of her absence and made themselves right at home.

She'd started the generator before unlocking the shed's doors so lighting wasn't a problem as she searched for something to sweep away the pests. Since the floor was made of packed dirt, there was no reason for a broom, but as soon as she'd had the thought, movement outside of the open doors captured her attention and delight flooded her for the first time in days. Vines grew from the ground and twirled as they wove themselves through each other. Those making up the brush head straightened, and those binding the brush together tightened. As if a season had changed, the vines dried instantly and their leaves hit the ground. Thicker vines danced and braided themselves but they remained long, creating what was clearly the handle. Dia watched the last of the process completely captivated, as the last strands attached head to handle.

"That's quite impressive."

Dia gasped and jerked back and then sent what she knew was a silly smile at her mother. It was good to see her, but more importantly, it was good to see her smiling, too. "Hi, Momma."

Rayne advanced on her daughter, and the broom danced to the side making them both laugh in surprise. "That is amazing!"

Dia nodded. "It is. I wanted to knock down spider webs and wished I had a broom, and it just made itself!"

Rayne looked her over speculatively. "And you were afraid you had no magic."

Dia nodded as her smile faltered. "Is everyone still mad?"

Rayne shrugged. "They aren't mad. They're concerned. Have you heard from him?"

Shaking her head, Dia held out her hand and the broom flew straight into it. She couldn't help but smile. "I don't even have to say anything. It's like the earth knows what I want as soon as I think it."

"That is some very strong magic."

"But to answer your question, no. Ryan hasn't come back for his car or his game system."

"Or for you."

Though not a question, Dia shook her head. "No, not for me either." To distance herself from the hurt she felt, Dia used the broom to knock down the webs before cautiously carrying each spider out the door. As much as she hated them, Cavanaughs didn't kill anything unless absolutely necessary. Once her shop was as it needed to be, she opened her hands and the broom made itself comfortable in the corner of the shed. Though she felt a smile again, this time it didn't develop. Instead she solemnly retrieved Camellia Cavanaugh's booklet and flipped to the place she'd used to cast the love spell. She looked over the words again, and sighed, amazed her mother hadn't demanded the little book back before now. But then, maybe that was why she'd arrived.

"This is the spell I used."

Rayne took the pamphlet but didn't even look down

before reciting the words:

> *"Three hearts of the precious wild growing rose*
> *Beneath the sun and starry sky, grows;*
> *Three silver drops of honey so gold*
> *Awaken the mysteries of bold, and old;*
> *Three silver spoons of blood red wine*
> *And thee shall be mine;*
> *Thee shall be mine;*
> *Until by will I set thee free*
> *This is my will, so shall it be."*

She smiled gently and then looked at her daughter. "Do you know what this book is?"

Dia nodded. "A book of spells."

Rayne nodded. "But did you know it is a companion book to Camellia's diary?"

"No, I didn't. I thought it *was* her diary."

Rayne handed the book back, smiling when Dia hesitated in surprise before taking it. "Her diary is quite long and details what happened as a result of each of the spells she created and tried. She was like you in a way, though ultimately her gift was more like Destiny's and Jewell's. She was of the *Divine,* but her ability to find truth took a while to develop, and in her impatience she made some mistakes.

"This spell was one."

Dia looked at the lovely words again ad then closed the book. "What happened?"

Rayne moved to the shelves containing the herbs, pickled items, and spices that made up Dia's treasure-trove. She searched the bottles and jars and began choosing this and that. "Camellia was born at the turn of the last century and by the time she was your age, the Roaring Twenties were in full swing. Her oldest sister was the one who carried the line, so her part in the family was that of teacher to her nieces."

Rayne glanced at her as she sat three small bottles in the center of the stove. "If you remember, before Destiny, Haven, and I destroyed the three-thousand-year-old love curse placed on our ancestors that was the way of it. It wasn't until my sisters and I were thinking about having babies and knew at the time that only one of us would be able to, I realized how emotionally draining that particular part of the curse was. The three of us didn't want the others to lose the chance at motherhood, but we were all fearful it wasn't going to be us." She smiled. "Well, at least Haven and me. Destiny claimed she never wanted kids, but after seeing her raise her boys, I'm sure she's forgotten that."

Dia nodded. She knew the story and knew it well. "So Camellia was dissatisfied with her lot in life?"

Rayne nodded. "Yes. By all accounts in her sisters' diaries, Camellia was always heavy of heart. Her oldest sister was busy playing mother and surviving the pain of losing the man she loved, which was also a given at the time. Few of the men before our generation ever survived the relationship beyond planting the seed for the next generation. Those who did live lost the Cavanaugh woman they loved to whatever fate had been decided for them. The men lost their children as well, because the aunts never allowed the babies to leave the protection of the family."

"So it was a damned if you do find love, and damned if you don't kind of thing."

Rayne reached for a large jar and pulled it down to look at the pickled frogs floating inside. "Yes. It was."

"So what happened?"

Sitting the frogs back on the shelf, Rayne continued her search. "Because she hadn't yet found her mystical feet, Camellia decided to force magic to come to her. She felt cheated by fate. Not only couldn't she have children, those she was responsible for teaching couldn't look to her for help in their training. So she decided to create her own spells, and like you, for some time thereafter, they blew up in her face both figuratively and literally speaking."

Dia grinned at that. Now that she'd found her own magic, her quest to have something other than what was hers seemed so silly. "Go on."

"Well, according to her diary, she met a man who appealed to her. Which wasn't all that earth-shattering, but what was is he didn't find her appealing at all."

"And the Cavanaugh women had never had trouble attracting the men they wanted, whether they could have children with them or not."

Rayne nodded, smiling. "That's correct. I'm glad you know so much of our history."

"Not enough, apparently. But in my defense, there are hundreds and hundreds of diaries to go through."

"Yes…" Rayne said on a sigh, "There are.

"So anyway, Camellia had already been dabbling in creating spells, which is why this particular one is so far back in her little book. She'd failed at all those that came before, but this time, she adjusted an ancient gypsy spell to suit herself, certain she'd succeed."

Dia groaned at that. How many times had she done the same thing knowing the next magical experiment would be the one to set her on the path of the *Celestial*?

Rayne laughed. "Yes, I know you can identify.

"What Camellia didn't know, however, was her own ancestral history, so after stealing a lock of the man's hair, she set about creating the potion to make him fall in love with her."

As frightened as she was of the answer, Dia was excited to ask the question. "What happened?"

"Oh, he fell in love with her, as she expected. But he became violent when she got tired of the constant stalking. He wouldn't let her out of his sight, and when she resisted him physically, he raped her repeatedly. Eventually it elevated to beatings, until he finally killed her."

Stunned, Dia shook her head in denial. "Ryan would never do that."

Rayne looked at her with sadness in her eyes. "We don't know that. He was very angry when he left here. But we've been watching, and he hasn't left Mystic Waters. Your Jeep is parked outside the motel in town."

Dia forced herself to calm down. "His father was in a mental ward at the hospital before he escaped. Ryan came here to deal with that. Everything that has happened since is my fault."

Rayne shrugged. "Well, there is another aspect of the story I haven't told you about, and it may be what keeps us from wiping his mind completely, if he comes around and can be reasoned with."

"What?"

"Had Camellia read the entire diary of the gypsy ancestor whose spell she was trying to replicate, rather than just taking the spell and trying to make it her own, she would have known the heart of the man must be pure before the spell is cast, or his deviant personality traits will only be magnified. The man she fell for must have had a black heart to start with, otherwise, she may have found at least a temporary season of happiness before the curse found some other way to part them."

Relief washed through Dia. "Ryan *is* pure of heart. He's the best person I've ever met outside of our own family."

Rayne smiled. "I believe you are right. So now you have to decide what you're going to do about it. You can hide away here like you have for the past few days and both of you mourn the loss of the other to the point it destroys your souls, or you can go to him and tell him who we are and what we are about, and see if his love for you is pure enough to sustain a lifetime of happiness."

Rayne's brows pulled together. "There is also a third option. You can try to undo the spell and see if he loves you for yourself, if the undoing doesn't stop his heart and kill him."

Dia stared at her mother before slowly nodding. "I think I have to try that one. I can't find my own happiness if I have stolen his right to choose."

Pleasure sparkled in Rayne's emerald eyes. "That's my girl."

"But you have to promise me my aunts will forgive me and keep him alive."

"You know we will all do our best."

Dia nodded, feeling foolish for even suggesting otherwise. "How will I survive if he stops loving me?"

Rayne moved closer and pulled her daughter into her arms. "If he stops, it means he never really did. But to answer your question, you will mourn your heartbreak as all Cavanaugh women before you have, and though you will wish yourself dead at times, you'll recover and embrace your gift to nurture the earth and sky."

Sudden nausea hit Dia with a punch. She pulled away from her mother and ran out the doors to vomit upon the ground. Shaking, weak, she was thankful when her mother's arms were once again around her. When she was able to fully stand, tears slid from her eyes.

Rayne looked her daughter over and then shook her head as she gently placed her hand on Dia's stomach. When she stepped back, there was caution in her eyes. "Do you know?"

Dia frowned. "Know what?"

"That a spark of life grows within you."

"*What?*"

Rayne's smile was sad. "Though barely discernable, life is knitting together within your womb. It's too soon for heartbeats, but warmth and movement are there struggling to create what is to come."

The earth spun and tilted. The ground replaced the sky. All Dia could do, her mother stooped at her side, was try to emerge from the fog blanketing her mind. Eventually sunshine lifted the haze and her heart burst with joy even as it shattered into tiny particles of dust. No matter what happened next, for now, all she could do was float in the wonder of a single word.

Pregnant….

****

Twenty minutes of sitting in a torrential shower did little to help with the turmoil in her mind. She'd been considering, and *reconsidering*, her options. Though all threatened to end disastrously for her, Dia knew she couldn't change her mind. Neither could she tell Ryan of her condition until all was said and done. If, in the end, he wanted nothing to do with her or their offspring, then she'd have no choice but to let him go.

Though she'd protested long and hard, Rayne finally left when Dia asked her to *please* leave her be, half an hour earlier. She'd needed time to gather her wits, time to come to terms with her situation, and time to question her motivation in making the potion to begin with, knowing to do so was taboo. Sure, she'd convinced herself it was nothing more than the simplicity of the spell, but all of Camellia's spells were modest in the making. But what rolled through her mind the most, was her own instant attraction to a man she hadn't even known. She played their meeting over in her mind, but none of it made sense.

Sure, he'd been cute with his dark rimmed glasses, and was easily hot as hell beneath them. His body was that of a man who took care of himself and she'd later learned delicious to discover. His personality was that of a gentleman, but she hadn't known that at first either. In fact, she'd run in and out of the other cabin so quickly that night, to get back to her potion, she'd really given him little more than a passing thought.

Dia's head came up sharply, causing water to run into her eyes and nose. *That wasn't true!* She had thought of him again when the smoke that choked her spiraled its way to his cabin when she'd flung open the shed's doors and ran outside to clear her lungs!

The smoke had filled *her* lungs!

Laughter filled her, overtook her, and made her eyes flood and her nose clog. She rolled into a ball on the tile floor as the hysteria increased and her tears flowed with the water down the drain. Of all the possibilities she'd ever imagined, this one had never occurred to her until now. She had no idea if she'd enchanted Ryan Steward, but she now knew for certain....

She'd enchanted herself.

Time held no concept as her mirth settled, reemerged, settled, reemerged, and finally died. She weakly dried herself and made her way back to the shed, so numb she couldn't even acknowledge Mother Mountain's generosity in placing soft moss beneath each barefooted step. The ingredients to break the love spell were still sitting on the stove in the shed where she'd left them along with the instructions her mother had carefully written out. She ignored them and closed and locked up the shed before cutting the generator's engine. She shuffled her way back through the trees to the little cottage she loved. With no energy or emotion left, she fell onto the bed and let it engulf her in a protective hug. Her last thought before giving in to sleep was she'd gotten exactly what she'd deserved.

Chapter Fourteen

Ryan sat in the driveway and stared at the large cabin that held so many good memories. For the first time there wasn't a crowd on the porch or meat cooking on the smokers and grills. He swallowed, wondering if he should have gone to Dia's cabin first, but he needed to get his game system and game, and then....

No, the truth was, he was procrastinating. He wanted to see her. He wanted honesty from her. But he wasn't ready to come face to face with her just yet. If she'd really enchanted him in some way, he wasn't sure he'd be able to focus on his anger, and demand the truth.

More than anything right now, he needed truth.

"Hey!"

Ryan jerked around and felt a smile coming on. Covered by a wife-beater T-shirt and running shorts, Heracles sprinted from the tree line to stop at the passenger opening of the Jeep. Bent over, he took a few minutes to catch his breath and wipe the sweat from his brow, before plopping himself into the seat.

"Thanks for coming back. I just won fifty bucks off my brothers."

Ryan relaxed, thankful normal was his first encounter with the mystical family. "Good. So how is the wind blowing around here?"

Heracles grinned. "The mothers were here all the time until today. They finally took Jewell and the babies back to her place. Then Rayne went to see Dia. No one had heard from her since she left right after you the other day."

Ryan digested that, wondering if she was okay. As lost and hurt as he'd been, he hadn't given a thought to her being hurt as well. "Any word on how she's doing?"

Heracles shook his head. "No. But that was a couple of hours ago. If there was reason for alarm, we would all know it by now." He looked Ryan over. "How about you?"

A long breath escaped through pursed lips. "I'm working it out."

"That's good to hear."

"I have lots of questions."

"That would be expected."

"I'm not sure if I'm in love with your cousin or if I'm only enchanted by a spell."

Heracles laughed. "Dude, seriously? What's not to love?"

Ryan grinned and nodded. "I know. That's what I don't understand. Why would she need to enchant a guy to have him? One look of interest from her would have us all falling at her feet."

Heracles looked around as if he were afraid the trees would overhear before turning back to Ryan.

"Dia is...*special*. She always means well, but she has a habit of screwing things up. What happened wasn't meant to happen, I'm sure."

"You shouldn't talk about her like that."

Looking more amused than chastised, Heracles nodded. "Got it. So why don't you head over there and sweep her off her feet?"

"I told myself I needed to come here first to get my game."

"You lied."

Ryan laughed. "Yeah."

"So what do you really need?"

The laughter died from the inside out. He shook his head. "I need a lot of things. Answers. Understanding. And your family's help."

Surprise lit Heracles's eyes. "What kind of help?"

Blowing a breath through his nose, Ryan shrugged. "I need to know if anyone here can help my father."

Heracles jumped from the Jeep and pulled his cell phone from a little pouch attached to his running shorts. He tapped its screen then held the phone to his ear. After a few seconds, his eyes intent on Ryan, he spoke into the phone.

"Emergency meeting. Two hours. Everyone who can. Mom and Dad's place."

He pulled the phone away and lifted a tweezed brow at Ryan as he punched another number. "Why are you still here? You have two hours to make pretty with my cousin and get her back here."

Embarrassed that tears were filling his eyes, Ryan nodded and started the engine, but he couldn't pull away as he looked at Heracles in wonder. "Just like that?"

Heracles nodded. "Yeah, man. Just like that."

Ryan pulled off, filled to the brim, yet he wasn't sure he identified the emotion. With a mother who had been grudging in her affections, he'd never been a part of anything bigger than himself, and now, amazingly, he felt as if he had a brother. It took too short a time yet much too long, before he was pulling into Dia's driveway. He smiled to himself as the earth decided to buckle here and there just as he'd reach a spot before he stopped the Jeep and looked at the smooth road ahead. Figuring, *what the hell*, Ryan voiced his thoughts aloud: "I'm not here to hurt her!"

When he started the Jeep again, he nearly laughed as it now felt like the vehicle was hovering above the dirt road and floating forward on air. As much as his mind rejected what was happening, his heart knew it was real, and he embraced the wonder of this as well.

The little cabin came into view and his heart rate

increased dramatically. As excited as he was to see her again, there was no guarantee she would be as happy to see him. He braced for the possibility she'd be angry and hate him, he just hoped she didn't try to turn him into anything before giving him a chance to make amends. The last thing he wanted was to end his life as a toad or something equally disgusting.

Ryan didn't allow that fear to settle as he exited the Jeep and made his way to the door, hoping it was unlocked. He intended to open it without knocking, not willing to give her a chance to lock him out. To his relief there was no resistance when he turned the knob. To his delight she was sound asleep, her nude body as beautiful as ever, which brought his own to full attention. Rolling his eyes at his completely male reaction, he closed the door quietly behind him.

It took all he had not to strip and join her on the bed, but he didn't trust her reaction and had little time to fix all he'd messed up by reacting the way he had. He gently pulled the sheet that balled at her feet and placed it over her body. She moaned and stretched and then jerked around, before a cry escaped her lips.

Naked, gorgeous female jumped up, clasping his body, as her soft lips collided with his. She moaned and whimpered, wailed yet devoured while pulling him atop her back onto the bed as she fought his clothing. As much as Ryan wanted to let her have her way, he wasn't entirely certain she was awake, so he pulled back and held her still as he looked into her eyes. They spun with color, with hunger, but with clarity, and he smiled in relief.

"You're awake."

Dia nodded. Her eyes searching his as they settled back to sky blue.

"You came back."

Ryan nodded. "I should have come before now."

Dia shook her head. "I'm so sorry. I couldn't tell you. To reveal ourselves places the entire family in danger."

"I figured that out. But there is so much I need to know."

Dia nodded. "I know. And you will. But for just right now, for just a few minutes, please, just hold me."

Ryan was more than happy to. He lay at her side and pulled her to him. Dia settled half on top of him, which made his desire for her hard to ignore. She raised up enough to look him in the eyes again. "I don't think you want me because I enchanted you. I was so afraid you did, but I don't think so now. I missed you so much. I'm so sorry!"

Though her words eased him some, Ryan shrugged, knowing the truth and knowing she needed to hear it. "I don't care if you did. I would have been enchanted anyway."

Dia searched his eyes, her own filled with doubt. "*Really?*" She frowned. "Why?"

"Because you are so beautiful, so sweet, so vibrant, and so everything I never knew I wanted in a woman."

She snuggled into him, fitting like she had always belonged. Ryan swallowed, realizing how serious this discussion had to be and knowing his mind wasn't going to stay on task if she didn't stop touching him. They needed to have more between them than sex. Right now that's all he could think of. He tried to ignore the weight of her breasts, the smell of her hair, and the fact he was engorged and throbbing to the point of pain.

It was impossible.

"I might have to stand on the other side of the room with my back to you if we're going to talk."

Dia ran a finger down the line of buttons covering his chest. "Or you could get naked and we could talk later."

"Tempting," he said, struggling with the tightness at

his zipper. "For sure. But I need to know something. I understand what it is about you that has me in knots. I just haven't figured out what you ever saw in me."

Dia's gaze flittered and she looked down so her lashes covered her eyes. A touch of unease cooled his ardor, some, but he knew he needed to get up if he was going to clear his head completely. He placed a gentle kiss on her forehead before rolling her over, to sit himself up. He kept his back to her, waiting until control was within his grasp. He glanced back, relieved to see she'd covered herself with the sheet. "Dia?"

Her chest rose and fell, and her voice shook when she spoke. "I think you are amazing. Everything about you."

"Then why aren't you looking me in the eyes when you say it?"

She glanced up then, her eyes filled with sadness. "Because when I tell you what I think happened, you aren't going to believe what I feel is real."

Her unexpected answer gave him a moment's pause. Ryan breathed slowly on purpose. "After learning my mind was wiped, you possibly enchanted me, and all the other stuff, what more could you say that would make me doubt...whatever it is you have to tell me?"

Dia frowned at his careful worded question. "Do you believe we are mystics?"

Ryan nodded slowly. "Yeah. But for reasons you don't yet know about."

She looked at him oddly. "What reasons?"

He bit his lip then released it. "We can get to that when we meet up with your family. I'm still trying to process everything. Just answer my question. Please."

"What are you talking about? *Why* would we meet up with my family?"

Frustrated, knowing she was dodging his question, Ryan rose from the bed. "Because I stopped by the

Whitehawk house earlier and asked Heracles for some help with a personal matter. He made some calls and we are supposed to be back there in about an hour and a half."

Dia stared at him. He knew she was offended when he didn't explain himself, but he was feeling a little offended as well. Even though she was happy to see him, something was off, and he had no idea what it was since she wouldn't tell him what he needed to know.

"I'm going to ask you this again, Dia, and I want an answer. Why are you so interested in hooking up with me?" At her hurt look, Ryan sighed. "I didn't mean it like that."

Dia rose, not caring that her nakedness was on full display. He looked away, not wanting to want her like he did. After everything he'd learned, he wanted her to open up to him. Once she pulled on a shirt and jeans, she turned to him, her eyes filled with sadness.

"The answer to your question is hard to explain without it hurting you. But I guess you have the right to know. I really don't believe I enchanted you like I'd thought, but enchanted myself instead. I don't know if this overwhelming need I feel for you is because I really love you, or if it's magic gone awry."

Ryan felt as if he'd been hit in the stomach. She had to be right. He'd always been logical in both thought and action, and nothing about their flash and burn relationship was. She'd breezed into his life like a sexy whirlwind, which never happened to guys like him. Even though he'd questioned it at the beginning, he hadn't allowed his concerns to manifest deeply enough because he hadn't wanted to believe it was anything other than what it was.

He swallowed and nodded and then turned toward the door. "Maybe you or your family can undo the spell. Then you'll know for sure." He smiled, sadly. "I won't hold it against you if you find it was all...*magic gone awry*." He shook his head, unable to believe such a thing was possible, but knowing nothing else made sense. "Let's just go see them, and if you find you don't really love me, I'll walk out of your life and go on with mine just like I always have."

Saying those words out loud nearly took his breath, but as much as he wanted and needed Dia in his life, he wouldn't hold her to something beyond her control. If she desired him as well, it had to be for all the right reasons, even if that meant his life was forced back into the loneliness of before. He knew it wouldn't be the same though, because he hadn't realized then he *was* lonely, just alone. Maybe he should ask if her family would wipe his mind again. This time, of the love he felt to the marrow of his bones.

He threw the small pile of dirty clothes into his suitcase and took one last look around the room. With his heart dragging, he swallowed back the emotions choking his throat. "I'll wait for you in the Jeep."

Ryan walked out into the afternoon sun, feeling his life had gone pitch dark.

****

Waiting around for the family to gather was torture. The usually boisterous group already assembled was quiet, looking at each other as if unsure what to say. Dia hated she was responsible for putting them in such an uncomfortable position and was relieved when her mother and aunts finally arrived from Jewell's house.

Rayne walked to the front of the room and looked around, her gaze settling on Ryan. She smiled slightly before telling everyone to take a seat.

"Before we get started, I want to say to you, Ryan, I am sorry for how this all played out. If you don't mind, I want to start by telling you who and what we are, and although I am technically a witch, if you want to use that term, we aren't all casters. We mostly call ourselves mystics."

Ryan nodded. "That would be great."

"Okay. First, my sisters and I are the daughters of Celestia Cavanaugh. She was from a long line of women who, for three thousand years, lived under a curse that caused all kinds of problems in regard to each one's ability to find and keep the love of a man."

Dia glanced at Ryan. Although she'd told him a little of their history, she hadn't gone into nearly the detail her mother was about to. She just hoped he could handle it.

"Though the details are vast and would take hours if not days to tell, what really matters now, is what happened when I was about the age Dia is now.

"My sisters and I came to Mystic Waters and we each met the man we are now married to. Because we still lived under the curse, there was no real expectation our attraction to these men would amount to what it has, which is an everlasting love we now believe will carry us to the end of long lives." She smiled. "Though Destiny, Haven, and I believe the love we feel for our husbands will take us into the next life as well."

Dia heard Ryan's deep breath and wondered if he was bored. When she glanced his way, she decided he was just overwhelmed but very interested.

"To make a very long story short, the point is it was the love of our husbands that broke the curse, not the magic we inherited from the ancestor who cursed our line." She smiled a little and shook her head. "I know this probably doesn't make a lot of sense to you now, but, if you decide you want to stay a part of our family, you'll have years to learn the details. If you decide this is too much to handle, then it won't matter anyway."

"So your husbands aren't...mystics?"

Rayne shook her head. "My husband and Haven's husband have no mystical abilities whatsoever, but Destiny's husband does. His line is as long and as strong as is ours."

"And they accepted all this without question?"

Rayne laughed a little. "Well, they've had a quarter of a century now to ask all the questions they've had. In the beginning, and in fairness I have to add, because of the circumstances of what was happening to their families at the time, their acceptance came easier than might have otherwise been the case.

"Having said all that, their love in spite of our mystical gifts is what broke the curse. And now we live a fairytale's happily ever after life."

Ryan turned to Dia, searching her eyes, her face, and Dia was dying to know what he thought and felt. He turned back to her mother, nodding. "Were these men ever enchanted?"

Haven moved to stand by Rayne and answered. "No. In fact, my Logan kept getting burned by me, and we fought about things, but in spite of that, his love was true, and we overcame every obstacle placed in our path."

Ryan frowned as he looked at her mother. "And Mr. White?"

Rayne shook her head. "No. He had no clue, until the day he did, and he accepted me without hesitation."

"Because he was already in love with you."

"Yes, Ryan, he was. Are you in love with my daughter?"

Ryan nodded, with a frown Dia feared meant this was all too much for him to bear.

"My daughter loves you as well. Is that not enough for you?"

Ryan stared at Rayne for some time before answering. "It would be if she really loved me too."

"I just told you she did."

Dia stood, not able to let things continue without catching her mother up. "Mom? I'm not sure if I do or not."

Several gasps filled the room, and Dia glanced from her cousins to Sapphire to her aunts. She swallowed, knowing she would once again have to lay a failure out for her family to see. "I don't believe my spell enchanted Ryan. I believe I ended up enchanting myself to fall in love with him."

Complete silence filled the room as everyone stared at her, until her cousin Soleli spoke up. "How is that even possible?"

Licking her dry lips, Dia turned back to her mother. "When I created Camellia Cavanaugh's potion, an eyelash fell into it. At first I thought it was mine, but then later, I remembered picking one off of Ryan's cheek that night and didn't pay attention to it when I brushed my hands together. So I thought it possible it may have fallen on me, then into the potion."

"You're not making much sense."

Dia looked at another of Haven's daughters, surprised Luna was speaking up at all. She did so rarely, and usually so quietly, one had to strain to hear her. "I'm sorry. I'm trying."

Ryan took a step forward. "Maybe it would be easier if you weren't all trying to be so careful about how you're explaining this to me."

Dia nodded as she looked down at the man she wasn't sure she loved, though she wanted with a passion it bordered on scary. "We are trying."

He nodded and then turned back to Rayne. "I overheard you the other day saying you'd wiped some of my memories. I'd like them back."

Destiny came to stand at Rayne's other side, placing the three identical matriarchs in a line Dia knew usually preceded them creating great power. She held her breath, knowing Ryan had no idea what kind of danger he could be in. Whenever her mother and aunts joined their power all things were possible, and that wasn't necessarily good. She hurried to his side and took his hand in hers and held on tight, not bothering to see if he cared. If their intentions were unfavorable toward Ryan, they'd have to go through her to get to him.

Rayne flicked her a look before a smile lifted her lips. "Down, Dia. No one is going to harm him."

Ryan looked at her with a frown, and then looked down at their joined hands. When he glanced up again there was a slight grin on his lips also. Dia relaxed a little and squeezed his hand. No matter what was to come, Ryan was a good man, and she liked him.

He looked from one woman to the next before his gaze settled on Rayne. "I'm serious, I'd like my memories back."

Rayne nodded. "That's fine. But before we make that happen, I want to explain a few more things.

"Throughout the history I've told you about, for each generation there has always been repeating themes. First we were all born identical triplets. Every one of us had red hair, green eyes, and were identical of face and figure. Of the three born, only one was ever able to produce the next generation." She smiled. "Yes, I can see by the look on your face, you find that shocking."

"Yeah. I do. Why?"

Rayne shrugged. "We've never fully understood. Maybe someday we will. That aside, another thing that always happened is each of us inherited one of three different types of…gifts. I received the ability to cast spells and conjure magic so I am known as *The Enchantress*. Haven's gift is elemental as she is able to control the weather in any given area and can, in fact, bring on a tornado with a thought, or stop a storm as quickly. She's known in the family as *The Regulator*. And Destiny is known as *The Divine* because she can leave her physical body to seek truth spiritually. I know what I am telling you makes little sense right now, but it's extremely complicated to explain. Since the curse was broken in our generation, our gifts have not only grown but have mutated. Now we have other powers as well and can even share them with each other."

"Mom, I think this is too much. You're only going to confuse him more," Dia said, appreciating her mother's desire to help Ryan understand but knowing even she wouldn't believe it if she didn't already.

Ryan shook his head. "No. I think I'm following pretty well. In each generation of Cavanaugh triplets you have had these repeating mystical themes: the Enchantress who is capable of casting or conjuring, the Regulator who is capable of controlling natural elements, and the Divine whose spirit is free to discover truth."

Dia turned to him, amazed. "Yes, that's right."

"In each generation the individual gifts were distinctly different," Rayne added, grinning. "One Regulator might only control the sky, another the earth, or the waterways, or all three, as in Haven's case. But that isn't what really makes her distinctly different. Her connection with the earth is what strengthens her gift of healing."

"What do you mean?"

With one look passing between her and her sisters, Rayne opened her hand and a small dagger appeared. She lifted it and cut her forearm in one quick motion. The gasp in the room didn't just come from Ryan, and Dia froze in disbelief her mother would make such a dramatic display to prove her point. Ryan started to rise, but she pulled him back down in his seat as Haven lifted her hands palm out. They pinkened and then glowed like a red flame had developed from within. As seconds ticked by the glow grew until it radiated from her hands. Smiling at Ryan, she placed her hand over Rayne's wound.

Ryan removed Dia's hand from his arm and rose. He approached the women slowly, stopping before her mother. Dia bit her bottom lip as she waited, wishing she was there to see the reaction on his face when Haven lifted her hand. This time only his gasp could be heard in the anticipation-filled atmosphere of the room.

"That's amazing." He looked up and then back at the line of family members sitting around the room before once again facing Rayne. "I get it."

Though his back was turned to Dia, she could hear the wonder in his voice. She relaxed back into the couch, knowing her family was safe no matter how things turned out between Ryan and herself. She tried to ignore the twinge behind her ribcage, but she knew they would have to face and address that soon, as well.

Rayne's smile was fully in place as Ryan returned to his seat. "I thought you would. A man who can create the world within a game the way you did, should be able to understand pretty much anything."

Pleasure filled Ryan's features. "Thank you."

Rayne nodded. "You're welcome. By the way, you shouldn't have left it the other day. The men in this family are all in competition to see who can get the farthest on it, and you're game is kicking their collective butts!" She laughed, as did everyone in the room.

He turned to Dia, looking into her eyes, his own filled with excitement. "What is your gift?"

Dia swallowed, knowing all eyes were on them. "I'm a Regulator. But I've only learned that since you've arrived. I was trying so hard not to let it show and was so scared you'd be afraid of me if you learned the truth. When we were in the cave...."

Ryan frowned. "What cave?"

"Yeah, what cave?" one cousin after another asked.

Dia ignored them and focused on Ryan. She knew there was no use holding anything back any more. He had to know it all. "The day we awoke late, it wasn't really the beginning of our day. Earlier I took you to one of my favorite places on earth, and there you saw the truth of my power. It frightened you so badly you backed away and tripped over a rock, hit your head, and passed out. My mother and aunts came to our rescue. Aunt Haven healed you, and they wiped the entire memory of that early morning from your mind."

He studied her in silence and then turned back to her mother. "Please, give me back my memories. Now."

Chapter Fifteen

It was obvious from his expression Ryan's mind reeled as one after another the moments of his lost morning played through his mind. He shook and spread his legs as an anchor. Dia was certain he was reliving the violence of the earthquake. He froze, his eyes wide and terrified, and she was sure he again saw the majesty of the lightning. He blanched, shaking his head violently, and she saw him relive the terror he'd felt when Dia had changed from a gentle woman into a powerful mystic. There was no doubt when the memories ended as he cautiously glanced from one pensive face to the next and then finally settled his gaze on Dia. She had no words to offer. His reactions had carried her into the memories he'd relived, and there was nothing she could say to ease the overload of his mind. He took a deep breath and expelled it, his emotions on display.

"Please don't fear us. We are your friends," Rayne said softly.

He nodded, his head jerking with the motion. "So the water *is* what cleared up my vision."

Dia nodded. "Yes."

"But not just the water," Rayne added. "It is the earth's desire to please Dia, and because of her feelings for you, to please you as well."

Ryan bit his bottom lip, keeping his attention on mother rather than daughter. "What if Dia is right about enchanting herself, and her emotions aren't real? Is there a way to undo the spell?"

Dia shook with emotion, certain her love wouldn't

change but knowing there was no choice but to find out. She turned to the matriarchs, and one by one they nodded. Her mother moved around Destiny to stand before her. "There is a way, but it will take your memories of Ryan as well. The only way the heart can forget is if the mind forgets first."

"No!" Ryan pulled Dia against his side. "You can't take her memories! It will destroy her in some way! My father has lost all quality of life because of this mind-sweeping thing you all do. He's even now in a mental facility because of it. You have to stop doing that."

Dia choked back a sob and pulled out of Ryan's arms. She didn't want to forget him, or their time together, but he deserved more than their love being a lie. She was so distraught, knowing what must be done, it took the long silence in the room to make her realize her mother was frowning at Ryan and not paying any attention to her. She looked at the other faces in the room, nonplussed before playing back all he'd said and finally, his exact words dawned on her.

"What are you talking about? What does my family have to do with your father's mental illness?"

Ryan looked from Dia to her mother. "One of your family members wiped his stepfather's mind when my father was a little kid. He witnessed magic and death, but no one has ever believed him. It's driven him crazy his entire life and cost me ever getting to know him."

"Who was his stepfather?" Rayne asked, her voice tight.

Dia frowned at her mother, but Rayne was intent on Ryan alone.

"His name is John Grammar, and from my understanding, he lives in Mystic Waters too."

Rayne swayed and her sisters were there in an instant, taking her arms. They made their way to the couch and sat her down before turning back to Ryan and herself. Dia looked from one to another of the stricken faces and wondered what it all meant.

Haven walked over to Ryan and smiled sadly at him, pulling him up and into a hug. When she stepped back, tears were streaming from her eyes. "You father is the last person to remember seeing our mother alive."

Dia rose as well and then felt her legs give. She caught herself by grabbing onto Ryan's arm. She looked at him through the tears forming in her own eyes. "John Grammar doesn't remember my grandmother. My great-aunts wiped his memory to allow him to forget he accidently killed Celestia Cavanaugh, in the hopes he'd live a long and happy life guilt-free."

Destiny approached them, her eyes dry, but her expression filled with pain. "Our aunts knew the little boy was there, but they must not have known he'd witnessed anything, otherwise they would have blocked it from his mind as well."

Dia kept her eyes on Ryan, her heart hurting for them all. Since he seemed frozen with shock, she turned to Destiny. "Can this be fixed?"

Rayne rose slowly as if suddenly old, to join them. Her face pale, her gaze sliding from one of her sisters to the other, she swallowed before turning to Dia. "We don't know. Taking your memories of Ryan after you two knowing each other a short time will be hard enough. Taking a lifetime of memories..." She shook her head. "It's too dangerous. He won't have any personal identity at all."

"What if you gave him different memories?"

"We can't do that, Ryan."

"Why not?"

Everyone looked at Ryan, but he kept his eyes on Rayne. Dia took his hand only to discover it was ice cold. When he turned to her, his desperation broke her heart. "It isn't that they can't, it's that to do so will involve him thinking he's had a different life with other people in it, and none of those people would exist, or if they did, they would still look at him the same."

"As if he's insane."

Dia nodded. "Yes."

Ryan nodded, facing Rayne. "What if you gave John Grammar his memories back instead?"

"That would only complicate the life of what is now a very old man," Sapphire said, stepping up to them. "I've seen him recently, and he's growing confused with age."

"At the police station," Ryan stated with certainty.

Obviously surprised, Sapphire nodded. "Yes. He's retired now but comes in a couple of times a month to visit. How did you know?"

"My mother told me a little about my step-grandfather, though she only met him once, when she was carrying me. And my father said he knew one of the witches was a policewoman. I guess he meant you."

Sapphire took a step back, shaking her head. "It was *him*?" She turned to Rayne. "It must have been him!"

Dia grabbed her sister's arm. "What are you talking about?"

"When I was transitioning into my Lycanthrope, Ryan's father must have been that crazed man who broke into the house that day!"

"*What did you just say?*"

Dia turned to a wide-eyed Ryan, knowing, after everything he'd already learned, this would likely be the thing to send him running. But full disclosure seemed to be the words of the day. "Um...my sister is a werewolf."

The room filled with Cavanaugh-Whites, Cavanaugh-Hansens, and Cavanaugh-Whitehawks was completely silent until Ryan broke into hysterical laughter. Dia tried to hold her smile back, but it was hard with him laughing to the point of tears filling his eyes. Even knowing he could be in the middle of nervous breakdown, and she in a panic because of it, she couldn't help but smile. "Ryan, stop."

He looked at her, his face contorted, and he started laughing again as tears let loose and ran down his face. Becoming truly fearful they'd pushed him over the edge, she looked at her mother, who nodded, and held up her hand palm out.

"Peace be with you, Ryan."

His laughter slowly trickled to a stop, and he took several cleansing breaths. He eyed Rayne warily and then nodded once. "Thanks."

Rayne smiled. "Come, let's reason this all out."

"I'm hungry."

Everyone turned to Heracles. He shrugged. "Seriously. Since when does this family hold a meeting where no food is involved?"

Ryan frowned. "Maybe that's a good idea. I need a minute here." He shook his head. "I think I need to take a walk and let all this settle before we continue anyway."

Dia nodded and watched him stroll to the door. He hadn't invited her to join him, and she knew from the pain in her heart, the only way she'd survive losing him, was for her mind to be wiped of his existence. She found her mother was watching her and shrugged. "Wipe my memories before he comes back."

Rayne's shocked expression was accompanied by the shake of her head. "Why?"

Dia looked at the doorway Ryan had taken and shrugged. "Because I want to meet him all over again. Only this time, I want nothing to stand between us but truth."

"You will also forget your gift."

Dia hadn't thought of that. "You can tell me what it is."

Rayne shook her head. "This could stop your heart, if

your feelings for him are true."

"What other choice do I have?"

"To love me forever, while knowing you really might not."

All heads turned. Ryan was standing in the doorway. He looked at Dia, with raised brows. "I thought we were going to take a walk."

Without looking to see what her family thought of his suggestion, she joined him, and they left the house in silence. Once outside he took her hand and led her to the trees. It wasn't until they were well into the forest before he spoke.

"The wolf we saw that day by the stream, was that a regular wolf?"

Dia tried not to smile. "No."

"Was it Sapphire?"

"No."

"So there's more than one?"

"Yes."

Ryan glanced at her. "As in a lot more?"

Grinning, Dia nodded. "They won't hurt you."

"I figured that. Otherwise I'd be dead by now."

"Most likely."

Ryan frowned. "What do you mean, most likely?"

"Sapphire survived the change when, according to her husband, none ever have before. But I guess that doesn't mean you couldn't."

Looking more than a little appalled, Ryan shook his head. "No, thanks. I'd rather stay human."

Dia grinned. "Jewell's husband is an ancient Egyptian. She went back in time and brought him into ours."

Ryan stopped walking, his brows pulled together. "So that would mean Jewell is Divine, and since you are The Regulator, that means Sapphire is The Enchantress?"

Dia nodded. "Looks that way. Sapphire has great

magic, though she rarely uses it. And Jewell, new mother of four, was learning to hone her out-of-body magic until she got pregnant. I'm sure she'll go back to it once she's up to it."

"What about you? Would you do something for me?"

Dia shrugged. "Like what?"

Ryan looked up to the blue peeking through the canopy. "Will you bring on a storm?"

Dia laughed, unable to believe he was really embracing them all. "Seriously? You want to see it?"

"Absolutely."

Swallowing, Dia opened her hands and splayed her fingers. The energy of the earth flowed from beneath her feet to surge upward throughout her body. The air pressure rose as well, sucking up oxygen, making each subsequent breath more of a struggle. Her hair rose with static electricity. Her eyes misted over and then filled with the vision of boiling clouds and lightning. She embraced it all as her vision cleared, and what had formed from within was now happening without. Ryan stood still, watching her intently, as his hair blew in wild abandonment and his clothing flapped against his body like a boat's sail caught in a gale. She grinned at him, and he grinned back. She knew, spell or not, she loved that man. Not wanting to soak them both, she closed her eyes and allowed the wind to settle and storm clouds disperse. Once she could breathe easier, she knew all was as the day was meant to be. She opened her eyes, only to find Ryan a hairsbreadth away.

"Don't let them make you forget me."

The sincerity in his voice matched the truth in his eyes. She searched their turquoise beauty, before nodding. "I don't think what I feel for you has anything to do with magic."

His brows lifted. "Why not?"

Dia smiled. "Because I know the *me* I've always been,

and there is nothing about you I wouldn't have fallen in love with anyway."

"Get away from that witch!"

Dia and Ryan swung around at the same time, but there was no time to react as a middle-aged man pulled the trigger on the gun in his hands.

Dia looked at Ryan in surprise as he screamed the word, "No!"

Pain slammed in her chest, and her hand went there automatically. She looked down at the red liquid seeping across her shirt and hand, confused. Her legs buckled. And then she realized she'd been shot.

****

Dia opened her eyes and stared at the blades of a ceiling fan as they leisurely made their way around and around. She almost closed her eyes again and then frowned. She looked to make sure she was seeing what she thought she was seeing. Her ceiling was not only *not white*, she didn't own a ceiling fan.

"There you are."

Something about the stranger felt familiar, but Dia was certain she must be mistaken. She smiled at him. "Hi."

A look of amusement lit his eyes. "Do you know where you are?"

Dia shook her head. "Not really. Am I dead?"

Blond brows rose as if he hadn't expected her question. "Not quite. But you're close. I'm Sabian. I'm here to help you make the transition."

Dia frowned. "Are you an angel?"

Sabian smiled. "Some would say I am closer to Satan. But, yes. I am the angel of death."

"So… What kind of place is this?"

Sabian frowned. "It's a holding room."

"With a ceiling fan?"

"That's just to set the mind at ease when you first

realize you're here." Sabian snapped his fingers and the ceiling fan disappeared.

Dia sighed as she studied his face. "What if I don't want to die?"

"That isn't your choice to make."

Realization dawned and she remembered where she'd seen him before. "You're him! I saw you. My sisters saw you, too! On the same day, but we were all in different parts of Europe!"

Sabian nodded. "Yes."

Anger brewed in Dia's gut. "So you've been stalking me just waiting for a chance to take me away from those I love?"

Sabian shook his head. "No. I just happened to be in the area looking for someone else and that man shot you. It wasn't your turn."

"Really? Well that's a relief."

"It doesn't matter. You're dying. That was a fatal shot to the heart."

Dia stared at him long and hard as a buzzing sound started and filled the air around them. Frightened, she shook her head, determined to make him stop whatever it was he was doing. "It isn't my time!"

"Like I said, doesn't matter."

"It matters to me!"

Sabian shrugged and frowned as he looked around nervously. "You aren't the only one annoyed. I was close to finding my target. It has taken your people's version of years! Which by the way is ridiculous. Now I'll have to start all over again... *What the hell is that sound?*"

As it had gotten progressively louder, and Sabian now looked as frightened as she was, Dia's own fear increased tenfold. "Make it stop, please," she begged, afraid she would disappear altogether.

"Hey! What the hell is going on?" Sabian shouted,

looking upward.

Pain flashed in Dia's chest, startling her. It came again, stronger, harder still, until it consumed. She panted through each hit, but couldn't speak as the white room turned to gray. She inhaled sharply before shouting, "What's happening?"

"You're fading! Dammit!"

Sabian reached for her but before he could take hold, Dia took a huge gasping breath. Her mother and aunts stood over her, hands joined and held above their heads, the cabin's ceiling now above them all. As soon as she cried out, relieved she'd made it back, their connection broke and Rayne was at her side, nearly smothering her. She struggled against her mother's chest as Rayne rocked back and forth, taking Dia with her.

"My baby! My baby! I thought we'd lost you!" She cried hysterically with great sobs that shook both her and Dia.

"Rayne, move over. I need to finish this!"

Rayne released her and moved back quickly. Dia turned to see Aunt Haven's hands glowing as they came straight at her chest. Dia shook her head, frightened, and prepared for the impact, but there was no shock, only soothing heat as the residual pain eased before it disappeared altogether. She took a cleansing breath and looked from one matriarch to the next, so relieved to be back she couldn't speak.

"Go tell the others, please," Rayne said to Destiny, before moving to her youngest again.

Only after Destiny left the room and several shouts of joy filled the air, did Dia realize the buzzing she'd heard while on the other side was in fact her sister and cousins, and more than likely the matriarchs, chanting from within and outside the room. She wanted to laugh that they'd defeated the angel of death, but all she could do was cry hysterically. Her mother cried with her, while begging her to calm down and telling her she still needed to recover, and then crying all the harder herself.

Dia tried to stop, but it took too much effort, so she gave in to it until her body was awash with sweat and exhaustion. When she could finally take jerking breaths, she curled onto her side and struggled to tell them all what had happened. But the words wouldn't come, and each second that ticked by, her memories faded until they were gone. She stared at her mother, confused.

"What happened?"

Rayne smiled at her as she wiped the tears from her cheeks. "You were shot, baby."

Dia looked down, realizing she was completely nude, as she tried to remember her last thought before awakening. "Ryan! Where's Ryan?"

Rayne took Dia's hand, her tired eyes sad. "He's in the other room. He was so distraught his father shot you, we had to put him under a sleeping spell."

Dia could barely breathe. "His father shot me?"

Rayne nodded. "Yes."

It was too much to process, but Dia struggled to understand anyway. "How?"

Sighing, Rayne looked down at her hands. "Because he escaped the hospital again this morning. They all thought him in a coma so they didn't lock him down.

"From the information Sapphire got from her partner on the force, Clayton Davis snuck out and jumped in the police car of an officer who had just brought in another patient. He stole the car, and because the officer was instructed not to carry his gun while delivering mental patients, he'd left it in the glove compartment. He hadn't taken the keys... He hadn't locked anything up... He claimed it was all he could do to get the man out of his car and into the building....

"Clayton apparently found everything he needed to come after us and because of processing time, the officer didn't know his car was gone for about half an hour. By the time they'd figured out what had happened..." She shook her head. "That man will likely lose his job, according to Sapphire's partner." Rayne looked at Dia, tears in her eyes. "We hold him no ill will now, but I would have probably killed him if I'd lost you to his carelessness."

Dia shook her head. "No, Momma, you wouldn't have. Killing is not in your soul." Dia smiled. "But I'm so glad to be here." She took a deep breath. "But what will happen to Ryan's father now?"

Sorrow filled Rayne's eyes. "He had a heart attack right after he shot you. Last we heard, he was being kept alive until Ryan comes to the hospital. Logan has taken care of everything there."

Dia's eyes filled and spilled over. "Ryan will never forgive any of us."

Shaking her head, Rayne agreed. "I'm not sure any love can overcome all this."

Epilogue

Numb, Ryan sat with his dry-eyed mother on one side of him and a teary-eyed John Grammar on the other as the minister read several biblical passages. He couldn't focus on the words of comfort, though he'd really tried to, out of respect for the father he barely knew and the elderly gentleman he'd only met before the service started. All he could think about was the multitude of Cavanaugh family members who were seated so quietly behind them in the sanctuary. All of them were present, except Dia.

He was surprised any had come, given the situation, but he was glad they had. He knew they felt responsible, but the truth was, he didn't feel that way at all.

They were who and what they were, which was the nicest, most loving people he'd ever met. None of them had anything to do with what had led to this moment, and he was glad they were here so he could tell them so. He hadn't seen any of them since hurrying to the hospital once they'd awakened him from the peaceful sleep they had put him under when he'd thought Dia dead.

Maybe it was because he barely knew his father, but other than regret, he felt no connection to the man in the casket, nor, in truth, to the man who was his step-grandfather. When the service ended, he rose and shook John Grammar's hand. The old man looked about to fall over, so he was led away by Ryan's mother, as the two of them had hit it off from the moment she'd arrived in Mystic Waters.

Ryan turned to those waiting at the back of the

sanctuary and smiled, happier to see them than he should have been, he supposed. He searched their faces one by one as he approached, allowing his attention to land on Rayne Cavanaugh-White.

"Thank you for coming."

Rayne searched his face and smiled gently. "You are at peace."

Ryan nodded. "I am. I hope my father finally is."

Rayne looked over his shoulder and nodded. "He is beside you, and he is very much at peace now he knows all truths. He says to tell you he is so glad to have met you, to be well and embrace life."

Not doubting Rayne would know such things, he nodded. "Thank you." He bit his bottom lip, wondering if he should ask, but he needed to know. "Why didn't Dia come with you?"

Sadness replaced Rayne's serene expression. "She doesn't know about the funeral, or anything that came before. I'm sorry, but she begged us to take her back to the day before you met, and so she has no memory of you at all. The love spell is broken."

Ryan nodded but couldn't help the tears that formed in his eyes. He blinked them away as he took several slow breaths. "Where is she?"

Rayne smiled at his reaction. "She's likely in her little shed trying to whip up some concoction that will explode."

"I'm going to her."

Rayne leaned forward and kissed his cheek. "I knew you would."

"I'm going to make her fall in love with me all over again."

"I have no doubt of that."

Ryan smiled. "I love you all."

Rayne's eyes filled with tears. "And we love you. Go get her. We'll be waiting at Destiny's to meet you for the first time, all over again."

Mystic Waters Books
By JC Wardon

The Cavanaugh Series Books Now Available!
(The Cavanaugh Sisters Trilogy)
#1 **Mystic Thunder**
#2 **Touch of Lightning**
#3 **Tempest's Embrace**

(The Cavanaugh Series continues!)
#4 **Jewel of the Nile**
#5 **Sapphire Blues**
#6 **Diamond in the Rough**
#7 **Luna's Landing**
#8 **Celestial Liaison**
#9 **Zeus:** *Unbound!*
#10 **Apollo:** *Unleashed!*

The Cavanaugh Series Books to come!
Heracles: Undone
Soleli's Secret
Gavin's Ghosts

Blood Moon Chronicles
Blood Moon Rising

Visit my website: **www.jcwardon.com**
Facebook pages: **www.facebook.com/jc.wardon** and
www.facebook.com/JCWardonNovelist
tweet me: @jc_wardon

Thanks for sharing my world. I'd love to hear from you!

JC Wardon

ACKNOWLEDGEMENTS

I would like to send out a special Thank You to all who have embraced the Cavanaugh women. May your lives be as enchanted!

Thank you all so much!

JCW

ABOUT JC WARDON

JC Wardon loves writing fantasy and spends her days weaving stories for those who love it as well. Though she has great appreciation for romances, a juicy and complicated plot is what she holds most dear. Danger, mystery, and magic are the life's blood for her Mystic Waters Books. She hopes you are captivated and stimulated, and your hearts become engaged.

If you enjoyed *Diamond in the Rough*, please consider telling others and writing a review.

Luna's Landing, *Book Seven* in the Cavanaugh Series, is now available!

Keep reading to get a sneak peek!

LUNA'S LANDING

Is the call from the depths her salvation, or will it lead to her demise?

With no previous memories of the wonderful mystical family who claimed her as a child of seven and nurtured her every day since, twenty-four-year-old Luna Cavanaugh-Hansen has always felt disconnected in every way. Now that she's fallen into the vast Mystic Lake, her memories return. But is it too late?

His young life was that of privilege and beauty, but his act of saving that little girl when he was a merchild cost his family everything. Now that they are both grown and she's back, he doesn't want to *want* and need her. But how can he not, when her beauty takes his breath, and she alone could be the salvation of his kind?

~~~~

Prologue

"Luna!"

Seven-year-old Luna Cavanaugh-Hansen looked back once, smiling because her sisters were once again frantically searching for her. Their game of hide-and-seek was a favorite. She was really good at it and always the last of the three to be found. Unlike her identical sisters, Soleli and Celestia, she didn't fear leaving her parents' close watch every time they picnicked with the other Cavanaugh families at the edge of Mystic Lake, and this time she'd ventured farther into the tall grasses than ever before.

Being the youngest by only minutes had always given her an advantage. Celestia, the oldest, was always trying to steal their mother's attention by being *Little Miss Perfect*. Soleli, the middle child, was more often than not glued to their father's side when he wasn't at the hospital fixing someone's health. Soleli had already decided she would one day be a doctor also, and he loved answering all her thousands of questions.

Which gave Luna the freedom to dream.

A moment of irritation flittered through her but she pushed those thoughts away, convincing herself she liked that the others often forgot to see what she was about...*sometimes*, even seeming to forget she existed.

"Luna! I'm going to tell Mom if you don't come out! *Now!*"

Stifling a laugh, she knelt at the lake's edge and peered at her reflection in the turquoise waters. She wanted to dip her hand in and take a drink but was afraid the sound would carry to her sisters, and then the game would be over. Movement in the water caught her attention, but Luna paid it little mind. All manner of freshwater fish made the large lake their home, and none of them would ever harm a member of the mystical Cavanaugh family. She smiled at herself and tilted her head from side to side as she inspected the chain of daisies she'd fashioned into a floral crown, ignoring her name being called again, though this time by Celestia's much softer voice. It was always her hope that her sisters would give up and one or the other of her parents would be forced to find the child they rarely noticed was gone.

A loud splash was followed by something painful latching onto Luna's arm and pulling her into the water. Stunned, she held her breath as she fought to get the large ugly fish with the hideous teeth to release her. Terrified, she thrashed about, her long red hair swaying in and out of her face as she jerked repeatedly to dislodge the lake creature, but it hurt like the dickens. It wasn't long before she started getting dizzy, and her lungs heated, feeling as if they were about to burst into flames.

A flash of blond hair suddenly appeared between her and the monster, blocking her view of the enemy. Only seconds passed, giving her little time to register the flash of thin muscular arms, narrow shoulders, and a back as small as her own, before her attention was drawn to what looked like a thin crystal spear being shoved into the side of the massive fish. The monster released her, sending out waves of rage before it turned and fled. Luna's savior faced her and she filled with wonder to find he was a child close to her own age. Dizzily now, she smiled at the beautiful face, and her heart filled with happiness and, she was certain, love.

Expecting immediate rescue, she was horrified when the arms of the little boy caught her around the waist and pulled her farther into the depths. Trying to stay conscious, she struggled to look back up to the surface, but all she could see as the last of her oxygen depleted was the sun shining through the water, setting off prisms of shimmering light over the iridescent scales of the child's *fishtail*.

Chapter One

"Luna!"

At the sound of tinkling coming from the bell attached to the front door, Luna looked up from the arrangement she was creating to smile at her cousin as he entered. "Yes, *boss?*"

Zeus Cavanaugh-Whitehawk smiled and pulled her into a hug, something he'd done every time he visited his shop, exactly once every week. She felt the heat in her cheeks as she stepped back, knowing the other women he employed would give their eyeteeth to have the amazingly hot Native American son hug them as well.

"How's it going?"

Luna grinned. "Sales have tripled since reopening, and we've gotten a great write-up in the *Mystic Sun Chronicles.*"

Zeus nodded and looked around the shop. "*Thanks to you.* I knew hiring you was the right thing to do. This place looks great. So much fresher and more modern than before."

Pleased with the praise, Luna took a deep breath and released it as she too surveyed the remodeling she'd done since being hired months before. Now all signs of the previous owner, who'd had the shop for fifty years before Zeus bought it, were gone. As was the smell of *old people.* "It's easy when your boss gives you unlimited funds and free rein."

Shaking his head, Zeus turned back to her. "No. This is all you."

Certain her freckled cheeks were are red as her hair, Luna looked toward the front of the shop again, on the pretense of seeing if someone was possibly entering the shop. Praise wasn't something she was used to and it made her uncomfortable, even coming from a *cousin*. Knowing she owed him a great deal for hiring her to get her out of the little house her parents had given her as a graduation present following college, she turned back to him and made herself make eye contact, which was always so hard for her to do.

Zeus was still smiling, and she felt one coming on herself. "So how was your week?"

Since their greeting had become something of a ritual—the hug, the compliment, the embarrassment—and then her inquiring of *his* week, Luna expected the usual answer, which was *fine*. But the look that crossed his strong Native American features alerted her to expect something different this time.

He sighed heavily. "It's been a week."

Not sure how to respond to the ambiguous response, she bit her bottom lip. Zeus wasn't a man any of them questioned. He'd always seemed so...*formidable*. Since she was the last person to question anyone about anything, she hardly knew what to say. But they'd gotten a little closer after he'd hired her, and she was concerned something seemed *off* with him. She wasn't sure why she thought so, or even if anyone but her had noticed.

"I...is there anything I can do to help?"

Zeus looked at her in surprise then smiled gently. "No. But thanks. You do more than enough to make my life better. What you've done with this flower shop makes me realize you've been hiding great talent all these years."

Luna was afraid she'd burst into tears if he didn't stop. So much praise in one day wasn't the only thing to have her so emotional. She'd grown up with him, his identical brothers, her supposedly identical sisters, and triplet female cousins, and for the first time felt as if she was actually a part of the large family.

"Luna, are you okay?"

Appalled there were actual tears flowing from her eyes, she nodded and quickly headed to the back room. She hated that she was such a ninny! Hated it with a passion.

But any time her *family* paid direct attention to her the same thing happened. She wiped her eyes quickly knowing the steps she heard were her cousin's. She turned to him with a bright smile, but his frown made it clear he wasn't buying her attempt at merriment.

"Is there something *I* can do for *you*?"

Luna shook her head. "I don't know what's wrong with me. It's been a long day." Zeus nodded, still frowning in that way that kept others from getting too close to him.

"After the endlessly long days you've put in getting this shop together, I can't say I'm surprised. I think you need a vacation."

Luna laughed, actually amused, as she tried to hide wiping her cheeks with the pretense of pushing her flyaway curls from her face. "After being employed only a few months?"

"You've done more work here than three people could have done in a year. I think you need some time off. How about a week at a beach somewhere tropical? My treat."

The thought of a week by herself wasn't intimidating at all. She'd made a point of being by herself physically and emotionally as far back as she could remember. But she had taken on this job and loved it. Going away for a week sounded like torture. All she'd do was try to remember who she really was, and she'd already spent too much of her life trying to do that. "No. I'm happy here. But thanks."

He stared at her for a moment before nodding. "Okay. The weekend then. In fact, let's have a family get together at the lake, and you do nothing but sit back and put your feet up while the dorks and I feed everyone. Heracles and Apollo need to work on their grilling skills a little, and we haven't gotten together since that thing with Dia and Ryan. I'd be interested to see how that's working out."

She'd wondered what was happening with them as well, but something about going to the lake gave her the willies. Unfortunately, everything gave her the willies, and she was tired of being poor little shy Luna where her family was concerned. Working with the other employees and the customers was helping to bring her out of her shell, *some*, and she liked it.

Since she hadn't responded, Zeus continued to try to convince her. "Besides, Mom was saying just last week it's been years since we picnicked at the lake." He frowned for a moment and then smiled again, but this time it didn't reach his dark brown eyes. "Close up shop whenever you want. I'm heading to my cabin to crash for a few hours. But I'll see if everyone can get together tomorrow." He sighed heavily. "Thank God, this week is done!"

Luna watched her cousin leave and, as always, wondered just what it was he did all week. He flew out on Sunday nights in his little plane and showed back up just before time to close the shop on Friday evenings. Shaking her head, she told herself to mind her own business. What Zeus did was his.

Determined to finish the arrangement she'd been working on before closing up for the night, Luna returned to the front of the shop and spent another hour making sure Mrs. Guthry's centerpiece was perfect before telling Macy she'd have to run the shop tomorrow, and that the elderly customer would pick it up early the next morning.

Now that the renovations were complete, she no longer planned to work seven days a week. Not because she didn't want to, but because she couldn't justify having her cousin pay her when the shop was supposed to be closed.

With one last look around, she bid the others farewell, closed down the shop and locked up. With her mind free to wander, she thought of the day to come and cringed. She'd always dreaded the boisterously happy family gatherings. Just thinking about it now tied her stomach in knots, making her realize her trepidation seemed stronger than normal. Luna shook off the chills and walked out into the warm evening air hoping this time she'd actually *feel* like she belonged with the wonderful people who claimed she was one of them.

Knowing it no more likely than all the times before, Luna again mourned that her memories, and thus her life, first began when she was that lost little waif who wandered into their lives, when she was but seven years old.

＊＊＊＊

Haven Hansen stared at her husband, her eyes holding fire. "I can't believe I let you talk me into coming back here!"

"We don't know that it happened here! You're being irrational!"

"Don't you tell me I'm being irrational, Logan Hansen! That is my child!"

"She's mine too. But stop this before *anyone* overhears!"

Luna tried to ignore the rare argument going on between her parents and noticed her aunts, uncles, and cousins were doing the same.

"Would you like something to eat, honey?"

Smiling at her aunt Destiny, Luna shook her head. "No, thank you." She was uncomfortable asking, but her parents' behavior was so out of tune, she felt compelled to anyway. "What are they fighting about?"

Destiny's lips pressed together in that way they always did when she was annoyed, as she looked to the tree line where the Hansens continued what they probably thought was a quiet conversation. She looked back down at Luna, her eyes filled with regret. "It isn't my place to tell you, honey, but I think you're old enough to find out if you want to ask them."

"Is it because I'm not really their child?"

The startled look Destiny sent her wasn't the only one, she realized, as she looked at those sitting around the campfire. Now they all watched her with forks hovering, or mouths frozen in mid-chew, as if she'd lost her mind.

"Of course you're their child. What would make you say such a thing?"

Luna shrugged, uncomfortable with everyone staring at her. But she was glad the topic was finally out in the open after so many years of her wondering. "When I was small. That day I found you all."

Destiny said nothing, but looked to the Hansens again. "Haven!"

Haven turned to face them, her face still filled with fury. "What?"

"You and Logan need to come here."

Haven looked from Destiny to Luna and then back up again. Luna turned back to her aunt. "I wish you hadn't bothered them."

Destiny smiled at her gently, making Luna realize she was once again being treated as a child rather than a woman of twenty-four. She hated that. *Not* because it was anything new. Which made it even worse.

She heard her parents approach and cringed that the entire family was there to witness the confrontation she'd always avoided having. But that was nothing new either. Whatever happened with one of the Cavanaugh clan always included them all.

Luna looked up as her mother stopped in front of her, though it was hard to maintain eye contact as Haven looked from Destiny to her.

"What's going on?"

Luna wet her lips, but found she couldn't say anything. She knew her immediate and extended family had always looked at her with curiosity, *or worse*, pity. Now she was going to sound more like a freak to them than ever before. It was a relief when her mother turned back to Destiny and she was saved from answering.

"*What?*"

"Your daughter doesn't think she belongs to you."

Haven frowned and looked down. Luna bit her bottom lip as heat fried her cheeks. She swallowed. "I just don't remember."

Haven squatted down in front of Luna, her emerald eyes filled with confusion.

"What are you talking about, honey? *Of course* you're our child. What is it you don't remember?"

Luna swallowed and then glanced past her mother to see the others weren't even pretending not to listen. She took a deep breath, knowing she had to put it out there. "The day I found you in the clearing."

Haven glanced up to Destiny, who shrugged before turning her attention back to Luna. "What day?"

Just say it! "The day you said you thought I was dead. The day you claimed I was your baby girl."

Haven stared at her until her expression finally changed into disbelief. "Are you talking about the day we were holding your memorial service? When we thought we'd lost you forever?"

Luna nodded, although she hadn't known then that was what they were doing. All she remembered was waking up in the woods and stumbling upon that large, tearful group of people who immediately, and nearly hysterically, embraced her before claiming her as their own.

Haven's mouth finally closed before she took a deep breath. "When you came out of the woods, you told us you didn't remember what had happened to you for the weeks you were gone. And because you were so little, and I feared traumatized, I didn't push it once you were examined and found healthy. But you never told us you didn't think you were ours."

Her mother's softly spoken words filled her with shame. "I was afraid to. I didn't remember who I was."

Horror crossed her mother's features before she carefully pulled her face back into concern. "Nothing? You remember nothing before that day?"

"Nothing."

Haven fell backward to land on her bottom, never taking her eyes off Luna's face. "You don't remember being a little girl, playing with your sisters? *At all?*"

Luna shook her head, hating that she'd hurt the beautiful woman who had been nothing but kind and loving to her since that day. "I'm sorry. I don't."

"Luna…."

Looking up, she stared into the face of the man who had claimed her as well. She tried to smile at him reassuringly, but she teared up instead, because he had too.

She'd never seen him cry before and hated she'd said a word.

"You are most definitely our child. I wish you had told us all this sooner." Logan turned to her aunt Destiny and aunt Rayne who had joined them. "Can you help her remember?"

Destiny and Rayne shared a look Luna felt certain meant they couldn't. It wasn't something she'd ever thought to ask of any of them, though she knew they could wipe away memories like they had for her cousin, Dia. From her understanding, they could also put false memories into someone, though she was told it was something they would never do.

"Can you?" Luna asked, looking at her aunts, then her mother as well when Haven stood.

"I don't know," Rayne answered. She turned to Haven. "We will have to look to the diaries."

Luna sighed. She knew from all the odd experiences her mother and aunts, as well as her Cavanaugh-White cousins had gone through, the three millennia of Cavanaugh family diaries were often consulted when something new came up. The problem was that there were hundreds and hundreds of them...and by the time anything was found, it usually didn't help anyway because the situation had been resolved one way or another.

Haven looked down at her daughter. "I am so sorry I didn't realize your shyness had nothing to do with personality, and everything to do with feeling like strangers had taken you in. If there is a way to fix this, we will find it.

"But you are my baby. I gave birth to you, and I have loved you every second since knowing I carried you. Don't you ever doubt that."

Luna nodded, hoping she could make herself believe it. But the obvious had to be stated now that everything was coming into the open. "But I'm not pretty like the rest of you. And I'm not particularly gifted in any way at all. There is nothing about me that makes me special except the silver in my blood, and I don't know if that is hereditary or simply because I was included in the ceremony with the others." She blushed, looking at the two women who called her sister. "I'm not even sure if my being there was what kept Celestia and Soleli from getting their hereditary gifts that day, like the cousins all did. I was afraid their sadness was all my fault because the *Powers-That-Be* were mad at you for bringing me along."

Distressed eyes stared at her from too many faces to count. Luna looked down to the ground, something she'd always done when afraid. She took a breath and forced herself to look back up. If she was going to get past this and be treated as an adult, she was going to have to start acting like one. "I'm sorry. All I'm doing is upsetting you all. Please, let's just change the subject."

Haven shook her head. "No, baby. Not this time. You are so beautiful it breaks my heart sometimes. Your gift is kindness. And you had nothing to do with anything that has happened, or not happened, to yourself or anyone else.

"When Rayne, Destiny, and I broke the three-thousand-year-old love curse, we changed everything. So we have no idea what is to come. But none of that is your fault. Not one thing!" Haven's eyes filled and spilled as tears ran down her cheeks.

Luna expelled a breath. "Okay, Momma, please don't cry."

She looked to the three powerful mystics who she knew were capable of nearly anything, yet always chose to do only good. "Mom, Aunt Destiny, Aunt Rayne, *please* find a way to give me back my memories. I need to know who I am if I'm ever going to feel like I belong."

****

Though it took a while, the usual teasing and tussling between her cousins had the rest of the family either laughing or rolling their eyes in exasperation. The antics of gorgeous and sometimes wacky Dia Cavanaugh-White and underwear model and unapologetic *diva* of the family Heracles Cavanaugh-Whitehawk was normal as far as their family gatherings went. There were, *however*, large differences regarding this get-together over and above her outing her lack of *familia* feelings and the fact the family now thought her stranger than ever before.

Glad the sun had set and only the campfire illuminated the area where relaxed family members lounged and chatted or stood off and did their own thing, Luna rose and walked to the edge of the large clearing, close to the tall grasses that eventually led to the bank of the lake. She stopped and looked back at each little group, relieved they now all seemed to have forgotten about her. The thought that it would be so easy to slip away unnoticed made her frown, though she didn't know why.

A strange sense of...*something* washed over her, sending chills up her spine and raising the hairs on her arms. She blinked in surprise as a strange scene flew through her thoughts and feelings of asphyxia nearly took her to her knees. Unable to grasp the thought fully, she forced herself to breathe in and out deeply until the spots before her eyes cleared and, though shuddering, her breaths returned to near normal.

Determined to push away the fear she felt, she focused again on those who called her family, this time giving each one determined attention to make sure that sudden bout of dizziness had cleared completely.

Dia's laughter and flashes of long white hair caught Luna's eye first, and she watched the way the man who'd entered their lives recently looked at her cousin so adoringly. *Her* oldest sister and husband, Sapphire and Nicolae, hadn't made it but sent their regrets through Sapphire and Dia's mother, Rayne.

Jewell, the middle Cavanaugh-White daughter, was busy with her new babies, as were her husband Amen-ra and the new grandma and grandpa, Aunt Rayne and Uncle Garrison. Luna's mother, now a great aunt, cradled one in her arms as well, making faces Luna suspected made the baby smile.

Luna slid a glance to her next oldest sister, who huddled with their father, as she always did. Soleli, a medical student and the most serious-minded of the three Hansen girls, put on her doctor face when deep in conversation with their surgeon father, and now it was no different. Earlier, the two of them had their dark-haired heads together and glanced her way often. Although she'd tried to pretend she didn't notice, it made Luna cringe even now, knowing she was the newest topic of their endless medical talks.

Their oldest triplet sister, Celestia, was almost ethereal with her long blond hair and gauzy white dress as she fluttered from one group of family to the next. This was completely normal, yet she seemed preoccupied at times and would occasionally look to the sky and stare at the clouds as if her mind were somewhere else completely, before blinking and once again engaging a cousin, aunt, or uncle in conversation. She stopped where Aunt Destiny was wrapped within the strong arms of her older but still gorgeous Native American husband. Destiny and Tom Whitehawk had also sent more glances her way than were comfortable earlier but, thankfully, now seemed otherwise occupied. Two of their triplet sons, Zeus and Apollo Cavanaugh-Whitehawk, had been in charge of cooking and serving the vast array of meats the family consumed at differing levels—depending on their relationship with the animal that had sacrificed its life for the meal. But now that the feasting was over, they were in mortal fisticuff combat with their youngest brother, Heracles, which was *the most normal* thing about all that had gone on during today's gathering.

Thankfully, everyone was busy doing something other than feeling sorry for her!

Luna inhaled and stepped backward, waited, then took another. Certain she was now outside the ring of firelight, she turned and made her way quickly, parting the grass as she moved forward. She knew she should be more careful but couldn't help advancing at a near run into the darkness. She needed to get away from them all. As much as she wanted to believe them, she still felt alone in the world, and their *knowing* her long held secret was even worse than she'd expected it to be.

The sudden loss of footing, the realization she was falling, and the ice-cold water flashing from sneakered toe to the crown of her head happened too fast for Luna to react, but the sight of the enormous sharp-toothed fish coming at her was accompanied by an explosion of memories.

She gasped great gulps of water, as terror filled her soul.

www.jcwardon.com